NEVER DIE TWICE

AN ACTION-PACKED HIGH-TECH SPY THRILLER

MARK CALDWELL JONES

SAMURAI
SEVEN
BOOKS

FOREWORD

BY CPT. NATALIE NICKS, DEFENSE INTELLIGENCE AGENCY

Since 1958, the American government has controlled the creation of future technology through an organization called the Defense Advanced Research Projects Agency or DARPA. Aided by their secret division, DR-Ultra, they fight a shadow war to make sure future weapons stay in the hands of the American military.

My name is Natalie Nicks. Like you, I had no idea about this hidden war until my first assignment as a newly minted Defense Intelligence Agency officer put me right in the middle of it. During a covert mission, I was targeted for assassination and killed by a suicide bomber. To honor my sacrifice, DR-Ultra used its secret TALON technology to revive me.

Now, equipped with several cybernetic enhancements, I work with an elite team of investigators called Reaper Force. We stand as a line of defense protecting the present from the weapons of tomorrow. We aren't just fighting a shadow war; we are fighting to save the future of mankind.

My codename is Viper and this is my story.

ALSO BY MARK CALDWELL JONES

REAPER FORCE: VIPER | The Natalie Nicks Thriller Series

Book One: NEVER DIE TWICE (2018)

Book Two: VIPER FATALIS (2019)

Book Three: MOONBASE ROGUE (2020)

PREFACE

The ideas and character in *Never Die Twice* and the Reaper Force: Viper series were inspired by *The Pentagon's Brain* by Annie Jacobsen and my subsequent research on the subject. Jacobsen's work is quite entertaining and disturbing at the same time.

Many of my readers have said the same thing about this novel. While this is a work of fiction, the technology in the story is quite real. Almost all of it already exists or is in the final stages of development.

The future is here and it's more dangerous than one could ever imagine!

For Hannah and Juliette,
my two little vipers.

I think it is no exaggeration to say we are on the cusp of the further perfection of extreme evil, an evil whose possibility spreads well beyond that which weapons of mass destruction bequeathed to the nation-states, on to a surprising and terrible empowerment of extreme individuals.
— Bill Joy, Sun Microsystems

"Generals gathered in their masses,
Just like witches at black masses.
Evil minds that plot destruction,
Sorcerer of death's construction."
— *War Pigs*, Black Sabbath

PART I

PROLOGUE

1

A wave of nausea washed over Director David Penbrook as he sat back on a stool near the doorway to the observation room. Despite the gentle breeze of sterile air flowing over his face, he was sweating. A bodily function he abhorred.

Project Starfire was gone.

It was impossible. Absolutely unthinkable.

Yet, someone had broken in and taken Starfire.

How did this happen?

The space, usually full of chatter or music, was hauntingly silent.

He forced himself to get up and look over the details of the room. He'd been in here a thousand times before. Nothing seemed out of place.

"Get our best forensics team to sweep this level and every other inch of this facility," he barked.

"Yes, sir, I'm on it." His nervous underling waiting beside him gave orders over her radio.

"Where is Echo Squad?" he asked.

"They were trapped in the freight elevator when the power went out. The guards cleared them to leave about an hour ago."

"Get their team leader on the radio. I want to know if they noticed anything unusual while they were picking up that equipment."

Marisol Flores paced as she hailed the team. Penbrook walked the room again. A small rubber octopus rested on one bookshelf as it had for years. He picked it up and played with it absent-mindedly while he considered the room one last time.

Blackwood Lodge was one of the most secure research facilities in the world. Like its name hinted, it was a *black* site for the Department of Defense's most advanced innovations—sensitive technology existed behind its veil of secrecy.

The base hid in the thick forest surrounding View Tree Mountain, on the grounds of Station B, at the heart of the infamous Warrenton Training Center. Warrenton was an open secret in the military world. Unacknowledged by the CIA and NSA even though it was well established their signal intelligence divisions were on site.

But no one knew about Blackwood Lodge.

The entire facility existed underground except for the entrance, which was the size of a double-wide trailer. It looked like a cabin you'd rent for a weekend in the woods. One way in and out for personnel. Along with a massive freight elevator that moved equipment between floors and in and out of the building.

It would take a brilliant mind to penetrate Blackwood, secure Starfire, and leave with no trace. This took meticulous planning. Months of it. Right under his nose.

He glanced across the room. "Marisol, what's taking so long?"

"I can't raise them, sir. I've tried every channel, even the emergency one Bishop Securities gave us. Nothing. They've gone radio silent."

Impossible. Unthinkable.

His mind, a train running on a track of hot-rolled steel, was always dependable. But now, panic crept up his spine, threatening to derail everything. He stared past his assistant trying to calm himself.

Everything he'd feared about his organization's vulnerabilities had come true. The entire world was in peril and, because of choices he'd made a long time ago, he was responsible.

Project Starfire was the most dangerous innovation his secret division of DARPA had ever created. Ironically, the breakthrough had been an accident. To this day, his best DR-Ultra researchers didn't understand the full potential and power of the discovery. However, he was sure if the technology turned against America, it could undermine her military might and safety for generations to come.

That was unconscionable.

"How is Natalie Nicks fitting in with the task force?"

"Fine. But, sir, there are concerns—"

"What kind?"

"Concerns about her psychological adjustment."

Penbrook was irritated by that assessment even though he shared the same conclusion. He'd insisted the issue be resolved. Now he'd be forced to rectify it himself. He pushed past his assistant and headed for the elevator. She raced after him.

"Get Colonel Byrne on the phone. I'll be in my office."

"What about Project Starfire, sir?"

Penbrook didn't answer. Too many horrible eventualities raged through his brain like an inferno burning away every other concern.

Only one team in the whole of the special operations community might have the intellect, technical knowledge, and operational skills to handle this.

He prayed they were ready for what was coming.

PART II

ELECTRIC FUNERAL

2

The man Natalie Nicks was sent to neutralize headed down the dark alley and disappeared into the building. The side entrance closed behind him but the sound of a lock never came. She was tempted to follow, but Declan Wilson was a trained special operations soldier, armed and dangerous.

He'd wait near the door until he was sure he wasn't being shadowed. To avoid an ambush, she'd have to find another way in.

Wilson and his partner, Edward Chapman—her other target —were the prime suspects in the robbery of some top-secret military weapons from the Department of Defense. The weapons were so advanced they were still off-book.

It had taken six months to hunt him down. Her team was the only intelligence group on the case. Nicks had to thwart the sale of the equipment, or dark minions from the Pentagon would crawl out of their spooky caves and come for her head.

This was a no-fail mission.

Around the back of the building, she discovered a set of doors secured from the outside. A large silver padlock was threaded through half-inch galvanized chain. Several feet of the heavy links were wrapped around the door handles.

She grabbed a handful of the chain and yanked. As if by magic, the handles—chains and all—broke away in one clean jerk. The doors swung open.

If there had been a witness, they would've been astonished. *How the hell did she do that?*

Natalie Nicks was a fit, athletic woman and, at first glance, nothing set her apart other than a streak of purple through her brunette hair. With her high cheekbones, green eyes, and olive skin, the twenty-eight-year-old was naturally pretty. Just like thousands of women in Los Angeles—where beauty was camouflage.

But the facade of a normal-looking, all-American woman hid more than first impressions could convey. Nicks was an operative for the Defense Intelligence Agency—the Department of Defense's very own CIA. At five feet seven inches, weighing in around one hundred and forty pounds, most of her weight was muscle. And she pushed her limits tenaciously. But at her strongest, she'd never been able to rip off door handles. She'd acquired that *skill* later.

She dropped the heavy chain and the door handles on the asphalt, pulled out her Glock 17, and slipped through the opening.

INSIDE THERE WERE no working lights and it was dark as midnight. The main room of the warehouse was crowded with machinery, equipment parts, and stacks upon stacks of unopened cardboard boxes.

Nicks moved in closer, read the labels, and opened one package. It was full of toys—hundreds of them, in unlabeled polyethylene bags. Plastic green army men, to be exact. She was too amped up to muse about the irony of that discovery, so she kept moving.

A man's voice spoke in her ear. "The locator's last ping was about a hundred yards ahead of you," he said.

"Copy that," she whispered and continued toward the back of the room.

Her team was a covert cell created by a rare collaboration between the Pentagon's top scientists and the DIA. The task force attracted people with unique knowledge in key areas like genetics, robotics, nanotechnology, and artificial intelligence. They were all former spec ops.

At present, the team leader was Colonel Jack Byrne, code-named Spartan. He was the guy in her ear, posted across the street in their tactical van. Nicks was second in command—their main tactical operator—point on this particular mission and the one cleared for chasing bad guys through decrepit warehouses.

Thus, she was here in this cold musty place that smelled like machine oil, dead rodents, and mold. She sidestepped past a rusty shipping container and over several frayed electrical cables. Then she stopped to listen. An almost inaudible hum of electricity proved the building had power. No sound from Wilson, but she sensed his presence. He was close.

All the public records on file said this business employed over fifty people and was still in daily operation. The owners paid their taxes regularly, and the building's exterior was in decent shape. They reported business was good. A small factory churning out toys and electronics, it netted millions a year. But, unless dead pigeons could manufacture knock-off action figures, all of those city records were a lie. The place had been abandoned a long time ago.

Nicks's intel said it was a money laundering front for MS-

13. The manufacturing only existed on paper. Dirty gang money went in; clean profits came out.

So far, that scenario held true. The only residents seemed to be rats and roaches. Even homeless squatters had steered clear of the place. So, why was Wilson hiding secret military technology here? It didn't make any sense. Why risk involving a dangerous gang?

Ahead of her, Wilson darted between two columns.

Nicks advanced, making damn sure no one, Chapman for instance, was flanking her.

She followed the sound of Wilson's boots scuffing across the concrete and echoing off the walls. He was on the move, weaving through the equipment toward the center of the factory.

Nicks jogged a few yards closer and took cover behind a rusty injection machine.

A black SUV was parked nearby on a sloped loading dock. Its nose pointed at a roll-down security gate, ready to take off at the first sign of trouble.

This entrance wasn't on the building's schematics. Surprises were inevitable on her missions, but they always triggered a deep frustration she had to suppress.

Poor intel had killed her once—a hard-earned lesson about espionage. Nicks tried to avoid surprises these days. But in her line of work, you had to adapt to changing circumstances.

Ahead of her, she heard Wilson throw a switch. At the click of the heavy electrical breaker, a motor activated.

Some distance past the van, Wilson popped up near a control panel. Pneumatic pistons hissed below his feet. He turned around and walked back to the SUV.

She moved closer and slid down behind a plywood crate to hide. As she listened, she scanned the stenciling on the wood sheathing and read the familiar acronym.

Five letters identifying the owner of the stolen tech. Five letters representing the organization she was here to protect. An acronym for the Defense Advanced Research Projects Agency.

DARPA.

DECLAN WILSON WAS SO CLOSE NOW, Nicks could smell him. During her time in the Army, her fellow Rangers called it FAN —the musky smell of sweaty feet, ass, and nuts. If she lost him again, she was sure she'd find him with her nose.

Despite needing a shower, he was handsome. A true meat eater who looked like an extra from a cop show. His dark head was shaved and he was dressed in a leather jacket, an AC/DC t-shirt, jeans, and one strange accessory—an old-fashioned eye-patch.

When he shrugged off his coat and threw it in the SUV, she could tell something was wrong.

"I have eyes on Wilson," she whispered to the man in her ear. "Looks like he's getting ready to move."

"What about Chapman?" he asked.

"No sign of him."

Nicks examined the crate more intently. Nothing indicated what might be inside, but the shipping number checked out.

DARPA was the preeminent military science agency in the world. It had no serious rival. President Eisenhower created it in 1958 to ensure the USA always maintained its military dominance. Since that time, DARPA had created the M16 rifle, GPS, Agent Orange, stealth airplanes, smart bombs, night vision, the computer mouse, and the Internet. It literally invented the future.

"Found one of the missing packages," she whispered.

"Bigger than a toolbox?"

"The size of a refrigerator."

"Has to be the MAARS system."

Nicks smiled. Most of the time Byrne was a light-hearted jokester, but when they were on a mission, he was hard-nosed and impatient. Right now, relief bubbled under his tough, sarcastic growl.

She was relieved too. The theft had included one UAV sniper drone, the MAARS breaching bot, and several battlefield surgical devices that were highly classified. Her team's mission was to manage the proliferation of this kind of dangerous technology and to keep the United States in control of it.

Chapman and Wilson were dumb enough to rob DARPA like they were lifting cheap stereos out of the back of some broken down delivery truck. Nicks's job was to stop said boxes from falling off those trucks.

She peeked at Wilson again. From her vantage point, Wilson looked vulnerable. He was acting more agitated by the second. Loading gear into the SUV, he worked as if he was preparing to bug out.

He stopped what he was doing and pulled a phone from his back pocket. After hitting some buttons, his expression changed. If he'd been texting, he didn't like the response or lack thereof. His face showed an emotion she rarely saw in an operator like him—panic.

Did he know her team was closing in? That she was in the building? No, that wasn't it. He appeared scared. Not because of her. Something else ... but what?

Adrenaline pumped through Nicks as she waited for an opening.

Wilson placed a call on his smartphone, held it to his ear. Whoever he was calling—Chapman perhaps—was not answering.

"Damn it!" Wilson slammed his phone down on a nearby

crate. "Where the hell are you?" He spit out another string of obscenities and threw more gear into the SUV.

She noticed he'd set aside his gun. It was out of reach.

Nicks stood up.

"Wilson!" Nicks yelled.

"The hell?"

"Don't move!" She leaned out aiming carefully. "I don't want to hurt you."

"Is that why you have a gun pointed at me?"

She had a gun on him because Declan Wilson was a former Marine Raider, the equivalent of a Navy SEAL, recruited by Joint Special Operations Command to serve with the 1st Special Forces Operational Detachment-Delta, also known as Delta Force. After receiving an injury on a mission, he was offered the gig with a private military company called Bishop Security.

Wilson's team had a contract to provide services to several secret DR-Ultra facilities across the country. Six months ago, they vanished with a truckload of equipment. It was speculated they were selling it to a contact in the international arms market. Penbrook wanted to know whom they were working for. He also wanted the tech back.

"I'm just here from the missing property department."

"Is that so? Well, you picked a bad time to show up!"

Wilson didn't seem to be in the surrendering mood, which sucked because Nicks didn't want to kill a fellow soldier, no matter how off the rails he'd gone. She hoped he would surrender and give up Chapman.

"There's an easy way to do this," she said, maintaining her cover. "Turn around, get on your knees, put your hands on your head."

"I don't think so."

"I'm here for the MAARS. No need for anyone to get hurt. Those weapons can't hit the black market."

The size of a riding lawnmower, the Modular Advanced Armed Robotic System was a war-fighting robot that moved on tracks like a tank. A crown of situational awareness cameras rotated on the top like police sirens. They scanned the terrain and used algorithms to figure out where it was and who to engage.

Marketed to the top brass as an Escalation of Force weapon, or EOF, it could be used non-lethally because it had a Taser attachment. But the feature was as useful as the corkscrew on a Swiss Army knife. Soldiers wanted it so they could use deadly force from a concealed and safe location.

A soldier could drop any military rifle of choice in the weapon's cradle and send it on its deadly way. As a bonus, it had a grenade launcher and the whole machine could be controlled with an iPad.

UAV's flew in the sky. The MAARS rolled on the ground.

"I was told if anyone came, they'd come to kill."

"Well, I'm here. And I haven't shot you yet." Nicks holstered her gun. "But I am going to take you in. So turn around—"

"—you need to understand, I never wanted things to go down like this," he said and lifted his eye patch. A faint scar around his eye socket revealed he'd lost his eye. But it had been replaced.

Nicks had seen images of the prototype, but she'd never seen one in the field. Not real enough to hide its artificiality, it moved too fast as it scanned the environment, adjusting to the change in light.

The eye patch made sense. The prosthetic would draw too much attention in public.

"Yeah, I wanted the money, but that chick lied about the

fine print," Wilson said. "That voice in my head, I couldn't take it anymore, none of us could."

His strange eye whirled up and down, out of sync with his other. He was scanning Nicks head to toe.

"Damn girl, you're more tricked out than me. How much did the doc charge for all that? I'd love to get acquainted, but I've got a friend to find and a buyer to meet. Don't have time for this shit—"

Wilson lunged for his gun.

"Don't do it," Nicks yelled.

Too late. He squeezed off several rounds forcing Nicks to drop behind the crate.

"If you knew what was really going on, you'd get out of town with us," he yelled, becoming more agitated by the second. "But now there's only time to save one ass, and it's gonna be mine."

Wilson fired two more rounds.

They whizzed over Nicks's head, nowhere close to her position. He was either Delta Force's worst shot, or he was warning her to back down. He must've shared Nicks's disdain for shooting fellow servicemen.

She held her cover for a few beats, hoping he'd see reason.

"Wilson, let's talk about this before things go off the rails."

No answer.

When she looked again, he was gone.

3

From her place on the roof, Scorpio looked through the lens of her Leupold Mark 4 spotter scope. She had good sightlines on the side and back entrances of the warehouse. She'd been in the building for several hours setting the trap, and now everything was ready.

The video feeds were recording from inside the building and from the cameras set up at her current location. The information these devices gathered was transmitting without interference back to the new base.

Everything was going according to plan when Declan Wilson turned into the alleyway and hurried to the side entrance.

Scorpio perked up. She felt the pleasant rush of adrenaline, accompanied by a strange, peaceful confidence. No one matched her skill level, no one could defeat her in hand-to-hand combat. But tonight, she might finally meet her match.

It wasn't Wilson. No, her orders were clear. Both Wilson, and his partner Edward Chapman, were to be eliminated along with everyone else in Echo Squad. They were merely pawns on a chessboard. Their deaths would be the first moves in a game that would change the world.

Studying her main target was the objective tonight. It had been suggested, she was potentially, the most dangerous piece on the game board. Even a serious rival.

Her codename was Viper.

She appeared seconds later. Instead of following Wilson inside, Viper circled around to the back entrance. With no effort, she ripped the titanium chains, and the handles, off the door in one clean jerk.

How the hell did she do that? Impressive!

Two months ago, Scorpio had received a comprehensive dossier on Viper. She had studied it obsessively.

While there were many gaps in Viper's early history, for instance information about her parents and birthplace had been scrubbed, the science behind how a one hundred and forty pound female could tear apart a reinforced door without breaking a sweat, was laid out in clear detail.

It read like science fiction, but now she had witnessed a convincing demonstration of how true it was. Viper, whose real identity was US Army Captain Natalie Nicks, did seem to be a formidable weapon, surely one of DARPA's greatest achievements.

Her story had started in Afghanistan. The purpose of her mission in Kandahar was heavily redacted. The medical reports showed she sustained life-threatening injuries during a suicide bombing called the Jehanni Market Incident. She was at the epicenter of the blast and was declared clinically dead on the way to emergency surgery.

Her left arm had been severed at the shoulder. Her right hand was destroyed and amputated at the wrist. Her left ear was ripped off and, both eardrums were destroyed, deafening her permanently in an instant. Her right and left legs were severely damaged. She lost vital muscle mass, and her fatigues had melted in such a way as to become a temporary layer of skin. Scars and amputations—the medals of war she could never take off and put away in her drawer.

Minutes after the bombing, she was getting the most advanced medical attention any person had ever received.

According to Viper's dossier, because the clandestine services had invested so much time and treasure in Natalie Nicks, they had flagged her as approved for a secret project called the TALON program. TALON was the latest advancement in the long dreamed of super soldier project. The primary focus of DARPA's secret branch called DR-Ultra. Because of her age, extraordinary health, and fitness level, Nicks was the perfect candidate.

When the unimaginable happened, DR-Ultra made good on that promise.

They rushed her to the nearest airfield and loaded her on a special C-130 Hercules containing a secret aeromedevac center. While in flight, they repaired and replaced all of her physical injuries with the experimental biomimetic components.

It wasn't exactly special treatment, because her chance of survival plummeted the minute they put her on that plane.

The surgical methods were untested. The bionics were experimental prototypes. Her chance of living through the operations and recovery were minimal. But luck was with her. From her vantage point, Scorpio could see Viper was a stunning success.

She turned on her computer tablet and fixed it to the ledge of the roof with a small tripod. The criminal syndicate she worked for had stolen DARPA's new AMEBA communication system. The device used ultra-low frequencies to send information through barriers that caused interference, like deep water, caves, or old buildings with concrete basements.

She transmitted the signal and information flowed halfway across the world at the speed of light. Her leader reviewed it with her in real-time.

Watch carefully. There can be no doubts.

She did have doubts. Natalie Nicks was vulnerable even if the technology that created her was awe-inspiring. She was sure of it.

The base's network assumed control of her tablet. Details of Viper's dossier flashed across the screen. Knowing the words almost by memory, she skimmed through the file pages.

The Talon Protocol System was the artificial intelligence that managed all of Viper's cybernetic parts. Her bionics had to be used efficiently, and managed carefully, to maximize their power. The best combinations were pre-programmed into tactical profiles.

However, the report showed Viper was resistant to using the protocols because she said it dulled her other training. According to her psychological assessments, the doctors felt she was having trouble accepting her bionics. Even after months of training, she was wary of becoming too dependent on the AI and had requested only a few profiles be available to her during her missions.

One psychiatrist theorized Viper was hiding symptoms from her medical team. He believed she suffered from PTSD, possibly complicated by childhood trauma that she'd never disclosed. There were off-the-record reports that she was having mood swings, flashbacks, and night terrors, and was abusing alcohol to cope. But she denied it.

She acknowledged having occasional migraines but rated those as being manageable and not affecting her performance.

The DR-Ultra leadership had flagged Viper for continued review. Her current assignment to the task force was another test. If Viper wasn't able to fully accept her bionics, all of the tech keeping her alive would be confiscated. They called this *decommissioning*. An interesting word choice, given the result would be immediate death.

Scorpio smiled.

It confirmed what she had suspected. Viper was compromised because she failed to embrace her new abilities.

The fundamental weakness of pairing machines with humans was the human.

Viper was the most successful test subject in TALON's short history. But DR-Ultra had picked the wrong woman for their experiment. Nicks wasn't a hardened warrior.

Scorpio found that ironic. DARPA thought they were the only ones who had an interest in their billion-dollar woman. Their arrogance was as impressive as their results.

What would Viper do if she found out her usefulness was still being debated? What would happen when she found out other organizations might want to add her to their arsenal?

At the moment, Natalie Nicks had no idea she had a target on her back.

Scorpio typed a line of code into her computer.

That was about to change.

4

Nicks searched through the maze of manufacturing machines for Wilson. He'd vanished like a ghost.

"Your signal is breaking up," Byrne said. "The plans show the entrance to another room about fifty yards ahead. Be careful!"

Nicks's coms faded in and out. Interference was scrambling the signal. She continued forward, but there was no entrance. No other room.

An odd hum vibrated in her ears. She twisted her head to find the source. It was coming from the floor.

No, that's not it, she thought. It was *below* the floor.

Nicks kicked some loose cardboard boxes out of the way, searched underneath, and found a rectangular metal trapdoor about seven by four feet.

"Got something here—a hidden storage area or basement."

"Make sure it's not rigged with—"

The signal crackled in and out. Nicks knew what Byrne was worried about. An improvised explosive was the last thing she needed. She had used all nine lives on the last one.

Nicks walked around the edge of the door. No wires. No

cables. Nothing indicating a bomb. No handles or locks. He had to be in that room but how?

Wilson had thrown a switch. She'd heard pneumatic gears. Remembering the control panel, Nicks jogged back and examined it.

The panel was a collection of electrical junction boxes with an array of machine controls. All the switches had a thick coat of dust, except for one.

She flipped it, and the metal trapdoor retracted, revealing a set of stairs. She walked over and stared into the unknown.

Turning on her flashlight, she stepped down and followed her gun into the darkness.

The room smelled of incense but it was masking something pungent, the sweetness of decay. A bad sign.

The ceiling was full of white Christmas lights. There were so many, they created the impression she was walking under a piece of the Milky Way.

Round Japanese lanterns dangled down at random intervals like planets. Plastic bonsai trees around the floor created a winding path through a miniature forest.

In the center of the room, she found a structure made of cardboard boxes and more carefully-placed Christmas lights. Each tier of the structure had a curved roof made of fabric, the ends suspended by fishing line. It looked like a child's playhouse built to resemble something one might see in a Japanese tourist book.

This was a distinct contrast to the trashed warehouse above. Someone had to be living down here. Maybe an obsessive homeless person or an eccentric artist—Los Angeles was full of both.

Nicks tilted her head, waiting for the cochlear implants to amplify the room noise.

She ducked into the cardboard temple. "Wilson?"

He was inside on his knees, in front of a small altar. He head hung down like he was praying. His eyes fixed on the altar.

"Chapman was the best of us. He would've put up a helluva fight."

He looked back at Nicks, laid his gun on the floor, and slid it toward her.

She kicked it out of reach and moved past him.

She found an odd bowl full of weird metal coins. Behind that, centered on the altar, was a plastic treasure chest. Nicks remembered playing with one in her youth. It was begging to be opened. Nicks flipped the lid and immediately regretted it.

"Shit—" She jumped back.

The treasure was a human head, severed with surgical precision. The flesh was cauterized and bloodless.

The victim was a young male. Late twenties. Clean cut. Short dark hair. The faint shadow of a beard. It seemed the back half of the man's skull was missing.

No, that wasn't right. It was missing. The bowl. The bowl was his skull, and someone had filled it with silver coins. Along with the coins, Nicks saw a set of dog tags, confirming this was Edward Chapman, Wilson's partner and Nicks's other target.

"Who did this, Wilson?"

Wilson reached forward and closed the chest. He was a hardened warrior, but despair had him by the throat.

"If they can get to him, they can get to any of us." Wilson choked back emotion. He pointed to the wall.

Nicks aimed her flashlight in that direction, revealing a bizarre bit of graffiti depicting a picture of a monster. Red skin. Three bulging bloodshot eyes. It wore a crown of skulls.

Underneath the image, the artist had written a message:
Cursed Creators! Your monsters rise!

As she considered the meaning of the message, a movement in the corner of the room caught her eye. There was a glint of silver, the scratching of metal on concrete, and then ... her eyes widened with surprise. What the hell was that?

To work for DARPA meant to live in the future. Almost all the secret technology developed in DARPA's labs was twenty years ahead of what was sold in the stores. If you could buy an iPhone 10 down the street, it was a good bet DARPA was working on the technology that would go into the iPhone 30.

That was the rule of thumb, and it matched Nicks's experience. When she started with Reaper Force, her constant exposure to new technology made her feel like she was living in a science fiction movie.

But what she saw crawling toward her and Wilson out of the dark corner of the room was beyond shocking.

Two silver-skinned spiders, each the size of the king crabs shown on nature shows, scuttling toward them. The only difference was, these creatures were machines.

Their metal appendages clicked like knife blades on the concrete as they skittered closer. Their menacing red eyes twirled, tagging the space and its occupants, filling the room with hypnotic red pulses.

"Did you turn these things on?" Nicks asked.

Wilson snapped out of his grief. "Hell no! I don't even know what those are!"

"Caduceus drones," Nicks said. "Battlefield surgeons. Robots created to crawl across an active battlefield and surgically treat wounded soldiers."

"If those things are medics, screw Obamacare!"

They backed up as the spiders moved closer.

"You stole tech you hadn't been briefed on? Genius move!"

"Do you think we took this stuff because we wanted to?" Wilson said. "It was an order. Move the crates; don't worry about what's inside."

"So, you don't know how many of those things you have?"

Wilson shrugged. "Our team leader, Tango, was in charge of that."

"Tango?"

The lead drone stopped and scanned Wilson with its laser eye.

"These fuckers are creeping me out. Can I have my gun back?"

Too late for that.

Without warning, another Caduceus tore through the ceiling tiles over Wilson's head. It half-leapt, half-fell from the aluminum ceiling lattice right onto the big soldier's back. The drone grabbed a web of his skin with its medical-grade grasping instrument. Another claw sank a stainless steel probe into Wilson's neck.

Wilson furiously tried to shake the thing off but the machine just tightened its grip. He couldn't rip it free without tearing his own skin.

A six-inch needle with a full syringe telescoped from another of the crab's appendages. The needle sunk into the left side of Wilson's neck, injecting the fluid into an artery. His eyes rolled backward, and he collapsed.

Nicks tried to catch him mid-stride, but he fell out of reach. As she bent over to help him, a metal spider landed on her back. Its legs clawed at her, climbing toward her leather belt, and she pictured it aiming a syringe at her spine.

Nicks reached back, trying to tug the thing away from her body. It readjusted itself and clamped onto her shirt, crawling farther up her back. Nicks grabbed at the spider but found it impossible to dislodge. The needle sank into her triceps and deployed its drug.

Nicks, off balance, stumbled forward. The Caduceus drone waited patiently for the drug to take effect. But Nicks wasn't going down. In fact, she felt no effects. The robot had injected her cybernetic arm.

The drone was re-tasking, computing what to do next, as if confused by the failure of its procedure. It refilled its syringe and got ready for another injection.

That small delay allowed Nicks to bring her gun up under her arm. Praying she wouldn't wound herself, she fired several rapid shots.

The drone's shiny silver thorax cratered in on itself, and it fell dead at Nicks's feet.

She turned her gun on Wilson's Caduceus drone. There wasn't a clean shot. The robot was sitting on Wilson's chest removing his eye.

He was paralyzed but awake, feeling every cut and snip the drone made. Nicks heard the squish and tear of tissue ripping as the drone pulled out the manmade organ. The bloody ocular prosthetic dangled from tweezers as the Caduceus analyzed what it had dissected like a thoughtful surgeon.

Nicks had had enough.

With a running start, she kicked the steel spider hard enough to dent its shell. The drone flew across the room, hit a wall, and burst into pieces.

The move may have saved Wilson, but the attack wasn't over. Several more spiders scuttled across the floor toward them.

"We've got to get the hell out of here," she said, unsure if Wilson could even hear her.

She fired again, destroying another drone. The remaining surgeons scurried away in the shadows, sensing the threat. She heard one more in the ceiling overhead. They were following their programming and avoiding the danger. But they remained hell-bent on getting back to their patients.

Nicks couldn't risk being paralyzed; she had to leave now. She tore several strips of fabric from the makeshift shrine and packed and bandaged Wilson's wound. Then, she dragged him across the room to the stairs.

The remaining Caduceus drones re-targeted the pair and sped after them. Nicks yanked Wilson up the stairs, and they cleared the opening.

The spiders were right behind them. She ran and hit the switch for the trapdoor. A metal claw reached for Wilson as the trapdoor clanged shut, crushing the Caduceus in its hinge.

They were safe.

Nicks hoisted Wilson on her back and moved them toward the exit. She was halfway across the warehouse when the MAARS unit burst out of its crate and fired.

5

Wilson's body jerked against Nicks and she knew he was hit. Another volley of bullets clattered to the right. Nicks dove behind an old conveyor belt and took cover. Wilson's body fell beside her.

"Wilson! Wilson! Talk to me." She pulled him closer. Blood poured from a wound on the back of his neck.

"Finally, it's quiet," he muttered. "Someone in your mind like that, it's worse than death."

"I'm gonna get you help, stay with me," she yelled. But it was too late. Wilson was dead.

Bullets continued to pepper the machinery all around her.

This was madness. Why were the drones attacking? "Byrne, I'm taking fire! Can you disable these damn things?"

"Trying to figure that out, now. Are you hit?"

"No, but Wilson and Chapman are dead. I'm bringing Wilson out."

"Leave him and move!"

The MAARS was coming like something out of a *Terminator* movie. Byrne was right. She couldn't risk carrying Wilson. She'd be lucky if she saved her own ass.

"What's the safest route out of here?"

"The east exit leads to another alleyway. Head out and run south. I'll pick you up on Santee."

"Copy that."

A spray of bullets ricocheted off the conveyor. Keeping as low as possible, Nicks lunged forward and sprinted for the exit. As the metal door closed behind her, it rattled from a new hail of bullets.

Nicks had escaped, but she wasn't in the clear. Halfway down the alleyway, hiding in the shadow of the building like a predatory animal, waited another MAARS unit.

She was out in the open—a perfect target.

The tank-like robot was designed for military reconnaissance, surveillance, and target acquisition, or RSTA. It was very good at it. It had picked the perfect place for a trap.

"Damn it, there's another one. I'm cornered!"

"I'm on my way!" Byrne yelled.

She could hear the roar of his engine as he gunned the van, racing to their rendezvous. No way he would make it in time.

Nicks dove behind a nearby dumpster. The tank treads creaked forward, opening up a better angle for its weapon and showing off its targeting ability.

The machine could carry up to 450 rounds of ammo and fire up to four grenades. Nicks peeked out just in time to see it was carrying a CAR-60 belt-fed machine gun, a favorite of the Navy SEALs.

The robot squeezed off its first burst of ammo. Bullets pinged off the big metal dumpster. They ricocheted in every direction. The MAARS advanced as it fired. A robot had boxed her into the perfect kill zone. Who was controlling these things?

Nicks noticed the dumpster had wheels. She cocked her arm back, flattened her palm, and slammed it into the dumpster. The dumpster vibrated violently and rolled forward.

She put her biomimetic legs into it and kept the momentum going, using it as a shield as she moved forward. Meanwhile, the machine gun was burning through its belt of ammo, trying its best to kill her.

As Nicks edged closer, the bullets punched holes in the dumpster, sounding like a slot machine that had hit the worst kind of jackpot.

Even with the augmented stimulation, her muscles didn't have enough power to crush the bot, so she rolled past it, forcing it to turn and chase her. Because it moved on a pair of roller-belts, it had the same problem regular tanks had: turning around wasn't easy.

Nicks was well past the unit by the time it swiveled enough to reengage. Her speed kicked in and she flew down the alley. The MAARS was having trouble recalculating her exact location, but it wasn't stopping.

She heard the distinctive *thunk* of a grenade launcher lobbing its projectile up into the air. The ordinance arced down and detonated a safe distance behind Nicks. It was off target, but the concussive wave made Nicks dive for the concrete.

"This damn thing won't stop!"

"Machines aren't programed to give up. Use the dazzler!"

Nicks remembered Maggie Quinn had upgraded her flashlight with a laser strobe. Its pulse was strong enough to induce flash blindness. She placed it on the concrete, and aimed it at the MAARS before she got up and ran.

"Forget Santee, cross the street, and meet me behind the next building."

Nicks looked back; the MAARS had lost its advantage. The strobe had rendered its laser-positioning computer useless. It careened off course and toppled over into a concrete culvert.

This terminator wasn't getting back up without some human help.

Nicks took a deep breath and let out a grateful sigh. Her eyes locked on to something coming straight for her that was the opposite of a guardian angel—the only piece of stolen tech that hadn't attacked her.

It was closing in and she had no place to hide.

"We have another problem," Colonel Jack Byrne said through the com.

"Is it the Sniper Drone."

Nicks's cybernetic ears picked up the buzz of the seven rotors and the faint burst noise of the drone's gears. Its robotic stabilization platform adjusted the attached sniper rifle, preparing it to fire.

"Yes! It's targeting you!"

"I hear it."

"You *hear* it?" He corrected himself. "Silly me, of course, you do."

Byrne screeched to a halt right in front of Nicks. The drone had dropped out of its higher trajectory. Despite wearing mechanical knee braces on both legs, Byrne sprung from the van, surprising Nicks. What the hell was he doing? Any delay made them an easier target.

"If this is a rescue, get me the hell out of here!" she yelled.

Byrne ignored her while he rummaged in the back of the van.

"Get down. I'll take care of this." He pulled out what looked like a rocket launcher.

Okay, at least he had some useful firepower. But they were in downtown Los Angeles, and this was a clandestine operation.

"You're shooting it with a *rocket?*"

The gunfire was bad enough, but this was ridiculous.

The drone buzzed closer and hovered, zeroing in on its targets.

Byrne fired. *Fffwhump!*

His strange missile arced out of its tube and exploded with a weak pop in front of the drone. A massive cloud of colored paper filled the sky.

Nicks heart sank. "A confetti cannon?"

"A *badass* confetti cannon!" Byrne smiled, impressed with his accomplishment. The man had lost his mind.

The drone's rotor revved higher. But they weren't strong enough to disperse the cloud and the rotors sucked in the confetti. Shredded paper wrapped around its blades. In seconds, all seven rotors jammed. The drone dropped like a rock toward the ground.

Byrne and Nicks ducked behind the van. Broken rotor blades hurled at them like throwing stars. One dinged the side panel and ricocheted off.

"Crap, I just had this thing repainted," Byrne grumbled.

"Better your shitty van than me. I'm much more expensive."

"Ain't that the truth." He laughed.

Byrne tossed his confetti cannon in the back and they climbed in. A tactical retreat was in order. He fired up the engine, and they drove off.

The plan was to reclaim the stolen property and neutralize the thieves. Instead, they'd walked into a trap. After hearing what Wilson said, Nicks knew there was more to the theft than they had thought.

Had Nicks spotted her new enemy watching as they drove away, that theory would've been confirmed. Scorpio was busy transmitting her last package of data about the ambush.

Viper had passed her first test. It was time for phase two. The next encounter with the DARPA detective would be much more deadly.

PART III

CHANGES

6

After the last typhoon, the monks shuttered the shrine due to its dangerous instability. When the pilgrims stopped coming, the monks left for other shrines on other islands.

In only a few years, the fertile evergreen forest grew around it. Hiding it among new vines, jisugi saplings, weeds, and animal nests, all of which encroached on what had once been a beautifully maintained refuge.

One faithful believer remained.

The tea seller, now eighty-four years old, couldn't bear to give up on the sacred shrine. Her pilgrim stall on the path to the temple had been a place for rest and food for over sixty years. It was also her home.

She refused to leave. Even after terrible things began to happen.

"Demons," she told the few who still visited her. "Emboldened by the lack of prayers, they've made a home in the shrine"

"Don't be superstitious!" her friends scolded.

She disagreed. The desecration of the shrine had to stop.

She believed the *kami*, or divine spirits, only remained benevolent when venerated.

So, she walked the path each morning and left offerings to the gods. Outside the shrine, she bowed twice, clapped twice, bowed again, and offered her prayers like the Shinto priest taught her.

But it didn't work.

As the days passed, the temple changed. The soft, natural aesthetic of stone and wood gave way to metal and concrete. The demons were turning the shrine into a fortress.

Now, they seemed angry when she approached. They fluttered around her, buzzing their wings until they chased her away. At night, they followed her home and harassed her there. Red eyes peered through the dark forest, watching her.

She convinced herself it was a test. She was the last pilgrim, the last of the faithful, and she couldn't let the demons win.

THE BATTLE STARTED before sunrise on the day of her eighty-fifth birthday.

An animal squealing in pain woke her. It was a beautiful raccoon dog. One she had fed during the rainy afternoons. A *tanuki*, who she believed was a mischievous woodland spirit, lay at her doorstep, partially disemboweled.

When she realized it was still alive, she gathered the largest stone she could find and killed it as an act of mercy. Its blood poured out, creating a dark circle of mud. The image haunted her for hours.

Beauty is so hard to find in our world, she thought, yet evil is so quick to destroy it.

It was the final straw. She decided to make a last stand against the demons.

She recovered her grandfather's sword buried behind the shack in an iron chest. She cleaned, sharpened, and oiled it back to life. Then, she strapped it to her fragile body along with a sack of handmade, oil-soaked torches.

She tied back her silver hair, like the ancient samurai, with the tail of the tanuki and set off.

Red eyes stalked her through the forest as she hiked up to the temple. She marched on. Strange wings buzzed like bees as demons zoomed past her to alert the others of her approach.

Reaching the temple's entrance, she found the main door barred. In her whole time living near the shrine, the door had never closed. The demons were frightened.

Good, she thought, as they should be!

The same was true of many of the front facing windows. The demons had covered them with metal plates. Long black cables, humming with energy, hung from the eaves like vines. Roots of steel pipe grew from the ground and into the walls of the building.

The desecration of the temple was complete. She felt no qualms about burning it to the ground.

After sorting the torches, she stuffed her first bundle under the main door. She circled the temple carefully, repeating the process until only one large torch was left. As she lit it, the first demon appeared.

She drew her sword and took a defensive stance as it buzzed past her and circled back around. It dove like an angry bird and, when it was within reach, she cut it out of the air.

Its strange body fell in pieces around her. It seemed to be angry; the buzzing grew louder as it tried and failed to take to the air again.

"For the tanuki," she said, "may your spirit return to hell."

"You inspire me," said a woman as she appeared behind her. She was dressed like the traditional Shinto priestesses called *mikos*. Her white kimono had metallic piping along its sleeves and pants. A hood covered her head.

"Young woman, you must help me stop this desecration!"

"Help you stop it? Why would I do that? I'm the one *responsible*."

The old woman's eyes widened. "Then you must die as well."

She swung her sword but the girl easily dodged it. The old woman tried again, slicing clumsily through the air. The girl swatted the weapon from the old woman's hands.

"No matter." The old woman coughed, catching her breath. "You may stop my sword, but you will not stop the fire!" The flames consumed the exterior of the temple with a greater ferocity.

"Activate fire suppression on the west wall and at the south entrance," the miko said to no one in particular. Jets of fire-retardant foam burst from small hidden nozzles all around the shrine. Within seconds, the fire was out.

Crestfallen, the old woman fell to her knees in defeat.

"If you do not enter the tiger's cave, you will not catch its cub," said the young woman. "I admire your bravery no matter how foolish it may be."

The girl stepped closer and lowered her hood. Her appearance was ghastly. It was obvious she was another demon.

The old woman hid her face in the dirt as she wept. Something cold pressed into her neck and bit her like a snake.

She looked up as an explosion of transcendent joy filled her mind. Light, *beautiful light*, encircled the young woman like a radiant halo. This was no priestess or demon. This was a *god*.

How wrong she'd been. So terribly wrong.

She heard the god's reassuring voice in her head.

I will remember you.

A smile of mystical bliss filled the old woman's face as the god slowly pushed the blade into her chest and stabbed her through the heart. The life drained from the old woman and she collapsed.

The priestess removed the sword and wiped away the blood. She admired its ornate handle shaped like a scorpion. It made her smile.

Another sign, she thought.

With the old woman gone, the base would go undisturbed. She could engage the real threat. She would kill that enemy the same way she killed the old woman—with its own weapon.

Project Starfire would destroy them all.

PRESENT DAY

Fatima Nasrallah hated flying and everything that went with it. The inevitable delays. The stomach-tossing turbulence. The frigid air blowing in the cabin. And, in most cases, no one to kill.

To add to her aggravation, Director David Penbrook was running behind which was a mistake. Showing up late to a meeting with an assassin was bad form. It gave her time to muse about ways to punish him for making her get on this damn plane.

She'd had at least two glasses of wine by the time he boarded the chartered jet. He was agitated and mumbling things to Marisol Flores as he took a seat. The nervous woman made notes on her clipboard and disappeared. The crew closed the doors and the director buckled in.

Fatima felt his gaze as they took off. She was okay with it. Universally, men underestimated her because of her appearance. It was an advantage she relied on.

Fatima had middle-eastern features. Thick round lips. Long lashes and thick black eyebrows. Most striking—her piercing green eyes that seemed to detect the slightest bit of falsehood.

She wore blue jeans and several colorful scarfs over a tight black t-shirt. A long silver chain with a leather pendant and matching bracelets added to her appearance.

A black soft-shell case, about four-feet long, was strapped to the seat beside her. It held her Zagros Sniper Rifle.

Fatima had built it herself from spare parts while fighting against ISIS in Syria. Its base was a 12.7 mm DsHK Russian heavy machine gun. The trigger came from an RPG launcher, and the bolt and barrel were milled down by hand.

The rifle looked like the monster Barrett M107 .50-cal many army snipers preferred. Fatima had tried that gun during her training in the United States and felt it didn't match the accuracy she achieved with her Zagros. She went nowhere without it.

"This flight is going to take a while. I'll brief you when we are an hour out."

That was fine with Fatima. She didn't care for details, anyway. Point her at the target and she'd get the job done. She closed her eyes to take a nap.

"Until then, read these files," Penbrook added.

He dropped a thick binder in the seat across from her. It was the size of an old phonebook. She could've killed someone with it, if she could pick it up.

"*Fucking mothers,*" she mumbled and reached for the binder.

After skimming through the intel for a half-hour, Fatima had a better grasp of her new assignment. She was going to work for a task force nicknamed Reaper Force.

Dr. David Penbrook was their boss. Officially, he was the

program director of DR-Ultra, a secret offshoot of DARPA, housed at the facility called Blackwood Lodge.

DARPA had a simple structure. The buck stopped with the Program Director. Under him were the Program Managers. PM's were the most senior scientists within the research group; they were the lead investigators who came up with and managed the experiments.

Performers were the scientists contracted by the PM's. They carried out the necessary functions within the research project. DARPA was decentralized so when performers were given a contract, they continued working out of their own labs and universities. It cut out the normal bureaucracy that slowed down other government agencies.

DARPA had a cozy relationship with the press. It fed the media a steady supply of stories about its innovations. It even had a website and an Instagram feed. That familiarity made it easier to keep their covert branch secret.

DR-Ultra was a parallel organization that explored the most dangerous and sensitive military research. There was no public relations office because no one knew about DR-Ultra. Penbrook's purview wasn't listed in any organizational chart.

Every program director and manager that worked for DR-Ultra worked out of classified locations. Penbrook watched over programs that were literally buried where no one would find them. The Reaper team helped him keep those secrets.

Reaper's investigation of the Bishop Security team called Echo Squad was the most interesting thing about the brief. There was a list of names Reaper Force had been looking for: Declan Wilson, Edward Chapman, Frank Hitchens, Dwight Johnson, Hal Simmons, and C.T. Williams. She'd crossed paths with some of the men before and had hoped fate would allow her to do it again. It seemed she was finally getting her chance.

Reaper was a small outfit. Fatima figured she was a free

agent being asked to suit up and temporarily expand the team. She guessed Penbrook had decided they needed her particular set of skills. Sounded fun. She closed the binder, threw it back into the seat, and asked for another glass of wine.

It was the first time Fatima had smiled since she stepped on the plane. Sometimes dreams did come true, even for assassins.

HALFWAY THROUGH THE FLIGHT, their jet hit turbulence and David Penbrook was jostled from his nap. He turned his face to the window and wondered how the team's operation was progressing. He hoped he had given Byrne the right amount of guidance. Times like this made him feel so utterly out of his depth. He'd never felt he was a good leader.

All the members of the task force called him "the Boss" because he supervised their team. But he wasn't a *boss* in the way men defer to each other out of respect. He had the masculine radiance of a six-foot earthworm.

His features didn't help. He had a bland, pasty look. If he had worn khakis with an outdated windbreaker and sat on park benches all day, he would've been suspect number one on the neighborhood watch list.

However, he'd somehow avoided those fashion mistakes. All of his clothes were expertly tailored and purchased from high-end apparel stores. His glasses had black box rims that gave him an air of authority. He swept his hair back with an expert amount of gel. Very Gary Oldman, minus the movie star's charisma.

Despite the great wardrobe, he was still awkward in a way that made people avoid prolonged conversations with him. At the same time, he was surprisingly kind, and would occasionally shock his colleagues by being extraordinarily compassionate.

Unfortunately, since he worked for DARPA in a quasi-military environment, this just made him even stranger.

Had anyone cared to know, Penbrook could tell stories that would make a grown man want to curl him up in a fetal position and rock him back and forth like a new baby.

DARPA tolerated his rise through the ranks because of one important quality—he had the strategic mind of a Vulcan. Plus, he wasn't exactly out of place. DARPA had a long history of working with misfits and weirdos.

This flexibility was their great genius as an organization. They operated as a centralized hub and, like the ringmaster in a circus, made sure all the strange projects they paid for, and the bizarre but brilliant minds they encouraged, kept doing what they did best—unlocking the secrets of the universe, so the United States of America could continue to live in safety and security.

Penbrook fit nicely into DARPA's world. Nothing suited him better. When he was given the directorship for DR-Ultra, it seemed his life had been arranged like components on a circuit board.

Then he met a little girl who had been injured. There were many ways to describe what happened when he met her, but he liked to call it becoming a father.

It was as if a dormant mutation rewrote every strand of his DNA. The child radiated an infinite list of needs, most profoundly the desire to be protected and loved. The minute he was exposed to that radiation, he transformed and swooped in to heroically use his latent nurturing powers. It was astonishing.

In those early days, the love he felt for the little girl had not clouded his judgment. That had changed. Like all flawed creatures, Penbrook had his share of vulnerabilities. And, while the best intelligence officers in the government would've never predicted it, he became a target. A target of an emergent threat that had grown in plain sight.

Accepting this realization was proving to be one of the most painful emotional events in his life—and he had a long history of those. How would he clean up this mess? Undoubtedly, he needed help.

Luckily, the first solution was in the chair next to him.

He cleared his throat and said, "I understand you fought with the Kurdish Women's Protection Unit in Syria?"

"Yes, with the YPJ. We fought against Daesh or, as you call them, ISIS." Fatima said.

"Your file says you were their best sniper."

"That's true."

"You're familiar with this Bishop unit called Echo Squad?"

"Yes, I met them in Syria. They were our contact with the DoD. They were the ones responsible for delivering a resupply of weapons. That never happened. We trusted them too easily."

"An unfortunate misunderstanding."

"I have another interpretation of it."

Penbrook paused, hoping she'd elaborate, but Fatima turned away and looked out the window.

"I recognized your codename as one of the operators who field-tested the EXACTO system."

"You mean the *magic bullet*?"

"Yes. I understand you used it in direct combat? But I couldn't find your final report."

"Perhaps you missed it. It was very short. Your bullets didn't work."

"Well, that is the nature of a field test on an active battlefield. Sometimes prototypes fail."

Fatima gave him a hard look as if to say she was sure he didn't understand the first thing about an active battlefield.

He decided to redirect the conversation. "Are you aware this mission involves Echo Squad?"

Fatima perked up. "Please explain."

"My organization used them to guard shipments of experimental weapons. Six months ago, they disappeared while moving a rather large cache of new equipment. The Reaper team found two of them. They are engaged in a recovery operation as we speak. I suspect they'll have two men in custody by the time we land.

"Custody?" Fatima asked.

"We need information," Penbrook said with a dash of apology in his tone. "I want to know who they are working for."

"Where do I fit into this?"

"I need you to help the team find the other members. DR-Ultra has concerns about our main tactical operator, Captain Nicks. I believe your experience will assure the success of the operation."

"Do you share this concern about this *woman?*"

"When the mission is over, and you've filed your report, we can discuss that and what to do about it."

She held his gaze until he felt forced to look away.

"I can't prove it yet. But I believe Echo was also involved in the theft of one of our most important projects to date. I want you to make sure Reaper Force recovers it as soon as possible. The remaining members of Echo Squad are our best lead."

"You said they were working for someone?"

"These are trained operators, but stealing Starfire required a certain strategic flair that I don't believe they possess."

"And this Project Starfire is—"

"—a present danger to us all. You are cleared to bring these men in by any means necessary, as long as it leads to the safe return of the project."

She seemed to love the sound of that. "Maybe climbing into this goddamned airplane was worth it."

Penbrook offered a brief smile and said, "The Reaper team often encounters enemies with advanced weaponry. You might need your own." He handed her a small tactical box. "The EXACTO system you tested has been perfected. I understand you prefer your own equipment, but if you change your mind, here's a token of my appreciation. These won't fail."

She opened the case. Inside was a small optical guidance mount for her rifle and a specially-designed box magazine with six 12.7 cartridges.

One bullet each for the members of Echo Squad.

8

PRESENT DAY

The temple was silent now. Fragrant incense burned on the altar. Black fingers of smoke reached through the candlelight out into the dark space as the temple maiden sat in front of the main shrine and breathed in the perfume. She closed her brown eyes and cleared her troubled mind.

Riza Azmara was twenty years old but her small frame—a few inches past five feet and barely one hundred pounds—gave the impression of a young child, not a woman in the middle of establishing one of the deadliest espionage organizations anyone had ever conceived.

She pulled back the hood of her white robe, exposing her strange appearance—a shocking blend of beauty and horror. Tan skin. Dark full eyebrows. High cheekbones reminiscent of her beautiful Afghan mother.

On the left side of her head, long silky strands of gorgeous black hair fell down over her shoulder. From a certain angle, you'd never guess she was disfigured.

Since the accident, the right side of her scalp was covered in scars and incapable of growing hair. Instead, she wore thick fiber optic cables rooted into stainless steel ports embedded in her scalp.

Each cable was capped with a micro-antenna resembling a metal bead. The cables looked like dreadlocks and seemed to be alive. Red LED lights within the antennae blinked like eyes. From her right side, she gave the impression of a young Medusa.

She relaxed and reflected on her progress.

Almost everything the organization needed was now in the temple. It was fitting that the base of operations would be a sacred site. To her, this war was a divine calling.

The organization would make itself known in several phases. First, she would gather allies, intelligence, and secure weapons. Second, she would implement a series of guerrilla attacks against DR-Ultra to plant the important psychological seeds of surprise, fear, doubt, and uncertainty. In the midst of that confusion, she would secure information about their most prized weapon. She needed to understand how to control the weapon properly. Finally, she would turn that weapon against them. This carried the most risk, because if the mission failed, the whole organization would be compromised. But Riza was sure this was the key to victory.

This was an attack on the United States, but also the preparation for a global war on the military industrial complex. This battle, decades overdue, could be the only thing capable of saving humanity from complete annihilation.

The preliminary work was done. She had established a secret base. Regular flights of hijacked drones supplied the temple at night. They brought equipment, tactical gear, rations, and other necessities that would allow a dedicated team to live in the hidden retreat for several years without resupply.

Her army, the pawns in her game, would come from the world of private contractors. She had no problem allowing these honorless mercenaries to die for her cause, as long as they fulfilled the mission.

The money to fund the syndicate would come from DARPA just like the equipment and weapons had. Military contracts were so fat, they allowed for a certain percentage of "unaccounted for" losses. Skimming funds from hundreds of dormant accounts had already filled the coffers with enough income to make the operation viable for decades to come. The money was hidden in the dark corners of the web and watched by a notorious accountant known only as The Rook.

Data transmission and encrypted access to the Internet was achieved by hacking into secure military networks, and piggy-backing onto classified NSA spy nodes. She controlled all of this, personally using the ingenious network she had created at her base.

The most difficult aspect of the preparation was the dedication it required. For inspiration, she'd remember the owner of the teahouse. The old woman proved it didn't matter the age or gender or class of a soldier. Warriors were born when people were shaken out of their apathy and confronted with the specter of real evil.

The old woman did everything to coexist with the forest, the animals, and the ancient temple. However, when the dharma was disturbed she sacrificed her own life to restore the balance. Riza would do the same.

If she didn't stop the rise of secret military technology, the entire world would suffer just as she had. She would destroy DARPA along with everything and everyone that supported it.

This was the purpose of her war.

This was her destiny.

Suddenly, an alarm sounded breaking her meditation. Riza opened her eyes and scanned the bank of computer screens.

Someone was walking up the path to the temple's main door triggering the perimeter alarms.

Recognizing the face of the intruder, she disabled the automated defenses. Then, carefully and methodically, disconnected herself from the elaborate web-like apparatus surrounding her. It was so important to be precise. Any variation from the procedure could cause lasting neurological damage.

Once that was done, she stood up, pulled her white hood back over her head and made her way to the main chamber of the temple. There she greeted her most important ally—the woman who had tested Viper.

Lida Laram was essential to their operation. Her loyalty and abilities proved she was the best choice for chief operative. If she was inspired, she would sacrifice everything to ensure their success. A set of orders wasn't enough. She needed a challenge that channeled her rage into meaningful action.

Riza handed Lida the sword with the scorpion handle.

"I put all my faith in you, as you have me," she said.

Lida bowed, as befitted the honor. "You know the plans. Establish the network among our allies. Eliminate the loose ends. Then draw our enemies into the open. This will be the greatest challenge of your life." She stared into her old friend's eyes. "I believe this sword is a sign of victory."

"Have you had another vision?" Lida asked.

"Yes, but part of it is unclear. This katana will return to the temple covered in blood. Whose blood covers the blade is the mystery—either the Scorpion or the Viper."

"I'll make sure it is the latter," Lida said.

Riza smiled and broadcast her thoughts into Lida's mind.

It will happen just as it should.

She was sure of it. They both were.

PART IV

WHEELS OF CONFUSION

B right California sunlight warmed the gentle breeze drifting over the lush garden and through the windows, of the Angelos Grove Estate—the place Natalie Nicks now called home. There was a distinct smell of fresh-brewed coffee on that breeze, tempting Nicks from her warm bed. She stretched and thought about what had happened in the warehouse.

She couldn't stop thinking about Wilson's haunting comment as he lay dying in her arms. What did he mean about someone in his mind? She definitely needed coffee if she was going to make sense of any of what had happened.

She rolled out of the covers, and scurried to the bathroom. After a quick shower, she threw on a pair of black jeans, a vintage Led Zeppelin t-shirt, and eased her way downstairs.

The compound was a multi-million dollar property owned by DARPA and hidden in the Hollywood Hills. It was their assigned headquarters, and the West Coast base for DR-Ultra. The team both lived and worked there. Nicks loved it. It was one of the few luxuries of her job.

The estate had been inherited from a researcher who bilked millions from DARPA, researching psychic phenomenon. He was infamous for his dubious experiments into ESP, telepathy, and remote viewing.

Named Angelos, after a goddess of the underworld, it was used for his bizarre studies into psychedelics and parapsychology. When the science failed to produce results, and the scam was exposed, the estate's deed was handed over to DARPA as repayment for an unfulfilled million-dollar research contract about the time Jack Byrne had been put in charge of the task force.

Because the library and adjoining labs were made exclusively out of metal, the structure was grounded, making it impenetrable to radio waves and other forms of electro-magnetic interference. This kind of room was called a Faraday Cage, named after the famous physicist Michael Faraday. The previous owner had built it to measure psychic phenomenon in a controlled environment.

When Byrne moved in, he made sure all the rooms that composed the Faraday Cage became their main workspace. It was a fantastic workspace for those dealing with sensitive electronics and provided another layer of security from electronic eavesdropping. Byrne joked it was their secret headquarters, The Cage for short.

After a stop in the kitchen, Nicks strolled into the Cage carrying a steaming pot of hot coffee and two mugs. She sat in the library at the big round table.

A welder in a dented metal helmet and a pair of tattered heat-resistant gloves appeared from around the corner. "Is Byrne up yet?"

"Yep. I heard him up there. He should be down soon," Nicks said. "Want some coffee?"

The welder lifted her heat shield. "Yes, please." It was Sergeant Maggie Quinn, the third member of Reaper Force.

Nicks filled a mug as Maggie flopped into the chair. She let out a big sigh. "I have the Ghostrider running. Cut the weight down to 150 kilos, and I've doubled the power of the engine."

"What about the sound?"

"Purrs like a kitten—even to those posh ears of yours."

Quinn's work on the new stealth motorcycle had taken months to get right. It had all the power of a normal dirt bike but none of the noise.

"When do I get to take it for a spin?"

"After I've broken it in. I wouldn't want you to bust your ass on my account."

"Come on, Mags. I'm the ideal test pilot."

"Don't you dare touch that thing, Nat, until I say so!"

Quinn's perfectionism made her vicious when others messed with her workshop, tools, or new projects.

"Okay, when you say it's ready." Nicks raised her hands in mock surrender.

They sipped their coffee and watched the clock. A moment's calm before the inevitable storm.

Quinn was the team's quartermaster and chief engineer with a specialty in advanced weaponry. Her number one project was Nicks. She was constantly helping her tweak the idiosyncrasies of the TALON technology. She was like a car mechanic and doctor rolled into one very smart, no nonsense woman.

After all the excitement of being processed through the TALON program, Nicks underwent a series of upgrades. Modifications seemed to go on forever. That's when she met the team.

First, it was Byrne. He hobbled in one day, a young man

with a cane, dressed like one of the medical staff, and read her chart. He asked about her morning, not bothering to listen to the reply. With no formal discussions or even asking permission, he went to work.

"Let's see it," he said. He pulled back the sheet exposing one arm and her near nakedness. She recoiled and prickled at his touch.

"I know this is a lot to deal with, I've been where you are. It's scary sometimes." He flashed her a reassuring smile. "Okay if I continue?"

She nodded. He proceeded more gently, and rolled back the artificial skin covering her forearm. He put on a pair of magnifying lenses and, like a wise-old watchmaker, tinkered with the controller board buried just above the wrist rotator joint.

That was the first of many times he made needed adjustments, all of which got her back in the game. He was critical to her recovery.

He carried with him solutions not only to her bioengineering problems, but her emotional ones as well. By accepting her unconditionally, he helped her begin the real healing. Their affair was short but passionate. As it came to an end, Nicks decided she needed more specialized help.

"Do you realize your engineers have no idea what it's like to be a woman?" she complained to Byrne one day.

"Well, none of them are," he replied.

"Yeah, why the hell is that?"

Byrne shrugged. "We don't have any on this team."

"Yet, your main guinea pig is one."

"They treat you like a soldier, with respect. Isn't that good enough?"

"I am a soldier and I'm a woman. The next person who touches any of my body parts, whether they are the pink, soft kind, or the hard metal kind, better know what it is like to have her tits flatten like pancakes behind body armor. I want someone who understands the job and knows how to give this robot an oil change with a little female finesse."

A few weeks later, Maggie Quinn appeared.

She was a rare breed with a rough background like Nicks. They made the perfect pair. At the time she was recruited for Reaper Force, she was one of the few female British SAS soldiers, a position that was classified and considered just as innovative as her genius for engineering. Working in the 21 SAS Reserve, she made a name for herself because she could tear down and rebuild anything from a helicopter engine to a predator drone. They called her the Gremlin.

The cherry on top—she was good with other important tools like bladed weapons and machine-guns—*deadly* good. It took thirty minutes and half a bottle of tequila for her and Nicks to bond like they had been serving together for years.

Quinn was a colorful woman. Soft around a titanium core. One of the toughest members of their team. She had blue eyes and dark red hair usually tied back in a braid. Tattoos that were homages to classic punk bands like the Sex Pistols covered her body.

She was stouter than Nicks and an inch shorter, standing about five-six. She gave off the masculine vibe of a dive-bar bouncer—it wasn't hard to guess she preferred women in bed.

She lifted weights aggressively, and it showed—that had been necessary growing up on the wrong side of the tracks in a shitty part of Southampton, on the south coast of England.

"I had a rough upbringing," Quinn told her when they first met. "If a dog in my town had two ears, they called him a sissy. But I'll tell you one thing, they *never* called me that or I knocked 'em on their ass!"

"Speaking of mutts with one ear, you think you're good enough to keep me tuned up?"

"When I'm offered a shit sandwich, I pour on the ketchup and get to it." She laughed. "In other words, don't worry, I can handle you."

Bond had Q. Nicks had Quinn. She became vital to the team and, over time, she became family.

Colonel Jack Byrne creaked into the Cage holding out an empty coffee mug like a beggar bumming spare change.

Nicks looked at him. Byrne was what her Uncle Wilco called a corn-fed bullet sponge. A thirty-something green beret that stood six-three and weighed about two bills. You could mistake him for your typical close-cropped Army meathead, but Byrne was one of the best soldiers the United States had ever trained. He excelled as an effective Special Forces Operator and held multiple degrees in medicine and biophysics.

Due to injuries he'd sustained, he wore special mechanical braces on both legs, had a long list of medical problems, and sometimes used a cane. Nowadays, he used his brain instead his brawn to lead the team.

He was ruggedly handsome when his forehead wasn't twisted in his infamous angry scowl. Seeing Byrne *problem-pissed*, as he called it, was rare because his mind worked like a super-computer. Give him the right input, and he'd have an answer in seconds.The prior night had been a rare exception. They'd both been caught off-guard.

As the processors whirled behind his blue eyes, he raked his large hands through his brown hair as if he might pull it out by the roots. She reached over and playfully tried to flatten out his furrowed brow.

"Easy Colonel, you'll break your pretty face."

"I hope not; it's the one part of me that still works." He chuckled as his grimace softened.

Quinn poured him a cup of coffee. Then refilled her own mug and asked, "You two bugger up the op?"

"More like, the op buggered me," Nicks said.

"Is that why Penbrook is making a house call?" Quinn asked Byrne.

"I thinks so," he said, as walked across the room and sat down at his own workbench. "He hasn't sent me the agenda."

"That's easy," Nicks said, loudly. "The agenda should be figuring out why the hell DARPA tech just attacked one of its own."

"Bloody hell, what happened?" Quinn asked.

Nicks leaned in and explained how they tracked Declan Wilson into the warehouse and found the stolen gear, how the Caduceus drones attacked them both in the basement, and how she was surprised by the ambush of the MAARS and Sniper Drone.

Quinn punctuated the dramatic parts with expletives and slapping the table with her welder gloves. She was shocked Nicks had made it out alive.

Nicks circled back to the moment where she carried Wilson across the warehouse and the MAARS unleashed hell.

"Jack already knows this, but it happened again, Mags. I lost control of my left arm. It went dead on me. I could've saved him if I'd moved faster."

"You had to look after yourself, didn't you? Or you'd be here on this table, tits up, waiting on a toe tag."

Nicks stared over Quinn's shoulder, lost in her own thoughts.

"I'll give you the once over before the Boss gets here."

Nicks stared Quinn in the eye. "So, no lecture?"

"What do I say that hasn't been said already?"

They moved over to Quinn's workbench, and Nicks laid out

for inspection. Quinn flipped the master switch on her setup and her whole side of the Cage lit up.

Her fingers danced over a keyboard and fired up her *Upgrading Viper Playlist*. The sound of Joy Division beating on a metal trashcan reverberated through the room.

The lyrics from *She's Lost Control* blared.

Nicks groaned. "Real funny, wise-ass!"

Quinn swung a scanner mounted on an articulated arm over Nicks upper body. The monitors lit up. Quinn enlarged the image and focused it on Nicks's left side. Every detail of her cybernetic arm appeared in beautiful high-definition. Quinn jokingly called it the NAT Scan.

"When were you having problems?"

"When I picked up Wilson and ran for cover. It started twitching and went numb."

Quinn responded with the tone of a disappointed mother. "So, the exact time you needed it to work the most."

"Shut up, just fix it."

Quinn turned to her computer. Nicks watched on the large monitor as she pulled up a secure terminal, and typed several lines of green code into the little black rectangle. Quinn waited. Nothing happened. She tried it again and got an error message.

"What the hell? I can't access the TALON database."

"Is that an issue?" Nicks asked.

"Not really, I have it backed up here. By the way, keep that on the down low, no one knows. But, to get the updates, I login to Blackwood almost every day." An error message flashed across the terminal once more. "That's weird. I've never had an issue before."

Quinn closed down the terminal and opened her backup. After a few minutes, a file about the TALON bionics appeared on the screen. Quinn read it over and turned back to Nicks.

"So what's the damage?" Nicks asked.

"Not a damn thing is wrong. This is signal loss. The TALON protocols for your arm, hand, legs, and ears prevent interruptions in your signal processing. There wasn't enough viable nerve tissue to rewire you completely. If you don't use the protocols, you'll keep getting in these jams. Your arm may stop functioning all together. And, since it's happening under times of immense stress, during missions, you'll be incapacitated at the worst moments. I understand your feelings but we always come back to the same argument."

"Engage the protocols?"

"Yes luv, engage the *bloody* protocols!"

Nicks turned away in frustration. Accepting a machine made her a better human was a pill she couldn't swallow. "I don't want a *computer* pulling my strings like I'm a damn puppet."

"It's an artificial intelligence agent, an AI, not a computer. Same code that controls the Cage."

"Flux?"

"Yeah, Flux."

"*Fuck* Flux!"

This wasn't Quinn's fault. The TALON team explained it to her ad nauseam during her rehabilitation. Nicks knew the nerves in a human body had a certain natural flow. The nerve endings created sensations, and those sensations became electrical signals that activated impulses throughout the body.

The artificial intelligence agent used algorithms to enhance her signal processing. It also made her more powerful and more skilled at combat. She could run faster, jump higher, and her reaction times were off the charts. But Nicks hated the loss of control she felt when the AI was operating. And, it seemed like a self-betrayal. Since losing her parents at a young age, people had insinuated, or flat out told her she had problems that needed to be fixed, handing the reigns over to this machine seemed to confirm they were right—she hated giving in —hated it!

But that wasn't the worst of it.

The bigger issue was the quantum cortex where Flux lived. It was the most advanced piece of tech in her body. The pièce de résistance. The masterwork of the TALON program. It had been implanted in her hippocampus. For storage, it relied upon the same brain circuits that encoded human memories. Her brain cells were Flux's hard drive. Heavy use of the protocols had the side effect of erasing her oldest memories. These included the few vivid ones of her parents before they died— experiences and feelings that made her who she was. This was where she drew the line.

"We've been over this a *thousand* times, Nat. You know where I stand," Quinn said.

Yes, she did.

Unfortunately, the one thing the protocols didn't do was help Nicks process the fact she wasn't completely human anymore.

"I just can't do it," Nicks said as she got off the table.

Quinn shrugged. "You are always going to be more powerful than a normal human. But without the computing help of Flux, you're only using about a third of your full potential. Even then, that power will only be available for five or ten minutes before it fails and you have more problems."

"I'll take my chances."

Nicks fumed for a few minutes and sat back at the table to finish her coffee. Eyeing the screen, she noticed Quinn was still trying to login to the database

"Any ideas about how those drones were hijacked?" Nicks asked to change the subject.

Quinn finally gave up on the database and joined her at the table.

"If you have copies of all the software, you could install the drivers on almost anything. A computer tablet for instance. You wouldn't have to be in the building just inside the acceptable range of the drones. But I don't see how that could've happened. This is DR-Ultra tech we are talking about. Nobody could hack it."

"Unless they worked for our organization."

"Yeah, but we know everyone on the inside. DR-Ultra isn't that big."

She thought Quinn had dismissed that possibility a little too easy. "We know everyone on the inside ... *yeah sure* ... then why can't you login to the TALON database?"

"You're out of your mind!" Quinn's mouth dropped open. "You don't think?"

Nicks gave her a steely look.

Yeah, she did.

Sabotage was always a possibility.

Across the room, Byrne's smartphone chimed and buzzed, threatening to vibrate itself right off his workbench. Byrne stopped typing on his computer and grabbed the phone.

Nicks watched him take the call. As he talked, his infamous corrugated scowl returned to his face.

He hung up and said, "The Boss is en route."

Nicks rolled her eyes. If she was lucky, that meant maybe a half-hour before they had to saddle up again.

"Hmmm ... he didn't ask about the tech," Byrne mused, as he put down the phone.

"Which means what?" Nicks asked.

"He's after something more important than that stolen equipment."

Nicks took that to mean one thing—the real mission hadn't revealed itself yet.

She thought about the night before. Who—*or what*—had

killed Chapman and spooked Wilson so badly? Who set up that ambush?

More importantly, why would this new enemy hunt her? She had no idea but she was determined to find out one way or the other.

10

THE NOMAD CARD CLUB, LOS ANGELES, CA

"You can count on my allegiance," The Rook said.

The modest Asian man had close-cropped silver hair and thick wire-rimmed glasses. He wore a cream-colored suit expertly tailored for his slim frame. He spoke softly and with courtesy. No one would have suspected he was one of the most notorious money launderers in the underworld. Only his most important clients met with him face-to-face.

Scorpio slid a jewelry box across the table as if she were placing all her chips on black. The man leaned forward to admire it.

"A gift for your loyalty."

He opened it carefully. It was a silver ring. In the light he saw the signet was a skull. Flames encircled the skull's head like hair. "Quite beautiful," he said taking it out. He noticed the band wasn't a complete circle. The shanks flared out like prongs.

"A very strange ring ..." He handed the jewelry back to Scorpio. "I don't understand."

"Turn around," she commanded.

The man bristled. Anyone else with that tone would have

lost their tongue. But this was a moment he relished. So, he stood and turned obediently.

Scorpio folded down his collar and traced her finger down his neck provocatively. She took out a small device that looked like a plastic handgun and loaded the ring into its spring-loaded chamber. Aiming it at his neck, she felt for the correct position once more, lined up the device, and pulled the trigger. The ring shot into his spine like a carpentry staple fastening itself to a piece of wood.

The Rook stumbled forward, more out of shock than pain. The woman admired her work, took a picture with her phone, and showed it to him. He was speechless.

Scorpio smiled coyly.

A look of bewildered euphoria spread across the man's face as he heard the voice for the first time. It came from within his own mind.

Welcome to the council, Mr. Rook. You are among the first. I hope your contribution befits the honor.

"Thank you, mistress," he said, rubbing his neck.

He reached into his suit jacket and pulled out a folded piece of paper. He broke its wax seal and opened it.

"These are the current balances on the organization's accounts. As soon as the new transfers are complete, I will notify you with utmost urgency."

No need. I'll be watching. Always watching.

The Rook didn't know what to do next, so he bowed to Scorpio.

"She's chosen you to organize several phases of our expansion," Scorpio said. "Starting with the operation in Mexico."

"It'll be my honor," he said. "I already have contacts in the Draco organization."

"Good. I also need a meeting with one of your associates but it must be handled delicately. He's been a reluctant recruit to our cause."

"Can I have his name?"

"General Marcel Bishop."

He paused and cleared his throat, "I'll take care of it immediately."

"I know you will," Scorpio said. She was already leaving the room. Her work was done. Another skull in the crown was secure and more would follow.

11

M ansions filled the Hollywood Hills. They teetered on the edge of unstable cliffs like the wishes and dreams of the people who lived in them.

This was a land of misdirection. The houses, made of mirrored glass and draped in curtains, sheltered magicians and their grand illusions. Establishing the headquarters of Reaper Force deep in the heart of such a place allowed them to hide in plain sight.

Helicopters hovered over the hills every day. Ghetto birds from the Hollywood Division chased suspected criminals high into the twisting streets. News choppers watching the traffic flew over the 101 highway. Entertainment reporters circled like birds over movie premieres at the Chinese Theater.

People living up here accepted such annoyances as if the machines were nothing but hummingbirds buzzing around their garden.

No one gave Penbrook's arrival a second thought—except Byrne. He'd been checking the helipad cameras every five minutes. When the proximity alarms finally sounded, he was on his feet, cane in hand.

"Look sharp, the Boss is on deck," he bellowed.

The team jumped up and headed to the roof.

Nicks respected Penbrook, but she didn't trust him. Did anyone trust their boss? If they were smart, probably not. They may want to please their supervisor. They may even like their personality. Trust, well, that was another story. Distrust was the nature of her chosen profession. Espionage was a dark art. She operated in the shadows where nothing was as it seemed and trust was a liability.

Shadow state? Yes, of course it existed.

Shadow government? That was real too.

Shadow military? No question about it. She was part of it.

These things were like the quantum particles her science friends had tried to explain to her. The minute you tried to investigate, they would vanish from existence, shadows spinning the polarity of reality, putting your own existence at risk. From that point, you'd be the one called into question.

Suffice it to say, she had suspicions about Penbrook. It was a personal hunch, not his notoriously weird manner. Penbrook was a spider in the corner she couldn't ignore. His secrets had secrets. But she made sure her skepticism didn't impede their working relationship. She took orders and carried them out with few questions.

After Penbrook's copter landed, a young brunette with a stylish scarf wrapped around her face climbed out. She directed two Delta Team soldiers to unload what they'd brought—two black body bags. She picked up her duffel which seemed to be a rifle case and followed behind them.

When Nicks and Byrne stepped out to greet her, she signaled to the soldiers to drop the bodies right in front of them.

"In my culture, you always bring a gift. Hope you like mine," she said, and walked right past them to the elevators like she owned the place.

"Who in the hell—" Nicks hissed.

"Our new teammate," Byrne muttered.

Quinn winked at Nicks and purred, "I love her already."

"It seems our investigation of Echo Squad has taken an unexpected turn," Penbrook began.

Everyone was sitting at the round table, all eyes glued to their leader.

"After the ambush at the warehouse, I directed two Delta teams to secure the building. As you saw, they recovered the remains of Wilson and Chapman. The rest of the equipment, whether or not it is operational, is being moved here as we speak. We'll use basement level two, since it is only accessible by Colonel Byrne, to keep it secure."

Penbrook handed Byrne a thumb drive.

"One of the Delta technicians was able to download the Sniper Drone's video. Colonel, could you play this on your monitor please?"

Byrne uploaded the video file. Everyone leaned in as the clip started. The first image was the corner of a rooftop. The drone lifted off vertically and hovered. The camera scanned the horizon, turning a full 360 degrees, before it targeted the warehouse where all the action had gone down. It flew toward the building, and settled into a flight path parallel to the east alleyway. Seconds later, it targeted Nicks, who was running in the distance. The team watched as Byrne arrived and took the drone down with his confetti canon. The transmission ended.

"Replay the feed from the point of takeoff," Penbrook said.

Byrne reversed the footage. The drone began its scan of the horizon.

"Stop it there, and play it back in slow motion."

"Who the hell is that?" Nicks asked pointing at the screen.

Someone was in the shadows, barely visible. You'd miss it at normal speed. Byrne paused the clip and zoomed in on the figure. The person was holding a piece of equipment watching the drone take off.

"Yes, indeed, that is the question of the moment," Penbrook said. "I had the footage cleaned up and analyzed. Our facial recognition software had a difficult time with it. But we got a result."

Penbrook pointed at the screen prompting Byrne to open the next file. It was a short but heavily redacted Defense Intelligence Agency profile of a woman named Lida Laram.

"Her codename is Scorpio. She's an asset DR-Ultra had a hand in developing. A decision was made to field test her earlier this year, against the advice of the PM's at Blackwood Lodge. She went rogue during the mission and we lost contact with her.

"It seems obvious from this small bit of evidence she was involved in the warehouse ambush. I feel sure Scorpio is connected to the disappearance of Project Starfire. But we need more intel. That's where Reaper Force comes in."

Quinn interrupted. "You mentioned Project Starfire. I'm not familiar."

"No one on this team is, and it has to stay that way. All I can say is it must be returned." Penbrook cleared his throat.

The team glanced at each other. Penbrook was odd, but he rarely held back information.

"The immediate mission is to find the other members of Echo Squad."

He pointed to Fatima, who was sitting beside Byrne. Her belongings were on the floor beside her. She didn't look like she was staying long.

"I'm assigning Ms. Nasrallah to your team to assist in this mission. She will help you track down the rest of these men. We need to know what they know about this operation. If you encounter Scorpio, stand down. She is a deadly operator, an expert in hand-to-hand combat, with kinetic scores superior to any asset I've ever encountered. Do not engage her. Let Nasrallah do that. She has the skills to handle her from a safe distance. "

Nicks tried to swing the conversation around to the ambush. She wanted to talk about her strange conversation with Wilson and the clues discovered in the basement.

Penbrook cut her off. "Captain, I think you misunderstand me. The *only* mission right now is finding Project Starfire. Everything else goes to the back burner. Is that *clear?*

Nicks stiffened. Penbrook had never openly challenged her like that.

"Yes, sir. Project Starfire. We're on it."

General Marcel Bishop regarded her silently with dagger-like eyes. He'd loathed her from the outset. Yes, he had built a career on bowing to distasteful authoritarians but that time had come and gone. He was king of his own kingdom now, and this upstart wasn't going to back him into a corner no matter how enticing the offer might be.

"I'm not discussing this any further," he said. "Those men have gone to ground, and if we can't find them, I doubt anyone else can."

"They were one of your best units?" Scorpio countered.

"Yes, that's true. But someone spooked them. I'm wondering if that someone was *you?*"

Scorpio didn't argue the point. Her orders were to tie up loose ends and she needed intel to find those men.

"Their counterintelligence skills are top notch," he continued. "I'm guessing they knew you wanted to take them off the board."

"They've drawn attention from the enemy."

"That has complicated things. But the equipment theft was

a good ruse. It will slow Reaper Force down. I'll see what I can do to find Echo."

"I need the files for anyone that's been associated with them. In fact, it would be best to have access to the records for all of your assets. A backdoor into your network would suffice."

"I'll deal with *her* on that, not you! I built this company from the ground up. I'm not handing over an entire army without a better deal."

"I thought you were a true believer, General Bishop?"

"If I have a seat at the table and your organization can deliver on what *she* is promising. I'm all in."

She took out a jewelry box and pushed it across the table.

The man opened it and admired what looked like a skull ring.

"What is this?"

"Your seat at the table. She welcomes you with open arms."

General Bishop grinned. It was the first genuine smile in years.

13

Quinn handed Byrne a Styrofoam box. Dry ice smoked through its seams. "It's evidence from the Delta Team. They found it in the basement."

Byrne accepted the box like it was a bomb and took it over to his examination table. "Neutralize the static on the table, please."

Quinn threw a double-pole knife switch and the static dissipated. Byrne placed the package down.

"We'll need this during the autopsy to make some comparisons, thanks."

"I'll give our new friend a tour and get her settled," Quinn said, as she led Fatima to the stairs. "Be back in a few."

"Take all the time you need," Nicks said.

Byrne could hear the irritation in her voice. When Quinn and Fatima were out of earshot, he needled Nicks. "What's wrong? Aren't you eager to socialize?"

"Not unless you're giving me an order," she joked.

They prepared Chapman's remains for an official autopsy. Byrne pointed at a sterile gown on a metal tray. She put it on along with a pair of surgical gloves and joined him at the table. Her venting continued.

"Do you know her? I sure as hell don't."

"Heard her codename mentioned a few times—goes by Cartwheel—she's trained at The Farm. No bad chatter about her that I know of."

"She's a spook, then?"

"She's one of us. DIA not CIA."

The Defense Intelligence Agency was smaller than the Central Intelligence Agency but just as skilled when it came to espionage. Intelligence recruits were assigned to the Defense Clandestine Services, one arm of the DIA, and trained at Camp Perry, aka The Farm, alongside CIA officers. Unlike the CIA, the DIA's main loyalty was to the Department of Defense. Other differences were apparent when it came to the missions they took on. For instance, the CIA didn't like chasing down lost weapons, even if they were straight out of the oven. The DIA made those assignments a priority.

"I'll try to cut her some slack," Nicks said. "But what's up with the Boss? That has to be the shortest meeting I've ever had on this team—and one of the strangest."

"I agree. Something's off. I'd like to know more about this Project Starfire. The Boss seems to be twisted up about it. Maybe he's under too much pressure from on high?"

"Since when do we go into the field not knowing what we are looking for?"

"Since never."

"What are we going to do about it?"

"We do what we always do—our job." He handed her a pair of surgical forceps and pointed at the box.

Inside the box was an evidence bag. Nicks extracted the objects from the bag and placed them under the focusing ring of their high-powered microscope. Monitors hanging over the table came to life with an analysis of the object.

"I remember these. They were on the altar next to the treasure chest," Nicks said. A memory of Chapman's severed head flashed through her mind. "I thought it was a bowl full of coins."

Byrne studied if for several minutes.

"Close. This is a *kapala*. Some call them skullcaps. Normally found in Buddhist temples. It is a sacred bowl carved from a human cranium. Not as nice as some I've seen. Usually, you'd polish it and stick a few precious jewels on it."

"You have a few lying around your room, do you?"

"Only a few," he said, sarcastically. "This one isn't as ornate. I guess the killer didn't have time to decorate it."

"If those Caduceus drones can remove heads and decorate them, I'm retiring."

Byrne stepped closer, amazed at the intricate detail. The skull had marks on it that looked hand-carved. A small metallic wire was fitted in one of the grooves.

"There's no way the drone did this, no way," Nicks said.

"I agree. It seems someone spent time with Mr. Chapman."

"What's up with the coins?"

Byrne took his forceps and placed them in a line next to the kapala. The imaging device hovered over each as it scanned the objects. A magnified image of the first coin appeared on the monitor.

Neither of them could make sense of the objects. Byrne rearranged them as if they were pieces of a puzzle. After trying several configurations, he found a way to fit the fragments into a recognizable whole.

Nicks let out a small gasp. Byrne gave her a knowing glance.

She'd seen x-rays of them in her own body. They were bionic components built to facilitate the brain and computer interface necessary to operate cybernetic prosthetics.

"TALON tech?" Nicks wondered. "Why would they have—"

"These men were both *enhanced*."

"By who?"

"I don't know, but we need to find out. Project Starfire may be the priority, but I'm not putting this on the back burner. This changes things."

Nicks turned her head as Fatima and Quinn entered the room. They joined them at the examination table.

Nicks glanced at Fatima suspiciously. "So, fill us in, *Cartwheel*. Why are you here?"

Fatima ignored her, walked over to the monitors, and studied the images.

"Who desecrated his body and put these things inside him?"

"*Desecrated?* That's an interesting choice of words," Quinn said, glancing at Nicks. "I don't think—"

"You don't think people should put machine parts inside their bodies? I absolutely agree!" Fatima locked eyes with Nicks as she spoke.

Nicks tore off the surgical gown and gloves and got nose-to-nose with Fatima.

"What the hell is Project Starfire, Nasrallah?" Nicks asked, each word dripping with venom.

Fatima was a snake waiting to strike. Nicks hoped she would.

"That's the wrong question, *Viper*."

"What's the right one?"

"Why am I here in the first place?" Fatima said, scanning Nicks's body like she had x-ray vision. "The answer is, somebody thinks you're a liability. Didn't you know that?"

She turned to leave the room, and added, "I don't give a damn about Starfire. Maybe it's another shitty robot, not quite up to the task. Either way, I'm here to handle the things *you* can't. For the sake of your team, stay out of my way!"

14

Nicks didn't bother undressing. She was exhausted, still shell-shocked from being attacked, and now, pissed off over the dustup with her new teammate. She rolled over and closed her eyes.

The nightmares were waiting. One of the most frequent —*the interrogation*—faded up from black, like a Netflix show on auto-play.

An invisible force wheeled her bed into the observation chamber. Disembodied hands hooked electrodes to various parts of her body. A blood pressure cuff wrapped around her arm and squeezed. A galvanometer crawled over the sheets and bit her index finger like a baby alligator.

When all the electronics were set up, a team of surgeons in blood-red body exhaust systems entered her recovery room. They looked like villains in a science fiction movie.

Six of them in their strange spacesuits stood in a semicircle around her bed staring and pointing. Their faces were obscured behind their mirrored helmets.

An intercom squelched overhead, and the man standing in the center of the group spoke. "Let the record show TALON

Test Subject 03 is present along with the executive surgical team."

"What is this? Has something *bad* happened?" Nicks asked.

"This is a debriefing about the program, Captain Nicks."

"What program?"

"Just answer the questions as candidly as possible."

Nicks glanced at the cuff and her finger and realized they were monitoring more than her vitals. This was a polygraph.

She challenged the leader. "Is this a debriefing or an interrogation?"

"What do you remember about the attack? Tell us every detail."

FALLING INTO THE SUN.

It was the main thing she remembered. The overpowering and suffocating heat that came with disappearing into the heart of a burning star.

She knew it was coming ten seconds before it happened, but that wasn't enough time to shield her from the blast. It flattened her into the earth like an anvil and hammered her into a different woman.

It was her personal apocalypse.

Months passed as she pieced everything else back together. The memories started with flashbacks. Then, the night terrors—long nights of wrestling in bed sheets drenched in sweat.

The taste of bubble gum was another strange sense-memory. Bazooka bubble gum, to be exact. Rock hard pink bricks twisted in wax wrappers with corny comic strips.

Why? No one had a satisfactory explanation. Her theory was a tiny piece of shrapnel was lodged perfectly in the childhood memory section of her brain. It was a small mercy. Better the candy than the nausea-inducing smell of her own skin melting and sizzling like a steak on a hot grill.

These strange injuries lingered. The other damage had been repaired. *Sort of.*

Nicks's transformation into the bionic woman known as Viper was possible through TALON's proprietary surgical procedures. The concepts of advanced myoneural interfacing, reconstructive muscle pairing, and cybernetic nerve mapping scrolled past as they were reviewed.

TALON's secret sauce that made all of its other advances work came from an unlikely source. It used an innovative amputation procedure that only its team could perform.

The curious thing about human prosthetics was that few researchers had ever tried to improve the amputation procedure. In fact, most amputations were still performed the same way they'd been done in the Civil War.

From that time forward, medical science had focused on improving the prosthetics but these devices were limited by whatever tissue, muscles, tendons, and nerves cells still existed after the routine amputations were completed.

TALON salvaged the undamaged tissues and mapped them to an advanced neural interface. This restored a natural feeling of control. In this way, Viper's artificial parts became indiscernible from her biological ones.

Her bionic left arm was composed of biomimetic bone, graphene, and boron carbide composite. Her right arm was the same, but her right hand was modular, meaning it could be removed without surgery and upgraded faster than her other cybernetic parts.

Special self-healing sleeves, indistinguishable from Viper's remaining skin, covered these components. Sensors embedded in the sleeve gave her all the sensations she had before with one bonus.

The artificial bone was made from some of the strongest material known to man. It allowed the arm to withstand high force pressures, and the artificial muscles were knitted together with carbon nanotubes that allowed for electrical conductivity.

When artificial nerves were mapped to remaining nerve cells, the computer produced a simulation that revealed all the missing pieces. That guided surgeons on what to replace and how to do it properly. Viper wasn't just given prosthetics that were identical in function to her lost body parts; they were better.

Because the damage to Viper's hearing had been so extensive, the TALON surgeons decided both ear canals would be restructured and the machine-brain interface would piggyback onto her left Mark I Cochlear Implant.

The tactical cochlear implants were also experimental. They delivered frequency information at two hundred times the capacity of most hearing devices, providing over five hundred thousand pulses per second. The level of sound detail was far beyond any modern hearing aid.

In sum, one might say all the king's horses and all the king's men put her back together again, but they took a few liberties.

WHEN NICKS FINISHED EXPLAINING the bombing she was raw with emotion. Quite the contrast to her interrogator. His response was about as antiseptic as the room they were in.

"That's enough about the attack." The man said from behind his strange red decontamination suit. "What was your mission in Afghanistan?"

Nicks explained what she remembered—giving Afghan children vaccinations. Her armed escorts were protection because they were operating in the most dangerous part of the country.

Her American accent, and her military equipment and fatigues, made an impression everywhere she went. She tried to blend in with the men. Her face was usually covered in the fine Afghan soil called moon dust. She cut her hair short enough to pass as a man and hid her breasts behind her heavy body armor. Still, everyone knew she was a female.

Her cover as a medic was suspect but believable enough to give her plausible deniability. The real mission was different.

Natalie Nicks was a newly minted clandestine officer for the DIA supervising a Human Terrain Team. They'd sent her to collect data about the population of the Zhari District in Kandahar.

The general wisdom was that those who controlled Kandahar controlled Afghanistan. The Pakistani border region was just past the grape and poppy fields. It was said to be the birthplace of the Taliban. Tarnak Farms, the urban training camp for Osama Bin Laden and his followers, was near the airport. Because of Afghanistan's unique terrain, you couldn't get to the capital without going through Kandahar.

While she gave vaccinations, she used the Handheld Interagency Identity Detection Equipment (HIIDE) unit to collect DNA, fingerprints, retina scans, and facial recognition data. Everybody was processed but special attention was paid to males over the age of twelve. Her real targets were the over nine hundred recently escaped prisoners—hard-core Taliban fighters.

One month prior, those brutal men had been freed during a well-planned assault on a dilapidated, poorly guarded Afghan prison.

The American government wanted those fugitives returned dead or alive. Nicks's job was to find them so special operation teams could pick them up or pick them off.

The assignment thrilled her and she was good at it. Hunting bad guys was a surprising skill she'd discovered after several months in the field. Only one problem—they were hunting her too, and they blew her to hell.

The leader of the blood-colored spacemen waited impatiently for Nicks to finish, cleared his throat and went into an explanation of TALON and its connection to DARPA's super-soldier program. He told Nicks she would be involved in their continuing research.

His presentation seemed to be directed at the onlookers behind the glass more than Nicks. He talked as if her participation was a given.

Another man took the floor to verify her consent. He spoke with a warmer tone. Nicks guessed this was the team shrink.

"Do you understand our offer? Are you willing to join our program?"

"I'm grateful you saved my life, but I think I've done my time. I *really* want to go home," she said.

The men in the red suits let out an audible gasp. They huddled together in the corner and whispered to each other in hushed tones.

"The whole purpose of saving her life was to test out the technology."

"What does she mean she wants to go home?"

"She needs more time."

"Maybe she's cracked."

Nicks tried to interrupt, "Excuse me—"

"We'll have to remove that arm ..."

"She's hot though—I'd bang her. Arm or not."

"Hey guys, can I interrupt—"

"Give the tech to a better soldier ..."

"HEY GUYS!" Nicks screamed.

The leader turned around and barked at her. "Captain Nicks, most of us out rank you, how dare you speak to us—"

"—I heard everything you dip-shits just said. I have *cybernetic ears*. Remember?"

In fact, the detail was so advanced she recognized several of the men in the suits just by their voice pattern. The Secretary of Defense was one. The director of DARPA was another.

The men in decontamination suits stopped talking. They stared at Nicks and she stared back. For the first time, the balance of fear shifted. Nicks was pissed.

"Give her arm to someone else?" Nicks repeated. "I heard one of you say that."

No one acknowledged the comment.

"Are you telling me, you think I'm hot enough to bang, but I'm not good enough to keep this bionic arm?"

Her verbal bomb exploded. The shrink retreated behind his leader who was foaming at the mouth. "That's not a *robot* arm, it is a TALON Cybernetic Arm, Tactical Class, Mark V*!*"

"I'm keeping the *fucking* arm! And all the other *bonus bits* that go with it." She glared at them. "Unless one of you thinks you're *tactical* enough to come and get it?"

Again, silence.

"Well, now that we've cleared that up, explain to me exactly what my job would be if I joined the program?"

The leader stepped forward. "No, I don't think so. This isn't going to work out."

Before she could say another word, a Caduceus drone dropped from overhead and injected her with a sedative. She was instantly paralyzed.

The red suits operated. They didn't use anesthetic and didn't seem to care. They took her arm first. Stripped her and began removing her legs.

Someone was drilling into the side of her head. The buzzing was incessant—the buzzing wouldn't stop—

She woke up.

The clock said she'd only had two hours of sleep.

If that wasn't bad enough, the buzzing was still humming outside her window. It was driving her crazy.

She got out of bed and stepped onto her balcony. There it was—a shadow on wheels, racing over the grounds of the estate.

The Ghostrider.

The source of the noise was the motorcycle's high-tech engine. No one else could hear it, but to Nicks's enhanced ears it sounded like a chainsaw. The bike zoomed across the grounds of the estate, but Quinn wasn't on it. Someone was stealing her prototype.

Not going to happen, Nicks thought.

Nicks grabbed the balcony railing and vaulted over. She landed in the garden, three stories down, and chased the thief. Whoever woke her up was about to get a beating they'd remember the rest of their life.

15

Scorpio dumped her scuba gear and most of her equipment on the ocean floor about three hundred yards from shore and swam to the beach.

The lights of Venice twinkled in the darkening sky as she emerged from the water.

She wore a skimpy bikini, making her feel naked. One old man sitting in a beach chair and drinking Coronas noticed. His eyes sparkled as they traced the curves of her sleek muscular body. He beamed like he'd discovered a mermaid.

"Excuse me, miss. You look like an actress from a Bond film! Have I seen you in anything?"

Scorpio let out a girlish giggle, a sound she despised but found effective.

"You speak English?" The old man asked.

Scorpio shook her head no.

"Well, at least have a beer. You've made my night."

As he reached into his cooler for another Corona, Scorpio stole the folding knife he was using to cut limes. She accepted the beer and thanked him with a grateful smile. She walked on, knowing full well his eyes were glued to her body, rewarding himself for his generosity.

Raylock Industries was a large conglomerate specializing in defense technology. It had some of the largest DARPA contracts in the United States.

The artificial intelligence division rented office space on Ocean Front. Snapchat was down the street. YouTube and Google were blocks away.

Raylock A.I. sat in a two-story structure next to a modest warehouse. The warehouse was the server farm, and it had a back entrance leading to a small parking area and the alleyway.

Scorpio had cased the office several weeks back. The security guard was perfunctory. His main job was making sure the homeless didn't take a piss in the parking lot.

As she had observed many times before, most of the Raylock staff left around dark. And, like clockwork, after the last employee left, the security guard locked the front doors and retreated to the back entrance for a smoke. Tonight was no different. There he was on cue.

Scorpio stumbled into the lot singing. She made sure she slurred the lyrics. The guard admired her with a lot less respect than the old man. Another drunken tourist girl. She knew he saw dozens of them every night.

"You lost?" he asked.

"You sing Karaoke with me?" she asked.

"I don't sing."

"Oh, too bad. You're so handsome."

He glanced at his watch like he was embarrassed.

"Give me a cigarette," she begged.

"Sure."

Scorpio walked over and leaned into the young man, pretending she was about to fall. He caught her, conveniently, by her damp ass.

"What's your name, handsome?" She took the cigarette.

"Hitch."

He offered her a light but she'd lost interest in smoking.

"Are you alone?" She whispered into his ear.

Scorpio pressed closer. He gave up on giving her the cigarette.

"Yeah." He grinned.

She slid her hand down his muscular chest. It was cold and Scorpio's brown nipples were hard against the still-damp white top. Her hand slipped into his pants. He reached up and cupped her breast. She purred as he groped her.

"Take me inside; it's too cold out here."

"Fine by me," he said.

He turned and typed his access code into a panel. The door buzzed open, and the guard stepped inside. Scorpio quietly unfolded the stolen knife as she followed.

16

Maggie Quinn had created an excellent stealth motorcycle. It had a lot of power. The rider sped toward the edge of an embankment and jumped to the garden level.

Nicks raced after it.

Her cybernetic legs were modified with the same tactical grade biomimetic bone and muscle found in her arms and hands. As she cut across the property, they went into overdrive as designed. She guessed the thief would head for the paved road leading down to the front gate. Her legs pumped faster, putting her on a direct course to intercept it.

The TALON scientists knew a human being's biomechanics would allow for maximum running speeds of around forty miles per hour. This was fast enough to out run a grizzly bear. But in most recorded races between bears and humans, the bears still won. Superhuman speeds were impossible because muscles were limited by contraction speeds and oxygen consumption rates.

Nicks's muscles overcame human limitations through augmented stimulation. The results from the *augstim* muscles was unmatched, giving her the potential of new physical strength and speed. She could deadlift a thousand pounds using the full power of her leg muscles, arm, and hand.

A file that reported on Nicks's tests after her rehabilitation showed she could now run at Olympic speeds with little effort. In controlled environments, and with maximal effort, she ran at over forty-five miles per hour—more than fast enough to outrun an angry bear or catch a motorcycle.

The rider changed direction and headed straight for her. The thief must have spotted her. When it was about ten yards away, the high beams switched on, blinding Nicks. She skidded to a stop.

The motorcycle sped by almost running her over. As Nicks twisted away to avoid it, the thief kicked her in the back, forcing Nicks to her knees.

"Oh no, you didn't just do that." She sprung back to her feet. "It's on now!"

Nicks chased after the bike, pushing her legs into another gear. The thief turned to see Nicks gaining. She pulled the throttle back, but it was no use. Nicks had too much momentum.

She overtook the thief and grabbed the back seat with her bionic hand. She ripped the motorcycle out from under its rider and threw the Ghostrider to one side.

The thief hurdled headfirst into a wall of manicured shrubbery. Nicks ran over and pulled the idiot out by the boots, and tossed the rider over her shoulder and into the air. The thief came down hard and crumpled on impact.

"You got me, I give," the thief said, rolling around in obvious pain.

"You're damn right," Nicks said, and ripped the helmet off her adversary.

It was Fatima Nasrallah.

She didn't look as cocky covered in leaves and mud. After she caught her breath, and spit the blood out of her mouth, she giggled uncontrollably. "I think I like this team."

Nicks diagnosed her on the spot.

The bitch was bat-shit crazy.

Nicks rolled the bike back to the house. Fatima came dragging ass behind her trying to make amends.

"I was going to put it back. I was just blowing off steam."

"You tried to run me over!" Nicks yelled.

"I kicked you to get you out of the way. I didn't want to hurt you."

"Do you realize the fork is bent? Quinn will be *pissed*," Nicks complained.

"Hey, you were the one who threw the damn thing across the yard." Fatima rubbed her shoulder. It looked out of joint. "How in the hell did you do that?"

"I *desecrated* my body with *ass-kicking* machines."

"Oh." Fatima said, and cleared her throat. "Sometimes I speak with too much passion."

Nicks stopped pushing the bike and turned around. "If you want to apologize, why don't we start with the truth about why you're here?"

Fatima took a flask out of her jacket and offered it to Nicks.

"Have a drink with me, and I'll bore you with all the details you can stand."

THEY PUT the Ghostrider away and sat by the pool. Nicks took a few swigs from the flask while Fatima explained herself.

Penbrook chose Fatima for the mission because she had prior experience with Echo Squad. She'd had a run in with their de facto leader. A guy they called Charlie Tango.

"I don't know any more than you about Starfire. Penbrook wants to make sure Echo Squad is interrogated. He's promised me a role in that. His offer made me warm and fuzzy so here I am."

Nicks believed her. Fatima didn't seem concerned with a cover story; she was in the game for the action.

She sized Nicks up. "Exactly what parts of you are—what do you call it—a *Terminator*?"

"That's Hollywood, not—"

"Well this is *Hollywood,* isn't it?"

"Touche." Nicks took another pull from Fatima's flask. "Both arms have been completely replaced. My two legs are partially modified."

"Fast enough to chase me down on a motorcycle going what ...?"

"Maybe thirty. You didn't have time to get up to speed. I took advantage of that. If you had opened it up, you could've beaten me."

"I'll remember that next time."

"When Quinn sees the damage to her bike, there won't be a next time."

Nicks passed the flask back to Fatima.

"So, what's your story?" she asked.

"The DoD found me in the desert killing jihadis," Fatima told Nicks. "They liked the way I shot. Offered me a deal."

"So, you're Iraqi?"

"Kurdish. I fought in Syria with the YPJ."

Nicks wasn't clear on the different Kurdish factions. "Refresh me."

"Kurdish Women's Protection Unit. All female fighters. We train ourselves and make our own weapons. I was their top sniper."

"How'd you end up in that outfit?"

"My brother was killed by ISIS. I joined to avenge him."

Fatima explained how the jihadis captured and killed many young Kurd fighters. They mutilated their bodies and dragged them through a nearby village. Her brother was one of the few still identifiable.

She couldn't get the image out of her mind until she replaced it with images of the dead ISIS fighters—the ones she took out with her Zagros rifle.

"They say I've killed over a hundred. I don't know. If I had had that stealth motorcycle, I would've tripled the count. I was best at night."

"They call you *Cartwheel?*" Nicks asked. "Why's that?"

"Ever seen a Daesh fighter take an anti-material round like the 12.7? They do a lovely little somersault."

Nicks smiled. "So, what do you know about Echo Squad?"

"Their leader is a bad man, only in it for the money," she said, disgusted. "I'm happy they're finally facing justice."

She explained how Echo Squad had been her team's point of contact in Syria. "They brought us weapons but one of them wanted something from my fellow soldiers for their effort. The women who met them at the checkpoint refused.

"One of them went a bit insane. She ended up injuring two of their men."

"Well, they deserved every bit of that. Good for your team."

"No, it wasn't good. The leader ordered the squad to take the weapons back and they never returned. The whole deal was called off. We suffered heavy losses after that. We'd become dependent on the DOD's weaponry, instead of relying on our own power. We needed the resupply."

Nicks understood that better than most. "A no-win situation, I'm sorry."

"My unit turned on the crazy one. She was banished. In the end, she was one of the few who survived the war."

Nicks was disgusted by the story. Shocked the soldiers would do it, but not surprised.

"Penbrook thinks I can use what I know to get information out of them. He thinks I know their tactics enough to catch them."

"Can you? What's the master plan?"

A grin as wide as the moon spread over Fatima's face.

"My master plan is to shoot them all."

THEY CONTINUED drinking and chatting for another half-hour. Nicks wasn't sure what to think about Fatima, but she liked her vibe—a casual strength she suspected was hard earned. She'd sensed the same thing in other soldiers she admired.

Fatima asked about the team. Nicks filled her in on some of their history. She explained her side of what happened at the warehouse.

"Why'd he send you in there alone?"

"Byrne is a good leader. We were both caught off guard."

"I saw the way he looked at you, are you—"

"He's protective of me," Nicks interrupted. "We've been through a lot together."

"Does he take care of your *classified* parts?" Fatima couldn't finish her joke without snorting. The liquor was kicking in.

Nicks mouth dropped open. They howled so loud, she was sure they'd wake the rest of the team. It had been a long time since she'd done that. Maybe having Ms. Bat-Shit-Crazy around would be good for her.

"I'm laughing so hard, my cybernetic hand is malfunctioning." Nicks rotated her left arm robotically, and extended her middle finger. "I hate when it does that."

"*Lakawa!*" Fatima said, grabbing her flask from Nicks.

Nicks guessed the insult was Kurdish for fuck off.

Byrne interrupted by walking out on the terrace overlooking the pool.

"A party and I wasn't invited?" he joked. He was relieved to see the two women getting along.

"Sorry, did we wake you?" Nicks asked.

"No, Penbrook called. There's been an incident at Raylock A.I. in Silicon Beach."

"More rogue drones?" Nicks asked.

"No. More dead soldiers. Come on, we leave in five minutes."

17

They found Frank Hitchens, one of the missing Echo Squad members, in a pool of blood between two server banks, about ten yards from the back entrance. His back was savagely ripped open.

"Did a *Predator* attack him?" Quinn asked, her black humor on full display.

"I'm not sure anyone deserves this kind of death," Fatima said.

Byrne knelt down to get a closer view. "These wounds are ragged but purposeful."

"Please tell me this poor lad wasn't dissected while he was still alive," Quinn said. "I can't think of anything more terrifying."

Nicks knew it was possible. She'd seen it firsthand.

"Everyone spread out and search for evidence. See if there's been any damage to the servers. Nicks, clear the building. I don't want any of us taken by surprise. You know what to look for."

Byrne reached into is gear bag and pulled out a video camera.

"Fatima, take this, record everything, and see if you can find any other evidence the killer may have left—a weapon would be helpful. He has some deep defensive wounds. This soldier put up a fight."

The team fanned out to process the scene.

NICKS DID a sweep of the entire building. The structure was barebones. There wasn't anywhere for a drone to hide, except maybe in the massive air-conditioning ducts.

She cleared the obvious places. Then, walked under the duct system listening with her cybernetic ears for any sign of a Caduceus drone. Nothing was there.

QUINN CHECKED the server terminal closest to the murder victim.

"Whoever killed Hitchens used this computer. They broke the encryption."

"I'm guessing it wasn't easy," Byrne said, studying the victim.

"No, this is very advanced," Quinn said. "Which makes me think this is an off-site for DR-Ultra. Penbrook requires the highest security possible on all of its projects."

"They don't allow offsite programs," Byrne reminded her.

"This says otherwise. Check out the files."

Byrne joined her at the terminal.

The intruder had transferred a substantial amount of data overseas. It wasn't clear where. But the files were tagged with a telling signature: TAL for TALON.

ACROSS THE BUILDING, Nicks found Fatima shining a black light on a wall.

"There's something here," she said. "And it doesn't look good."

Nicks helped her push aside a piece of equipment obscuring the view.

"Can you believe this?" Fatima said. "What kind of animal—"

"Is that—"

"His spine!" Fatima answered.

It was glued to the wall with a rubber epoxy.

"I don't understand what this means, other than the killer is *Cuckoo-for-Cocoa-Puffs*."

Nicks wondered if they were dealing with a serial killer. Something they'd hand over to other agencies.

Fatima disappeared, then returned with Quinn's tool kit. She grabbed a pair of large tweezers and inspected the wall.

Nicks heard fizzing like the sound of a carbonated drink. It was coming from—

"Fatima! Don't touch that!"

She was leaning against the epoxy when it exploded with a giant *FA-BOOM!* The small shockwave knocked both women off their feet.

Nicks felt the heat wash over her but it was strangely benign. She shook it off and got up. Fatima looked hurt.

They checked each other for shrapnel wounds. Everything was okay except for Fatima's hand. It was burned and swelling.

Nicks helped her as the rest of the team circled around.

"What the hell happened?" Byrne asked. "Are you guys okay?"

"I'm not sure," Fatima said. "I barely touched it."

The spine was still stuck to the wall. The human tissue and blood were burning as the epoxy smoldered. Pieces of the spine clattered onto the concrete floor as the glue gave way. One piece in particular rolled in a different direction like a ball bearing. It was completely metal.

In her mind, Nicks was already rehearsing what she would do to the sicko who had set the trap. But that daydream faded the minute she noticed the image.

"Guys, do you see what I see?"

Everyone backed up to take in the view.

The explosion had created a unique burn pattern on the wall—a charcoal image of a demon's face. Three big eyes. Scary fangs. It wore a crown of skulls.

SEVERAL MINUTES LATER, as the team recovered from the explosion, Penbrook called wanting to be debriefed. He was still on edge, so Byrne was cautious with the details. The team was sifting through the clues, but a pattern was emerging. Someone was killing members of Echo Squad.

"It's the Frank Hitchens we were looking for. He used an alias to get that job," Byrne said.

"Colonel, your team needs to move faster," Penbrook said. "Find the rest of these men before they end up like Hitchens."

"Yes, sir," Byrne said, and the call was over.

AFTER THE CALL the team setup a workstation near Hitchen's corpse. Quinn unpacked a laptop and something with a rotating head of lenses that she called the CageCam. When she plugged that into the laptop, and networked into Flux at Angelos Grove, their portable lab was fully functional.

Next they circled around Byrne helping him prep the victim for a closer examination. Nicks wanted to know what Penbrook had said.

"Like Quinn discovered, Raylock AI does have a contract with DR-Ultra. Travis Raylock called Penbrook directly," Byrne replied. "All of this evidence stays in-house. I don't want LAPD or any other agency getting a whiff of this."

"Travis Raylock. Seriously?" Fatima seemed impressed.

Raylock was a celebrity inventor who seemed to be in direct competition with Elon Musk.

"Will we all be getting electric sports cars if we solve the case?" Quinn joked.

"Not likely, but I will buy a few pizzas and a six-pack," Byrne said. "In the meantime, do a final sweep of the building but please avoid getting blown up. If anyone has something to report, let everyone know over our coms. I'll be right here with our unlucky friend."

He pulled on a pair of surgical gloves and went to work.

ABOUT THIRTY MINUTES LATER, Byrne was well into his autopsy. Quinn was examining the metal spine, and Nicks was using the Cage's database to read through Hitchen's military file.

She flipped the page to his psychosocial history. It impressed Nicks he was more healthy psychologically than she was, and his service history was respectable.

Hitchens earned a Bronze Star for his actions during a snatch-and-grab raid on a high-level terrorist cell. When he returned stateside and left the military, he joined Bishop Security. The private military outfit was owned by the controversial three-star general Marcel Bishop. General Bishop sold Echo's services to the DIA as his most elite squad. The DIA assigned them to DR-Ultra.

The contract was incredibly lucrative, and a good portion of the money trickled down to the men. Hitchens pulled in six figures and had good performance reviews until he disappeared.

The new evidence showed Hitchens had adopted a false identity, moved to Venice, and called in some favors to land the position at Raylock AI.

It was a plush job for Hitchens. Solo gig. Important title. No other staff to supervise and a very large salary. He rented a small craftsman near the beach and walked to work. Seemed they questioned him about drinking on the job, but he had no other issues with his employer. He was a well-paid ghost living the good life.

Nicks looked through the emails and texts he'd sent from his company phone.

"Get this," Nicks said. All ears perked up. "Wilson and Chapman attempted to contact Hitchens, weeks ago. They tried to warn him. Said they were all in trouble and he needed to watch his back. Apparently, he never responded."

"Frank Hitchens wasn't some lightweight. Whoever killed him must have spec ops training, or how in the hell would they've overpowered him?" Fatima asked. "How could one person, like this Scorpio for instance, take out all of these bad-ass operators?"

That was a very good question, but Nicks knew it could be done. If the killer was using DARPA weapons like she'd encountered, taking out one operator wasn't implausible.

When Nicks was finished, Quinn took control of the display.

"My turn for show-and-tell," she said, and pulled up photos of the wall where the explosion had occurred.

"This epoxy is a classified plastic explosive."

She zoomed in on a sample of the glue that had held the spine to the wall.

"It's a thermomorphic solvent that catalyzes when you apply direct heat to its surface. Fatima's body heat activated it."

The chemical formula for the substance filled a sidebar. A large red classified icon flashed over the information.

"In its inert state, you can mold it into any shape with ordinary rubber molds," she said. "Once it's been formed, you spray it with a thin coat of chemical primer and it sets. Apply a little heat and it goes boom!"

Byrne looked up to study the formula. "Who makes it?"

"Wanna guess?" Quinn asked. "Anyone? Anyone?"

A name flashed across the screen—DR-Ultra.

"Of course," mused Nicks.

Fatima read over Quinn's shoulder. Quinn liked that. "Is this explosive in the list of stolen DR-Ultra tech?"

Quinn pulled up the list.

"No, it's not."

That intrigued everyone.

Quinn switched screens and continued. "As for the servers, a pro hacked them for sure. Penbrook sent me some analysis of what I found. Our killer used that facility as their own personal Dropbox. They transferred over one hundred TB of data overseas. No one can figure out where it went. Hong Kong possibly. The original file wasn't left in Raylock's system. Because of the logs, we have the exact file size. And that particular file size matches the file size of a certain Blackwood Lodge file I use all the time—the TALON database. All the research and history. Everything."

Nicks noticed Quinn's conclusion stunned everyone except

Byrne. He was zoned out hunched over his work examining pieces of Hitchen's spine.

"Byrne did you hear what Quinn just said?" Nicks asked.

"Yes, I'm listening."

"What else are you doing?"

"Great investigative work, if you ask me."

Byrne swung the portable CageCam over what he'd found and hit a switch. Images filled the monitor.

"Apparently Mr. Hitchens and his team members were much more than they seemed. This is the same type of brain-computer interface we found at the warehouse. It looks like a next generation TALON component. Far more advanced than anything inside you, Nicks."

Nicks stepped closer and marveled at the strange design.

"This proves my theory," Byrne said.

"What is that?" Nicks asked.

"Our killer isn't murdering soldiers. He's murdering *cyborgs!*"

PART V

THE WIZARD

18

Dwight Johnson couldn't see the keyhole and the porch light wasn't working. Why in the hell didn't the landlord repair it? He had called the cheapskate at least five times. Nothing was ever fixed around here. Probably never would be.

Damn it. He couldn't get his key in the lock. He shouldn't have had that last drink, but he'd needed it to relax.

The call from Wilson had been the first bad sign. The drunken call from Hitchens added to the drama. Now, he couldn't get Simmons or Tango on the phone. After two days and about fifty unreturned texts, he couldn't deny it any longer. His old team was in trouble.

He kicked the door in frustration and it swung open. Did he leave it unlocked? Damn, where was his head? He was losing his edge, and this was a bad time to do it.

He stumbled inside. Fumbled for the lights. Nothing.

Okay, so it wasn't just the porch light. The power was out.

Find your bunk, soldier.

Unless his landlord stole it, it should still be there. He took a piss, shuffled into his bedroom, and collapsed on the bed. The room was spinning but not fast enough to make him sick. Dreamtime baby. He'd figure out what to do tomorrow. Right now he needed—

"A shitty life on the shitty side of town. Is this the *glorious* end a warrior like you deserves?"

Johnson sprung from his stupor, reached for his gun. It wasn't there.

Scorpio leaned forward out of the dark corner and pointed the barrel of his Sig Sauer squarely at him.

"When did Echo Squad lose their honor, Sergeant Johnson? Or are you too drunk to remember?"

Johnson looked around for a means to fight back. There was no move to make. He was cornered. "Get it over with, you got me."

"Don't worry, this won't take long," she said.

He leaned against the headboard. He'd faced death a hundred times but never thought he'd go out like this. Defiance flashed through him.

"Why the hell are you after me? Huh? We did what we did. Got the package out like you wanted. But none of us agreed to have that witch take over for good. Watching, creeping around in our fucking minds, controlling us. It ain't right. Kill me or get the fuck out!"

"Are you so eager to die? I was hoping you'd entertain my proposition."

"Proposition?"

"One more job. After that, I swear to you I'll set you free."

"What's the job?"

Scorpio smiled and leaned closer.

"Do you like *birds*, Johnson?"

19

Nicks sat down at the round table in the center of the Cage with a blank legal pad and drew a picture. Fatima strolled in drinking a Mr. Pibb and watched her.

"Our cyborg hunter—what's your best guess? Is it this *Scorpio*?" Nicks asked.

"She's high on the list," Quinn said, from her corner of the room.

Was Scorpio hunting her too? Nicks wondered.

Nicks laid out the basic pieces of the design as she remembered it. A monster's face. Three eyes. Skulls around the forehead like a crown. Flowers above the crown.

No, they weren't flowers. They were stylized flames like hair on the skulls.

"That's really good," Fatima said. "Are you an artist?"

"More like an overly confident doodler."

Nicks took the drawing and hung it on the bulletin board she'd pushed into her corner of the Cage. Next to the board was a table with red yarn, pushpins, photos, black markers. She hung the symbol in the center.

"A case board? I thought your team did everything electronically?"

"A don't like relying on computers for everything, especially when it comes to things my brain should be doing."

Fatima examined the drawing. "You've captured the details pretty well."

"Is this something you recognize?" Nicks asked.

"Yes, it looks like my step-mother," she said, trying not to snort soda through her nose.

"Seriously, though. It's important to our killer. We should know what it means."

"I've seen it before. Wait here."

Fatima rushed over to one of the oldest and dustiest bookshelves in the Cage. She swung the library ladder over to one of the higher shelves. There were hundreds of books from the former owner's esoteric collection. Most of them were about mystical subjects and the occult. Parapsychology. World religions. The one Fatima grabbed was a guide to Middle Eastern Symbology.

After dusting the old hardback off and climbing down, she dropped it on the table next to Nicks and thumbed through it.

"Here," she said, pointing to the index. "Mythic Figures in Buddhism."

Fatima flipped to the center of the book full of colored plates. Among the images were several old photos of monastery walls. One had a close up of something a bit similar to Nicks's drawing. Fatima read the label.

"The Dharmapala," Fatima said. "That's it!"

"You're right," Nicks leaned over for a closer look.

Fatima read from the description, "In Buddhist myths, the Dharmapalas were wrathful gods known to be the defender of the law."

"Of what law?"

"Dharma itself."

She explained her understanding of the topic. Dharma was hard to pin down, but generally it meant living with a reverential attitude toward all life and a commitment to maintaining the natural order of the cosmos. The opposite of dharma was deception, greed, chaos, evil, and death.

Dharmapalas were enlightened beings, like the Buddha, who protected the dharma and sentient beings through their wrath. They manifested as angry demons. They were always depicted with fierce expressions. Blue and red skin. Fangs. Strange weapons in their hands.

Some were female and the crown symbolizes that they were queens of wisdom. They taught through fear to shock non-believers into faith.

The skulls on the crown represented the lords of wrath the demon queen controlled. Traditionally, there were six lords, and the flames on the skulls represented the six distinct powers they wielded.

Nicks listened intently until Fatima was done.

So the killer saw themselves as a dharma demon restoring the natural order by killing cybernetic humans. This wasn't your run-of-the-mill logo. It was a symbolic threat.

Next, Nicks did some research on the phrase that had accompanied the first image of the Dharmapala. The graffiti had read: "Cursed Creators! Your monsters rise!"

It only took a few minutes of searching the internet to find that was a reference to Mary Shelley's *Frankenstein*. It was a paraphrase of an exchange between the monster and Dr. Frankenstein.

Nicks read it aloud: "'Cursed, cursed creator! Why did I live? Why, in that instant, did I not extinguish the spark of existence which you had so wantonly bestowed? I know not; despair had not yet taken possession of me; my feelings were those of rage and revenge."'

Fatima wondered, "Who are the creators? And who are the monsters?"

"I guess that's what we need to figure out."

Something about this cut a little too close to home. Nicks turned off the computer and stood up.

"I need a drink!" she said, eyeing Fatima's soda. "But it's gotta be stronger."

WHILE NICKS OPENED a new bottle of El Tesoro, Quinn, who was printing out documents, gazed over her shoulder.

"Sweet Mother Mary, you've solved it, and you're making margaritas."

"No, just deeper down the rabbit hole." Nicks groaned. She mixed her secret blend of lime juice and simple sugar, poured in a generous portion of tequila. Added the ice.

Quinn pinned six black and white photos on the board, in a semi-circle around the dharma demon symbol. Three men on one side. Three men on the other. She joined them at the table where one of Nicks's cocktails waited for her.

"From the top down, that's Edward Chapman, Declan Wilson, and Frank Hitchens. Our victims. Three dead soldiers. Each with some kind of cybernetic enhancement."

Quinn pointed at the three photos on the right.

"Those men are the three still unaccounted for: Dwight Johnson. Hal Simmons. And their team leader, Charlie Williams. I printed out their last known addresses on the bottom of the photos. I think we should divide these up and check them out."

Fatima reacted like she'd seen a ghost when Quinn pointed at the last photo. She stood up and grabbed it.

"What did you call him?"

"Charlie Taylor Williams, goes by C.T."

"You know this guy?" Quinn asked.

"They call him Charlie Tango," Fatima said. Her voice was soft, and she stared through the photo to another place, a million miles away.

"Okay, let's split up to make this faster. I'll track down Dwight Johnson," Nicks suggested. "You pay Charlie Tango a visit."

Fatima laughed. It was the same crazy laugh Nicks had heard a few nights before. "I promise you, I will find this one before the dharmapala even gets close."

Quinn and Nicks snuck glances at each other. Eyebrows rose.

"What's so funny?" Byrne asked from the doorway.

He strolled in and sat down smiling, primed and ready for the joke. They weren't sure what to say next.

"Have to be there," Fatima said, fumbling the expression. "Excuse me."

She finished her drink, got up, and left the room.

"What's up with her?" Byrne asked. He was developing a bad habit of showing up a few seconds too late to these meetings.

The women feigned ignorance and went back to looking at the evidence board.

"So, these are our targets?" Byrne said, inspecting the photos.

"How did your analysis of the components go?" Quinn wondered.

"Glad you asked," Byrne said. "Flux, display the new data on the main screen, please."

The screen came to life with an image of Hitchen's brain-computer interface.

"Flux, center the photo and zoom in," Byrne said.

The computer acknowledged the command and refocused the image.

Byrne nudged Quinn with his shoulder.

"What do you see?" he asked her.

"Looks like a manufacturer's stamp? Or serial number?"

"Close, but no cigar."

"Flux, zoom in another twenty-five percent," Quinn said.

When the image refocused, she saw a cartoon mouse making a rude gesture next to the component number. The mouse was flipping his middle finger at the team.

"That little fucker," Quinn exclaimed. "Mouse! *Mouse* made these parts?"

"Proof's right there," Byrne said.

"I'll kill the bastard. What in the hell is he doing mixed up in this?"

"I don't know, but I think we need to find out, do you agree?"

"Hell-freaking-yeah," Quinn said. "Koreatown here we come!"

20

F atima remembered Charlie Tango clearly. There had been jokes about *doing the tango,* and she didn't know what the reference meant. Now she did.

She found his house, and parked a bit down the street in the car she'd borrowed from the estate's garage. Her Zagros was in the floorboard behind her, begging to be used. She settled in with a hot cup of coffee and prepared to make a night of it. She didn't have to wait long.

The front door opened, and a pretty Hispanic woman in her early thirties stepped out onto the small porch. She had several empty reusable grocery bags in hand and a toddler on her hip.

The young mother made her way over to a luxury SUV in the driveway, strapped the kid in the back, got in, and took off.

Fatima watched her drive down the street, then turned her attention back to the house. The lights were off. No movement behind any of the windows. No one appeared to be home, and the mother would be awhile shopping with a kid in tow.

She waited for the dusky sky to darken. When the coast seemed clear, she slipped out and headed up the driveway.

A six-foot fence surrounded the backyard, but the gate was

unlocked. In seconds, she found a cracked-open bedroom window. She took the screen off, raised the window, and climbed inside.

This was the child's room. On the dresser was a picture of the happy family. Mom. Kid. Charlie Tango.

She crept through the house, room-by-room; in minutes she'd cleared it. The master bedroom showed no sign of him. Only a few shirts his size hung in the closet. The other bedroom —no sign of him at all.

On the computer desk, in a pile of legal paperwork, she found the reason he wasn't home. A divorce decree with child support documentation that included his forwarding address—a PO Box. His employer was still listed as Bishop Security.

The courts had given Cynthia Williams full custody and— no surprise here—a restraining order. She'd forced him to move out months ago. A police report included a claim of domestic violence.

Further evidence Charlie Tango was a bad guy.

This was the right man, but he was in the wind.

Across town, the news wasn't any better. Nicks found Dwight Johnson's apartment in disarray. The scene wasn't encouraging. She called Fatima.

"Any luck?" Nicks asked.

"Moved out and off the grid. What about Johnson?"

"Looks like he was in a fight. Blood on his pillow. Blood in the sink and gauze in the trash. But he's gone."

"You think they know about their teammates?" Fatima asked.

"They're scared for a reason."

"Hal Simmons is a ghost. None of his leads check out."

"We'll dig deeper and start the search again tomorrow. Right now, Byrne wants us to meet him in Koreatown. I'll text you the address."

"Copy that, we'll find these men soon. Dead or alive." Fatima had an edge to her voice.

Nicks hung up. She felt a wave of concern for the men of Echo Squad. What was the worse fate—being found by the Dharmapala or her new teammate? A toss-up. Best if Nicks found them first.

Byrne texted her again with an address.

"We're at Mouse's building. Meet you there."

The first skull in the crown had always been the most problematic recruit to the cause. Dr. Victor Vargas was one of the most important members of the council because of his knowledge of DR-Ultra's progress into the world of cybernetics. It made him essential in the quest to harness the power of Project Starfire.

However, the man was morally unstable, and that instability raised questions about his reliability. New intelligence suggested he was lying about his work outside the syndicate. That suspicion was now confirmed.

Eventually, the man would be dealt with accordingly. First, he would be allowed to serve his purpose, and when he was no longer valuable, he would be disposed of—that's why Scorpio was here, doing what she was doing.

She finished setting up the surveillance equipment and hacking into the navigation system. If it was needed, she could activate it remotely and take control.

When everything was in place, she made a sweep of the lab to make sure her visit was undetectable.

Satisfied she'd left no trace, she walked outside and admired the view. As the bright orange sun sank into the Pacific Ocean, beautiful pink clouds appeared over the horizon.

What is your assessment?

Riza's voice crawled across the surface of her brain, clawing and coiling around the nerves.

"Looks like he's playing both sides. Echo Squad paid him to alter the design of the sigillum," Scorpio said. "That's why they stopped responding to your commands and slipped out of your reach."

Find him.

"Yes, of course," she said. "We need to establish the high cost of such betrayals."

I'll be watching ...

Scorpio strapped on her scuba gear and equipment pack and lowered herself into the water. Her next destination wasn't that far away. She'd be there as night fell—the perfect time to attack.

22

The Reaper team checked the side-entrance to Mouse's building and found the door locked. Nicks called him up but he didn't answer the phone. A few minutes later, she received a text.

"*I'm laughing so hard. Who the hell calls people these days?*"

It was Mouse. He wasn't home, but he was watching them. Remote cameras swiveled in their direction and shook their little heads up and down.

Nicks texted back, "*Get your ass over here and open this door.*

"*I'm not there right now.*"

"*Open up anyway.*"

"*Hellsno I'm in the middle of a meeting.*"

"*Quinn is here!*"

"*Is she still single?*"

"*Get over here and ask her.*"

"*Meet me at Breakroom 86 in two hours.*"

"*One hour! Where is it?*"

"*Back of the Line Hotel. Bring Quinn!!*"

Nicks texted him the Middle Finger emoji and stuffed her phone in her back pocket.

"I guess we break for dinner," Byrne said.

"Lovely," said Quinn.

"That dude has the biggest crush on you," Nicks teased with a grin.

"Lucky me."

Nicks patted her on the back. "Well, consider it mission related. If you weren't here I doubt he'd meet us. So, thanks in advance for dealing with his awkward male gaze."

It was Quinn's turn to use the middle finger.

"I deserve that," Nicks quipped. "Okay, who likes chicken? Dinner's on me, let's go!"

POLLO A LA BRASA had a permanent B-rating from the health department. No matter how diligently they followed the last inspector's recommendations they never got the coveted letter "A" to hang in their window.

Why? It was the woodpile stacked haphazardly as high as their dingy shack, undoubtedly a home to all kinds of little creatures. The set up didn't impress health-conscious inspectors.

The unfair demerit was a sign of their greatness. They clung to the old Peruvian ways defiantly and cooked their delectable chicken on an open fire. Everyone who cared knew *it was the wood that made it good*! Not to mention the universally-loved, lime-green aji sauce for smothering the beautiful charred meat.

Health inspectors be damned. The food melted in your mouth. The team relished the opportunity to treat themselves.

Lee "Mouse" Park worked down the street out of a defunct Korean shopping center. Most people assumed the quirky twenty-five-year-old was a squatter, but that wasn't true. Mouse owned the building.

He had paid in cash. The source of the cash was money he earned from licensing a patent to the Department of Defense. The DoD was now dependent on that piece of tech and Mouse had more cash than he knew what to do with. With his reserves, he'd funded several more startups, which made even more money.

Mouse could buy half of Koreatown if he wanted it.

Thing was, the kid didn't care about the money. He was a gear head like Quinn and equally talented.

Nicks had seen him work. She considered him a wizard, literally. But he was a naive wizard and that may explain why he was manufacturing knock-off TALON parts. Nicks wanted to know every detail about his involvement. But Mouse kept everything close to the vest. His crush on Quinn would be very helpful when it was time to dig for the truth.

Outside Pollo a La Brasa, a bird on a wire watched the team.

The bird was alone but content. It didn't care that other birds were ostracizing it from their flock. It enjoyed watching the people trying to find Lee Park.

It had been sitting on the wire, the one running from the large transformer into the shopping center, for thirteen hours, twenty-three minutes, and thirty-two seconds. The electrical wire filled it with energy so it didn't have to leave.

It sat there as if warming eggs on a nest and didn't squawk in complaint—it didn't know how.

The bird resembled a small pigeon or perhaps a dove. Occasionally, it fluttered its beautiful wings to appear lifelike. Its feathers shimmered with the orange California sun as it sank into the ocean west of its perch.

When Reaper Force finished their dinner and headed down the street to meet Mouse, the bird received a new command. It took flight and followed the interesting people. It did so with such precision that, had anyone noticed it, they would have wondered who created such a perfect machine.

23

B reak Room 86, like most Koreatown bars, was a karaoke bar. Its one redeeming quality was that it was 80s-themed. It was always packed.

You had to know someone, or know someone who knew someone, to break the line and walk in. Luckily, Nicks knew the bouncer. In minutes, a hostess escorted the team through a maze of service halls, past busy hotel staff, to the break room snack machine.

"You guys ready?" she asked.

The team nodded cheerfully.

The hostess pushed the machine, and it swung out. It was a door on hinges. A secret entrance. It gave the club a hip, speakeasy vibe. The team shuffled through into a swarming mass of drunken patrons.

The place smelled like cheap body spray and spilled beer. Prince's guitar riff from *When Doves Cry* roared over the speakers. Nicks had a sudden urge for a shot of tequila. She whispered her order to Byrne and shoved him toward the bar.

Byrne made his way there only to be disappointed when the

bartenders suddenly stopped taking orders and stepped away from their post.

A gust of fake smoke plumed from behind the bar. The mechanized top rose a few inches and expanded, magically converting into a stage.

A Michael Jackson look-alike materialized from within the smoke and a crew of backup dancers took the surrounding stage. The iconic snare and high-hat of *Billie Jean* pounded through the speakers. Michael snapped his fingers in time and the crowd went crazy.

Nicks's team watched the show for a few minutes while gradually pushing to the south wall of the club. There, they found Mouse, glued to a Galaga machine, trying his best to beat the high score—an exercise in self-mastery given that he had all the high scores on the machines.

An alien ship shot Mouse with a laser.

Nicks wished she could do the same.

The kid had artfully dodged them for the last few hours. She didn't like wasting time like this. The only score she cared about was the Dharmapala's growing body count.

Galaga was trying to capture Mouse's ship in its tractor beam. He tried to avoid it, but Nicks hip checked him right off the console. She grabbed the joystick and moved the ship right into the beam.

"Damn it, Nicks. That's such a noob move; it'll cost me a ship!"

Nick broke the handle off with her bionic hand.

"Shit!" Mouse yelled.

She handed him the joystick. "We need to talk, don't have time to watch you beat up on imaginary aliens. Much more exciting things to hunt."

"Yeah, let me go get a drink. I'll be right back."

Mouse tried to squeeze by Nicks. Byrne intercepted his flight path. "We need your help, bud."

"Of course you do. *Everybody does!*"

Nicks closed in, "Quinn's buying us a round."

"Quinn's here?" He couldn't hide his excitement.

"Yes, why don't you unplug yourself and go talk to her. IRL."

Mouse finally acquiesced. "Okay, you win. Karaoke room number two. I already reserved it for you punks. Follow me."

OUTSIDE THE CLUB, the odd bird was burning through its battery.

Night vision pulled more amps and its creator was overusing the feature. Also, the audio enhancement filters were maxed out. Soon, it would be time to find another electrical wire to perch upon and recharge, or it would need to fly back to its owner and plug into its rapid recharge battery cable.

The bird turned off the orange LED and fired up the red LED.

As always, its creator knew best, it commanded the bird to transmit its video feed to the squad of operatives in the black Cadillac Escalade parked in an alleyway behind the karaoke club. It had just enough power to transmit the information, and it complied.

Once the operatives confirmed receipt of the intelligence, the bird took flight, careful to hover over the Escalade as the men dressed like club goers got out with their guns.

It would be fun to watch these strange men shoot those weapons, but its battery was low, and it had a long way to fly. It didn't want to die.

The humans in the club were the only ones scheduled for

termination. The bird circled over the club one last time and disappeared into the night sky.

"You like to sing, Quinn?"

Quinn took a swig from her drink. She was painfully mute. Mouse just stared at her with a goofy thousand-watt smile.

"I bet you're a great singer!" Mouse was twenty-something. A handsome, fit Korean man with a lot of money. His hair was combed in a perfectly styled pompadour, and he dressed like a hip K-Pop star. He turned heads, especially in this club, but Quinn was hilariously immune to his charms.

He fumbled pathetically with the equipment, trying to impress the one person in the room that did not want to talk to him. "Let me get this going for you."

Quinn was giving Nicks quick glances and rolling her eyes.

"What's your favorite song?" The kid couldn't shut up.

"Here's the mic. You flick this switch, and when the song starts, belt it out. Okay, everyone be quiet, Quinn's about to sing. Listen, she has the best voice."

Mouse was hopeless with women, but he could build almost any machine known to man. After seeing a machine once, he could tear it down, redesign it in his head, and rebuild the new version on the spot. He didn't need computer-aided drafting programs. His brain was far superior. In fact, he'd built many of the systems at the Cage at Byrne's request.

Nicks was a hundred percent sure he could build TALON components. But why would he do it? And for who? That's what they needed to know.

Thankfully, Quinn could handle him.

She surprised everyone by grabbing the karaoke microphone and standing up right in front of Mouse. She bent over giving him a clear view of her cleavage and sang to him like she was seducing a lover.

"We know you've been up to no good, baby. Oh, baby ..."

She spun around, shaking her ass in his face.

"... we aren't leaving until you tell us everything, baby, oh baby, you gotta tell me, everything..."

She turned around. Ran her hands through his hair.

"... if you want me ... baby ..."

Mouse was in heaven.

"... if you want me ... to ... not stick my boot up your skinny little ass ..."

Quinn dropped the microphone right on the sensitive part of his lap. Mouse doubled over in pain.

His face contorted into a pout. "You guys suck ass!"

A waitress knocked at the door. Michael Jackson had gone back to Neverland. The bar was buzzing again. "Who needs drinks?"

"No one!" Mouse said. He dismissed her with a wave. "These losers aren't getting drunk on my dime."

"Sorry honey, it's bottle service, got to bring something."

"Shit! The usual then."

The waitress smiled and spun around and disappeared back into the club's main room.

Mouse looked at the team. The smiles had disappeared. It was time to talk, and he knew it. Byrne confronted him about their findings.

"I haven't done any work for anyone involved with DARPA in a very long time. I don't know what the hell you're talking about."

Byrne reached into his jacket and pulled out a plastic evidence bag with Hitchen's brain-computer interface.

"I'm pretty sure it's your logo on this BCI."

Mouse ripped the bag out of Byrne's hand and eyed it closer.

"How in the hell did you get these? The man who needed it is—"

"—dead!" Nicks interrupted.

"What? How? Well, it's not because of my work. I promise you that. This thing is sheer elegance."

Byrne agreed. "It's very impressive. You've improved upon some military technology that, according to the Department of Defense, doesn't even exist."

"Oh, it exists, and I'm not the only person who knows about it."

"Which means you're in danger," Nicks said.

"Of what? Quinn singing off-key and teasing me with her money-makers?"

"Enough bullshitting," Quinn roared. "Tell us everything you know. Someone is killing people involved with this tech; do you want to be next?"

"Look, I helped this guy perfect a few designs. We hammered out several ideas over one weekend and did the rapid prototyping at my lab. That was it. I asked for more details but he was tightlipped. I mean, I researched his history, and it was easy to see he was making a move. Turning his time working for DARPA into a big payday. He didn't blink when I quoted him my price, and he paid when I delivered the components. I never thought he would install the hardware. Damn, I'd love to know how well it worked."

"Oh, it worked—until it didn't," Byrne said.

"What's that suppose to mean?" Mouse asked.

"Who was this client?" Nicks demanded.

"You know I can't tell you. Ever heard of an NDA?"

"It won't hold up if this guy stole the plans from the government," Byrne said.

"Well, I can say the guy was a creeper, if you know what I mean."

"No, what do you mean?" Nicks asked.

"Just a strange vibe, like he's one of those dudes. All brain and zero emotional intelligence. Y'know, someone who touches the cadavers inappropriately when the rest of the lab isn't watching."

"I'm going to vomit," said Quinn. "And not because you mentioned necrophilia. This vodka is way too sweet. It's terrible."

Mouse corrected her. "That's not vodka, it's Soju. A Korean thing."

"Here's a Quinn thing: I'm going to beat you senseless with this bottle if you don't give us a name."

Nicks chimed in. "Who the hell was working with you, Mouse? Spill it."

Mouse opened his mouth, then closed it and swallowed. Maybe the weight of their seriousness was finally hitting home.

"Vargas. His name was Dr. Victor Vargas."

The team stared at each other. The name didn't seem to mean a thing to anyone.

"Now, it's your turn, what has you guys so spooked?"

Before Nicks could respond, the power in the building went out. It was as if a switch had been flipped on cue to punctuate the seriousness of the situation.

Everyone froze.

Nicks whispered, "Does that answer your question?"

24

T he power surged and a backup generator kicked in.

The lights came on again. The bar crowd cheered.

Then the backup failed. Screams and expletives followed.

"That's not good," Nicks said.

It was pitch black in Karaoke room #2 until the team lit the room with their smartphones. Byrne looked apprehensive. Nicks listened with her cybernetic ears. The club-goers had stress in their voices, seemingly on the edge of panic.

Maybe it was her training, or even her trauma, but something told her to move. "Let's take this outside," she said.

Quinn opened the door, and they filed out. The club was chaotic. Using their cell phones like torches, the crowd headed for the south exit that led to Wilshire Boulevard.

To the north, Nicks heard radio chatter. She focused on the source. By her count, at least three men using tactical language were coming through the break room door.

"Find cover now!" Nicks screamed.

Everyone except Mouse responded instinctively by dropping as low as possible. Seconds later, two men with automatic weapons burst into the room.

The first round of bullets strafed the bottles lining the bar. The next burst hit *rat-a-tat-tat-tat* against the red high school lockers, part of the club's decor. It was inches away from their position.

Nicks swept Mouse off his feet and pushed him down next to Byrne. The team moved behind a sectional couch.

The two gunmen expanded to five and headed their way. Three broke off and went right. The remaining two went left.

As the attackers advanced, the gunfire came in controlled bursts. *Blatt-blatt-blatt.* A sign they were professionals.

Patrons scrambled past them. The gunmen didn't seem to care. They worked the room like they had a specific target in mind.

"It'll be open season if we stay pinned down like this," Nicks said. "Who has weapons?"

"Did you forget? You are our weapon!" Byrne said. No one had come armed.

The two gunmen advanced down the west wall of lockers, one behind the other, moving toward the karaoke room. The others were coming down the east side searching under the tables and in the alcoves.

Nicks whispered to Byrne, "Michael Jackson didn't appear out of thin air. Somewhere behind the bar is an exit. I'll clear a path. You get everyone over there."

A waitress was hiding nearby. She was crouched behind a divider a few feet away still dutifully holding her tray with empty champagne bottles. The bottles rattled as she trembled.

Nicks slid up to her and politely took the tray.

"Stay right here," Nicks said. The girl nodded.

Nicks stood up with the tray of bottles and rushed toward

the two gunmen as if she was a panicked waitress. As she closed in, she tilted the tray and the bottles slid off and shattered at their feet.

"Please, please don't kill me!" she screamed, hysterically.

The first gunman swung his rifle at Nicks, trying to move past her.

"Get the hell out of—"

Using the tray as a shield, Nicks exploded into the gunman like a battering ram. She heard the first man's ribs fracture and he stumbled backward into his partner. Nicks kept moving forward.

She grabbed the end of his rifle, ducked under the barrel, and pulled it her direction. Using the man's own momentum, and her enhanced power, she threw him head-over-heels into a nearby wall.

He hit the corner at an odd angle and collapsed.

Nicks kept low, rolling forward; when she came up she had a rifle in hand. She shot the second gunman in the face before he knew Nicks was there.

Nicks signaled Byrne to run for the bar. The team rushed for the secret exit.

The three remaining gunmen stormed toward Nicks.

One rushed forward, firing. Nicks swiveled and dropped to her knees and shot him through the right eye. He tumbled backward. She swept the room for his two partners. They had disappeared behind the club's furniture.

WHILE SHE SEARCHED for the remaining gunmen, Nicks's team made it across the room. Her bionic ears amplified their concern.

"What are these guys after?" Fatima yelled.

"I'm guessing Mouse," Byrne said.

Mouse panicked. "Why in the hell would they be after *me*?"

Quinn blasted him. "Did you hear anything we said in that room?"

He wilted. It seemed he'd never imagined helping Vargas would put a target on his back.

Byrne grabbed Mouse. "The stage. Can you activate it?"

Mouse zeroed in on the control panel. Flipped a few switches. The stage rose, revealing a hidden door to the backstage.

"Everybody, c'mon," Byrne pointed them to safety.

Fatima looked back. "What about Nicks?"

"She can handle herself, let's go."

NICKS HAD HIDDEN UNDER A TABLE. She was out of bullets and one gunman was coming her way.

When the gunman stepped close enough, Nicks grabbed his boot and gave it a bionic squeeze. The gunman screamed like he'd stepped into a bear trap. His bones fractured under the pressure. It sounded like she was breaking a handful of twigs.

She let go and the man's foot couldn't support his weight. His leg crumbled under him. Tripping forward, he fell on top of his rifle.

Nicks pounced on his back. Grabbing his chin with one hand and the back of his head with the other, she wrenched his head sideways with maximum power. His neck snapped. Then she grabbed his sidearm and slinked off to find the last gunman.

He was hiding behind a support column aiming squarely at the bar.

Nicks snuck up behind him.

"Drop it asshole!" she yelled.

The gunman froze, but he didn't drop the gun or turn around.

Several yards away, Mouse was fiddling with the bar's controls. He was terribly exposed. The gunman had him dead to rights.

"*You* drop it, or I take out the kid!"

"You're a dead man if you even graze him. Just lower your weapon. No one else has to die."

THE GUNMAN WANTED to do what Nicks was saying. It was the right move. But the voice in his head was much more compelling. The voice had complete faith he could finish the mission. All he had to do was believe.

Take the shot.

He fired. Nicks fired. Mouse spun in place and rag-dolled to the ground. The gunman fell.

NICKS SPRANG on top of him, pushed his gun out of reach and pulled off his mask.

It was Dwight Johnson. Nicks couldn't believe it. She'd been at his house hours ago, trying to save his ass.

She snuck a glance at the bar. Mouse wasn't moving. Enraged, she grabbed Johnson by the throat and squeezed.

"Tell me who sent you? Why are you after the kid?"

Johnson was fading. He had a nasty chest wound. She'd hit an artery.

"Who told you we were here?"

"Lady, you won't believe me." His voice was hollow, his breath unnatural.

"Try me."

Johnson mustered the energy for his final words.

"A strange little bird."

PART VI

PARANOID

25

Riza Azmara stretched her mind out into the virtual world. Her reach was growing. The rig she'd designed did seem to be working. It wasn't quite as elegant as she envisioned the final version would be, but it was getting closer each day. Would it be possible for her to expand her powers throughout the entire global computer network?

Cables of all sizes and shapes dangled from the ceiling. It had taken months to calibrate the neural interfaces. Her abilities were now amplified a hundred fold, maybe more. Once she had DR-Ultra's primary encryption key she'd be able to take control of any weapon they'd built. When she took over, unimaginable fear and panic would flood through Blackwood Lodge, and then spread to the Pentagon until the entire American military was living its worst nightmare. It gave her pleasure to imagine it.

The temple had been outfitted in such a way that it was a giant transmitter—able to exploit the various intercepts that had been planted for her in key fiber optic hubs like the one just placed by Scorpio at Raylock AI. From the base she could broadcast her reach everywhere at once, watching as the organization grew.

This was an ingenious design, but it created a new vulnerability. She was the critical node of the network, and the syndicate could be compromised from her location. But she wasn't afraid to sacrifice herself to protect what she had created. Failsafe measures ensured that if she was removed as the prime node, no one else could gain access.

Riza could see the seats of her war council filling up. More allies were embracing her vision every day. They shone like beacons amidst the storm of information.

Others were hidden from her, like pricks of light in a snow flurry. Vargas had found a way to shield them from her.

She wasn't the danger but she understood why they were fearful.

Danger and death lurked everywhere; the tentacles of the war machine seemed to be ubiquitous. DARPA, empowered by its dark heart in DR-Ultra, was like an old god lurking in the deep, souring life with its poisonous soul, biding its time, growing in power until it was ready to destroy everyone and everything that opposed its tyranny.

She was the new god on the block.

No time to waste. She would soon have their secrets. They would give her control of the old god's weapons—including the most dangerous one of all.

Scorpio would finish building the council. Then, Vargas would be found and dealt with. Betrayal was expected but it was still a surprise when it happened.

She recalled how much she once loved surprises and moved past the cacophony of mechanical voices that normally clouded her mind and passed into the deeper interior of her own darkness. Down a hallway filled with her worst memories, she found several gates.

These memories were purposely sealed. But circumstances had changed, and it was time to revisit them. She reached into her heart, retrieved a key, and slid it into the lock. The first gate opened and she stepped inside.

IMAGES of her childhood came into focus. She was seven, and she adored ...

Surprises.

Her father was full of them. His unexpected gifts were a fun ritual. As the family gathered around their table for dinner, Abdul would talk to Riza's mother, Safara, about the market.

Inevitably, he would ask some outlandish question. The more bizarre the better.

"Riza, have you fed the octopus?"

A smile wider than the horizon would appear, and her eyes would fill with magic. Her father seemed the happiest when he was delighting his daughter.

"Baba." Riza giggled. "We don't have an octopus!"

"What? Please child, don't tease your old father. The octopus must be fed, or he will get very hungry and grab us with his tentacles."

"Where is this octopus?" Riza asked, frantically searching her father.

Usually, the surprises were small. Tucked in his pockets, tied in a small piece of cloth, or even hidden in the folds of her mother's apron.

"Surely he's here somewhere!"

Safara gathered the dishes, but watched out of the corner of her eye. Riza, overcome with the giggles, searched for a strange creature that had no business being in their little home.

"Where is it Baba?"

He feigned ignorance, barely able to keep a straight face. "That is for you to find out, little one."

Finally, she did. It was under his hat, a small box with a red ribbon. Riza ripped it open to find a rubber octopus. A child's toy worth a penny at the most.

It was the last gift the man would ever give her, making it the most cherished gift she'd ever received. She thanked him with a million tiny kisses.

Riza watched the memory fade. Time had only intensified the pain it caused. It was time to repay injury for injury, and she would do it with a *surprise*.

26

On Hollywood Boulevard, the night started around nine.

Even then, it was a feeble beginning. The magic took time to simmer and stew. The stars had to bake away the kitschy facade of the earlier hours. The tourists retreated to their overpriced hotel rooms, exhausted from the frenzy of the hustlers, the street performers, the CD swindlers, the tour bus scammers, the spray paint artists, and the masked super-heroes slinging Instagram photos for a few bucks.

First, the young Orange County girls arrived in tight dresses and high heels and tried their best to look like they'd walked the boulevard a hundred times. The cooks fired the gas grills. The waiters took orders. The Uber drivers dropped off their fares. The nightclubs queued their clientele. And the bartenders poured the drinks that loosened the tension of the anticipation.

Then, the magic rose from the Walk of Fame like sewer gas and induced the illusions.

Nicks intended to take full advantage of that magic tonight.

She walked down the sidewalk, past the line, to the bouncer. She whispered the name of the eccentric owner, Alabaster Jack.

She'd done a favor for him a few months back. Part of his return payment was making sure her name was on any list in town. She was past the velvet rope in a blink of the eye.

Before joining the DIA, Nicks was too self-conscious to enjoy the club scene. Now, she walked in with the assuredness of a woman that knew how to weave her own illusions.

A tight black dress. Makeup applied like war paint. A bit of effort with the hair. Glamour could be worn like body armor once you learned how.

Heads turned. Male and female. Tonight, she gave off the glow that made people wonder, because it was Hollywood— *she's that girl in that thing, right?*

If they only knew.

Nicks picked a place at the bar that let her surveil the entire room. She ordered a tequila on the rocks and settled in.

The first person she took notice of was a punk-rock blonde. Platinum heat and electric eyes. She wore a dress that clung to the exact right parts of her athletic body.

Ms. Platinum made sure Nicks noticed her. Nicks made a mental note. This one was a snake in the grass. She'd keep an eye out for her.

The man she was waiting for arrived five minutes later. He walked in like it was his private party, glad-handing the staff and slapping the backs of the regulars. Surely he didn't understand how much danger he was in. This wasn't the behavior of a cautious man; Dr. Victor Vargas invited attention.

"Black looks good on you ..."

Nicks turned toward the voice she assumed came from beside her.

It was the blonde. Halfway across the club.

She stared defiantly at Nicks, a coy smile on her face. She spoke again, mouthing the words carefully.

"He's all mine."

Nicks laughed with surprise. Did the blonde know she would hear her? No, that's impossible; she was being paranoid.

Nicks swirled the ice in her drink and flipped through her cellphone, playing the part of a woman waiting on her date to arrive. She texted Byrne to check in.

Mouse was in the Cage recovering in one of the medical bays. Dwight Johnson's bullet had winged him. There had been a lot of blood and pain, and he'd hit his head on the bar when he fell, but the kid was okay.

Nicks was grateful for the luck. She would've felt very guilty if the outcome had been worse.

Needless to say, once Mouse was patched up and enjoying an expertly mixed morphine drip, he became more cooperative. He accepted he was in danger and he spilled the beans.

He explained, in great detail, how he manufactured the knock-off TALON components. Penbrook was briefed and it turned out Vargas had worked for DR-Ultra. In fact, he'd been involved with the TALON program. He'd been one of their best surgeons, but he was removed from the program after disagreements with the executive staff over credit for the creation of a new neural interface.

The team decided the attack on Mouse meant Vargas was next on the list. They also wanted to interrogate Vargas about his use of the technology. Had he enhanced the members of Echo Squad? Were they all enhanced? Why?

DR-Ultra would want any unauthorized use of the tech shutdown. They needed to know what his game was and where he'd set up his lab.

To find him, Nicks questioned Mouse about Vargas's lifestyle. He explained they partied together on occasion to grease the wheels of collaboration. He knew the man's favorite haunts, which gave her some good leads.

The rest of the team needed a break after the gunfight in

Koreatown, so Nicks volunteered to find him. The first lead panned out. Across the room, Vargas was still the center of attention.

Two waiters tended his table. It was a big one that filled with more women and wine as the night went on. Regulars stopped to chat. The DJ took a break and came for a visit. All the while, Ms. Platinum slowly but surely weaseled her way next to Vargas.

Nicks pivoted her head to catch the chatter at the table. It was hard in such a cacophonous space, but the filters in her implant were powerful enough to extract snippets of their conversation.

Vargas was regaling the table with a story of his last trip to Greece. The blonde was fawning over him, each playful response full of innuendo. If he wanted her, he could have her.

VARGAS WAS a man with a big appetite. Eventually, he took the bait.

Zen was the main dining attraction on Selma. It sat where the old Piano Bar had been before they demolished it. The Dream Hotel towered over all of it now. You could walk from the dining room into the lobby of the hotel and to the main elevators to access your room. And that's exactly what Ms. Platinum and Man-Of-The-Hour did.

A hotel manager greeted Vargas warmly and handed him his room key.

"Your suite is ready, sir."

Vargas palmed the manager a wad of bills and headed for the elevators.

Nicks followed discreetly.

27

Nicks gave Victor Vargas and Ms. Platinum a head start. Let them get comfortable. Once their guard was down, she'd pop in for a visit. Nothing too violent, but rough enough to scare the blonde off and get Vargas alone.

She wanted to convince him of the imminent danger he faced and the need for her protection. Once he saw things her way, she'd arrange for a car to take them to the Cage. He'd be safe there and easier to interrogate. Also, he might help find the rest of Echo Squad.

Nicks liked her strategy. But the minute she stepped off the elevator and headed to the suite, the plan went off the rails.

First, she heard shattering glass. Screams of shock and confusion.

A raised voice gave commands to Vargas and Ms. Platinum. The commotion ended with the unsettling pleas of Vargas begging for his life.

Times like this made her wonder about using the full power of her body. She could hear Quinn telling her: engage the *bloody* protocols! But she wasn't going to be a puppet to the machine inside her. The middle road was the sane choice. Stay in control and use the power that was available.

She tried the door. It was locked.

A struggle was going on in the room. The blonde was fighting back. Nicks could hear the effort she gave. Someone hit Vargas.

Nicks felt a surge of adrenaline, the anticipation of combat buzzing through her blood. She kicked the door next to the hinges with the full force of her augstim muscles. It burst inward like it had been blown off by an explosive.

Wooden splinters filled the entrance alcove. Nicks leapt over all of it like an Olympian and landed in the middle of the living area—and the danger.

A woman about Nicks's size stood in front of a shattered glass door leading out to the balcony. She wore a tight-fitting black outfit with a high-tech climbing harness around her mid-section. Her face was covered with a crimson silk scarf. She looked like a stylish ninja. She held a samurai sword with a handle in the shape of a scorpion.

Her sword had horrifically skewered Ms. Platinum.

Nicks could see the shiny end of it protruding out of the woman's back. The ninja admired the placement of her blade and waited for her victim to die.

Vargas stood a few feet away, trembling. He'd been roughed up. His right eye and lower lip were swollen. In shock, he stared at the gruesome scene with a bewildered expression on his face.

When Nicks appeared, the ninja's eyes widened with a mixture of surprise and delight. She jerked the sword out of Ms. Platinum, who collapsed.

"Viper." The ninja removed her mask. "Finally, we meet!"

"Scorpio," Nicks said, in recognition.

She was a beautiful middle-eastern woman with an aura that radiated danger. Nicks felt this from her best opponents.

She wasn't imposing, but she channeled the confidence of an experienced fighter, someone that enjoyed using their training to inflict pain on their opponents. Someone that could kill you easily.

Nicks knew any hesitation would be a mistake.

In one fluid movement, she grabbed the arm of a nearby chair, lifted it off the ground, twisted like a discus thrower, and flung it straight at her. Scorpio dove for the floor, tucked, and rolled out of the way. The chair hurtled through the already broken glass and exploded against the balcony railing.

Scorpio grabbed a wine bottle from a nearby side table and threw it at Nicks. The projectile forced Nicks to duck. The bottle sailed overhead and shattered onto the hard tile floor behind her. It was a diversion. Scorpio was right behind the bottle and plowed into Nicks like a linebacker.

The attack had little effect. Nicks planted her legs, bracing for impact, and absorbed the hit. Nicks's hand sunk into Scorpio's arm like a vise. The other grabbed a handful of her hair and Nicks twirled, using her own momentum to propel Scorpio across the room, back where she'd started.

She crashed into Vargas but got right back up and shook it off.

"Such a disappointment. You aren't using your full power, are you?" Scorpio sneered. "I consider that an insult."

Nicks fired back. "If I had, you'd be a bloodstain. Fifteen stories down."

"You fear your power. That is a mistake."

Nicks saw something in the woman's hand. A black cylindrical device with a perforated grip. It looked like a flashlight. Scorpio pulled the clip and tossed the device at Nicks.

Nicks had used them herself. It was a military-issue M84 stun grenade with a two second fuse.

The bang was deafening but, in this case, the magnesium

flare was worse. Nicks turned away to protect her face in the crook of her arm as it exploded.

The blonde screamed as best she could, "Watch out!"

Nicks turned back into Scorpio's next attack—a devastatingly accurate kick behind her left ear. It was an illegal move even in MMA fighting because it was so dangerous.

Nicks's body exploded in pain. Darkness closed over her and she fell backward, tripping over the sofa. She landed on the glass-covered tile floor with a dull smack.

When she regained consciousness, Scorpio and Vargas were gone. Nicks's audio input was distorted, coming in and out. She had trouble getting up because both of her legs were trembling uncontrollably.

Flux came online. *"Critical Warning. Engage protocols for optimum performance."*

She ignored the warning and followed a trail of blood into the bedroom and found the blonde on the bed. Her face was whiter than the sheets. She had a cellphone in her hand.

"My people are coming—you need to get out of here," she said.

"Your people?"

"An extraction team, courtesy of Her Majesty."

"What? You're—"

"MI-6."

That stunned Nicks, but it made sense. The competition for Vargas had been real for a different purpose. Ms. Platinum was a British spy.

"There's no time for us to get another operative on him. Take my phone. I copied the data from his."

"The location of his lab?"

"Yes. That's where they're going. But, understand, Vargas is just a pawn in a much bigger syndicate."

"Whose syndicate?"

"We call her The Demon Queen. Dramatic, but we like queens, you know."

The Dharmapala, Nicks thought.

The blonde pushed Nicks away and pointed her to the door.

Nicks hesitated. "But I could help you—"

"No time. Vargas. The lab. That's the priority," she said with a last defiant breath. "And, if you see that bitch again, don't pull your punches, kill her this time!"

The blonde passed out. Nicks checked for a pulse. It was there ... barely.

She grabbed the phone and headed for the door.

"I promise you, I will."

28

R iza Azmara's hair cast snake-like shadows on the wall as her meditation deepened and she moved down her hallway of memories to the another locked gate. Perhaps, it was her most traumatic wound. She pulled out the hidden key and opened it.

Time rewound to her childhood. She was happy in the cocoon of her Afghan village. Then the war brought soldiers. This spread fear and concern through her community. But for her, it sparked curiosity.

One of the American soldiers was a woman!

This amazed Riza. She hadn't known such things were allowed. But her friend Lida swore to it, and the two of them made plans to find her before the morning was over.

Riza pulled a traditional green scarf over her dark hair. Lida combed a few strands with her tiny brown hands and tucked them behind Riza's ear.

"You're so pretty, Riza," Lida said.

Riza's eyes widened as if shocked by the comment. "Of course, I am!" she said jokingly.

The girls burst into laughter.

"She wears her hair short like a man," Lida said.

"Do they make her do these things?" Riza wondered.

"They say American men cannot make American women do anything—it is against the law!"

The two girls, on the verge of becoming women, were small for their age; they looked like elementary school children as they left their house and joined the bustle of the busy neighborhood.

"Perhaps the army pays you to cut your hair?" Lida guessed.

"I would cry for days!" Riza said.

"No, Riza, you would be angry and scream. That is what you do. You always get your way."

Riza smiled. That was true. She had a way of imposing her will on her family and friends. She had always been strong like that. That was why the female soldier fascinated her. How much more powerful must she be? The villagers said she knew Dari, and she had American candy. How could they not seek her out?

"I hope she has bubble gum!" Riza said.

"If you want candy, you have to let them vaccinate you," Lida sounded concerned. "You know what my father says, we cannot trust their medicine or their machines."

"I think he's wrong. My father says American medicine and American machines are the best, our people are foolish not to take everything they offer," Riza replied.

"But they hide sickness in the vaccines, to kill us. They think we are all terrorists," Lida insisted.

"That's not true either, I bet my life on it. Everything they do, they do to help make the world better, make us safer. Why would a woman join the army if this was not true?"

"See, you always make yourself right, no matter what others say."

"I *am* right, don't be foolish."

"Well ... I do want some candy."

Riza laughed and said, "I want to touch her hair. Hurry; let's run!"

She grabbed Lida's hand, and the two rushed through the busy Jehanni street market.

They didn't have to go far to find the Americans. A squad of soldiers stood watch near one entrance to the market. In the adjacent alleyway, with a group of tiny children flocking around her, they found the female soldier.

Her hair was dark like a movie star, her eyes green like Riza's mother's.

She waved and gave the girls a soft smile, then called to them in their language. She was handing out bubble gum.

Riza beamed and ran over.

Lida was unsure and kept her distance. Riza wasn't scared. She buried herself in the soldier's arms and hugged her with all her might.

The female soldier hugged her back, and Riza felt a comforting truth pass between them. It entered her like a spirit and nested deep inside her heart—settling in like a promise.

Seconds later, the bomb exploded and tore the two of them apart.

For years she'd endured that severing. But through meticulous planning she'd worked a plan to heal their bond. This was the moment to restore that connection. She opened a channel and stretched across the miles with her mind, patiently waiting for the soldier to answer her call.

29

SANTA MONICA BAY, PACIFIC OCEAN

M s. Platinum's information led the team to the Port of Los Angeles and the Long Beach Harbor, specifically Truman's Yacht Center. Hacking their unsecured database turned up the final clue.

Vargas rented a slip for an expensive one hundred-foot Ocean Alexander yacht—called the Abraxas there. Recently serviced and fueled, it had left the harbor less than an hour ago. Now, Nicks was on a direct path to intercept it.

"I've got her!" Quinn yelled.

Quinn was communicating with Nicks through her cybernetic ears. The implants sent and received transmissions over an encrypted frequency. That was cool, but it wasn't cool when Quinn screamed.

"I read you *loud* and clear!" Nicks said.

"Oh, sorry 'bout that," Quinn said. "The Abraxas is headed north by northwest at twenty knots toward Santa Cruz Island. That means they're running full throttle if you factor in the wind speed."

"I can't see a damn thing. Maybe if I crawl back out—"

"Claustrophobic are we? Don't worry. You'll be underway soon. Your rig will catch her."

Nicks was in a jerry-rigged torpedo, which was in the belly of a small ship called the Sea Dagger. She heard the engine and the sound of the ocean smacking the hull, but she was blind to her surroundings.

The Sea Dagger was a Class III Unmanned Surface Vehicle. UAVs operated in the air. USVs operated in the water. This one was a three-hulled trimaran that looked like a child-sized destroyer.

It was a submarine hunting drone. Created by DARPA's Anti-Submarine Warfare Continuous Trail Unmanned Vessel Program (ACTUV), it was the smallest and fastest version of its class.

DR-Ultra held one back to use for clandestine missions. They'd added a personnel carrier to the mix called Threadwell. It could deliver a covert agent to an underwater target at unmatched speeds. They based the design on the Russian's VA-111 Shkval torpedo, one of the world's only supercavitating torpedos.

Nicks, ever the guinea pig, was becoming intimately acquainted with the insides of that system. This was the first time they had used it on a mission.

Since Quinn helped design it, it took her thirty minutes and two phone calls to get access. Now she was piloting the Sea Dagger from the team's pursuit helicopter.

"Okay, listen up, Viper," Byrne said. "You're locked on course and cleared for launch. Get ready."

Nicks tucked her head down and listened to the countdown.

A normal torpedo traveled around fifty-five knots or sixty-three miles per hour. Through the magic of supercavitation, Nicks's torpedo vaporized the surrounding water and enclosed itself in a bubble of air. The air bubble reduced the torpedo's drag by seventy percent and tripled its speed to over a hundred and fifty knots.

Shhfoommmm.

The torpedo shot from the Sea Dagger at a blinding speed.

As it closed in on the Abraxas, the tip of the torpedo fired a grappling projectile into the hull of the ship. Charges along the torpedo's body exploded, and its outer shell spilt open into four sections. When those fairings fell away, Nicks and her grappling mechanism were all that remained. The Abraxas was unknowingly dragging her along through the water.

She threw a switch and the device reeled her up to the stern with ease. She grabbed the swim platform and pulled herself onto the yacht.

It was quiet onboard. There was starlight but no moon. The chilly air off the ocean came in rolling gusts. Nicks snuck up the teak stairs to the aft deck.

The first thing she noticed was the security equipment. It was already disabled. The cameras dangled limply from their sockets, pulled or shot from their housings. The ship was ghostly quiet. Her intuition was buzzing but she kept moving.

She cased the main deck. A dinette and wet bar were next to two sliding glass doors that led into a salon. It was luxurious and decorated with high-end furniture, orchids, candles, and expensive art. She slipped inside and proceeded into the galley.

The galley was clean and undisturbed. She wondered if they had the correct yacht until she noticed the contents of the wine cooler. It was stocked with blood, enough for several surgeries. Disturbing to say the least. What the hell was going on here?

She crept up to the sky deck. The door to the bridge was ajar. No one was piloting the ship, but three monitors at the com station were alive with activity.

The navigation software was plotting the ship's course. The other monitors displayed the gauges showing engine speed, thruster activity, wind speed, and oil pressure. Everything was working perfectly.

Like the Sea Dagger, it was operating like an unmanned vehicle. That was unexpected, because the Yacht Center had reported it left with its normal crew.

Nicks took the spiral staircase down into the lower deck slowly and carefully. The haunting lack of a crew gave her pause. But once she cleared the passage she found what she was looking for. Several staterooms had been converted into a laboratory and surgical suite.

It was Vargas's secret lab and another gruesome scene.

Nicks reported to the team, "I cleared the yacht."

"What did you find?" Byrne asked.

"It's bad. Bring the body bags."

Nicks killed the engines on the Abraxas and the Sea Dagger and her team caught up. They roped down onto the yacht and the helicopter flew back to shore to refuel.

Quinn discovered someone was operating the yacht via a satellite feed. Who? She wasn't sure. She hacked into the system, took command of the ship, and set a course back to Long Beach Harbor.

Below deck in the lab, Byrne, Fatima, and Nicks studied what they had found.

"When I first saw this, I thought it was a joke—*a very bad joke*," Nicks said.

Byrne agreed it was twisted. Fatima was equally disgusted.

The lab was purposefully arranged to look like an electronics store—a product launch conceived by a madman. Two corpses lay on pristine metal tables covered with surgical drapes. Black computer monitors were positioned behind their heads like obsidian tombstones. Instead of iPads, human body parts were expertly arranged around the room. Each one had its analog, a matching bionic component, displayed next to it.

The lab was a showroom demonstrating which human parts could be replaced with cybernetic upgrades. The only thing missing was the right clientele and a geek squad with credit card terminals.

"I wonder how long he's been in business?" Nicks asked.

"One day is too long," Byrne said. "This is insanity."

Nicks lifted one of the drapes. The corpse had a long thoracic scar. It was fresh, as if he'd just had open-heart surgery. A code was written in black sharpie on his arm. It was a social security number. It matched one of the Echo Squad soldiers they couldn't find. Now they knew why.

"Major Hal Simmons," Nicks said with a defeated tone.

Byrne uncovered his face. Yes, it was Hal Simmons. The other man was—

"—Vargas!" Nicks gasped.

She'd failed to save either of them.

Their hot lead was as cold as the corpses in front of them.

WHILE THE TEAM continued to examine the lab, Nicks poked around the rest of the ship. She was the first to find something significant.

Vargas had taken the captain's room in the crew quarters. There were only a few personal items. Clothing. Swimwear. Toiletries. Hidden under his bunk, Nicks found a loaded Ruger .380 Light Compact Pistol, an iPad, and a large stash of Percocet.

Quinn walked in as she was going through the stash. She turned the iPad on. It was unlocked and filled with hundreds of documents, including Vargas's research for the TALON program, along with many new designs. There were also personal pictures in the Photos app.

They took it into the lab to share with the team. Everyone crowded around as Nicks flipped through the photographs. It was a lesson in how much the dead doctor loved himself.

Vargas with his research team. Receiving awards. Glad-handing the president of UCLA. A posed shot of Vargas peering into a microscope for the alumni magazine. Vargas in Vegas doing things they wished they could unsee. And one of him shaking Schwarzenegger's hand.

"The Governator. That's ironic," Byrne said.

"No shit," Nicks quipped. "The Terminator meets the terminator *builder*."

"He's traveled a lot," Fatima said. There were pictures of him at the Eiffel Tower, Barcelona, Rome, and Berlin. A younger Vargas partying with a team that looked a bit too straight. Not his normal crowd. Nicks studied the photo.

"Military, for sure," she said.

Byrne nodded in agreement.

Nicks stopped on a picture of him in front of an ornate building with a domed roof. It was some kind of temple. She shuddered as a wave of anxiety passed over her. She had avoided all images of the place for so long, it was a shock to see it again.

"Where is this? India?" Quinn asked.

"The Tomb of Ahmad Shah Durrani," she said, the dark shadow of her buried trauma chilled her blood. "Khandar, Afghanistan."

The place Nicks's life as a normal woman ended.

NICKS NOTICED Byrne had made a discovery of his own. On one side of the lab, Vargas had a collection of prototypes laid out in order of creation. They were different versions of the brain-computer interfaces, or BCI's, they'd found in the dead soldiers. Following the work, from left to right, Byrne showed her how Vargas had redesigned the device over time.

There were several more kapalas with metal wires fitted in the skullcaps suggesting an embedded antennae. Vargas seemed to be creating wireless BCI's that would have an expanded range, or perhaps a method of shielding a person from the BCI's signaling. Byrne handed Nicks a notebook with some notes by Vargas about bidirectional information flow and signal interruption to the central nervous system. He called the device the sigillum.

Byrne picked up one of the newer versions and gave it to Nicks. It looked like an integrated circuit—a black rectangle with several metallic prongs around the edges. The prongs were long and barbed like a roofing stable.

His final design had an ominous decorative detail—*a silver skull.*

"Dwight Johnson had one of these implanted in the back of his neck," Byrne told the team as they gathered around him.

Nicks watched as Byrne used a small flathead screwdriver to pry the ornamental face of the skull off the device. She leaned closer. "It looks like the same components we found in the other BCIs."

Byrne agreed. "Do any of you recall Bozkurt's experiments with moths?"

Quinn said she knew it. "They inserted integrated electronics into the insects prior to metamorphosis. They wanted to turn them into controllable UAV's, right?"

"Bio-bots is what they called them. They inserted micro-electronic payloads in the insect's thorax hoping it would naturally grow into the moth's nervous system as it continued to mature."

"You had me read that," Nicks said. She remembered it too

well. It was another example of cybernetic science that creeped her out and added to her reluctance to willingly give up control of her own body to the protocol system. "Didn't they patch into the flight muscles hoping they could control the wings?"

"Yes, exactly."

"What's the connection?" Nicks asked.

"Looks like Vargas was riffing on that experiment. He's expanded the testing pool. Jumped from insects to humans."

Byrne examined the last version on the bench.

"Once this is implanted, I'm not sure you could remove it without killing the host," Byrne said.

"DARPA would never approve something like that, would they?" Nicks asked.

"I don't think so, but I've been wrong before."

"I'll bet you this is why he was pushed out," Quinn said. "He found someone else to fund his research. Set up shop on the high seas."

Fatima turned Hal Simmons's head to one side. He had one of the skulls implanted in the base of his neck.

"So Echo Squad wasn't targeted for murder, they were being experimented on?" Fatima asked.

"Maybe the Bishop Group is paying Vargas to upgrade his men? To turn them into remote control bio-bots?" Nicks theorized.

Byrne had moved across the room. He was examining some of the other cybernetic components Vargas had laid out. "All I know for sure is these men were not willing participants."

Nicks flipped through the last pages of Vargas's notebook. There were references to Starfire everywhere. "This is it —*Project Starfire*—it has to be!" she said.

Her conclusion interested everyone except Byrne. He was hunched over a table mesmerized by another device.

"Byrne did you hear what Nicks just said?" Fatima said. "Do you agree? Could this be Starfire?"

"Quinn," he yelled, "grab the FLIR meter and get over here."

Byrne picked something up that looked like a hockey puck with several flexible cables attached to it.

"What in the hell do we have here?" he said. He lifted the device off the table with a pair of forceps. The ribbon-thin cables dangled like kite tails from the center of the device.

Nicks watched Quinn turn on the FLIR, an infrared imaging camera, and the screen on the back of the device filled with color. She waved it up and down Byrne's discovery.

"What do you see?" he asked.

Quinn turned it so Byrne and Nicks could see the screen. It was filled with strange colors. Byrne's hand was red. His forceps showed as purple. The center of the device was red-orange on one side and blue on the other. The attached ribbons dangled like yellow noodles.

"That's a power source," Byrne said excitedly. "A next generation power source to be exact."

"Is it bio-thermal?"

"If it is, that means it would be free of toxins."

"Fantastic," Quinn said.

Nicks noticed Quinn was giving Byrne side-glances, monitoring his reaction to the discovery. It was odd. She wasn't sure what was going on between them.

Byrne said, "Vargas seems to be obsessed with improving older TALON components."

"Penbrook will want to know about this ASAP," Nicks said.

Someone's phone rang, surprising everyone.

"Speak of the devil," Fatima quipped.

Nicks's stomach clenched. This was a covert mission. No one had a personal phone with them.

"What the hell?" Fatima said, zeroing in on Hal Simmons's remains.

Quinn looked ill. "Please tell me that's not—"

It was obvious the sound was coming from *inside* the corpse.

"Simmons is receiving a call," Nicks said, grimacing. "Who wants to answer that?"

Byrne unleashed a string of obscenities as he marched over to the corpse. He snapped on some surgical gloves and began impromptu surgery—reopening the thoracic incision by cutting away the sutures. Quinn held the chest cavity open with a pair of retractors. Byrne dug through Simmons's chest cavity until he found it—a Ziploc freezer bag stuffed in the right lung.

Byrne pulled it out and handed it to Quinn who extracted the smartphone and passed it to Nicks.

One of Nicks's trainers at The Farm often quoted a Japanese proverb: "The crab lies still on the chopping block, never knowing when the knife falls."

In this moment, she felt like that crab. All eyes were on her as she swiped her finger across the phone.

A strange symbol materialized on the screen. It was a mesmerizing animation of a demon with bulging eyes and fangs. It was wearing a crown of bloody skulls. Nicks watched it, somewhat hypnotized.

The Demon Queen, as Ms. Platinum had named her, was calling.

The knife had fallen.

31

"Hello, Natalie."

Nicks was confused why she was the one being addressed.

"I'm here," she said. "You have my undivided attention."

"I'm grateful for that."

"How about we start with introductions; you seem to know me, who in the hell are you?"

"I think you know. I'm the one making sure the weapons of the future are no longer in the hands of DR-Ultra—and your corrupt government."

Nicks didn't like the cat-and-mouse nature of the discussion, but she suppressed her natural inclination to be a smart-ass and played along.

"You admit to stealing this technology?"

"If by that you mean the *sigillum*, yes. But it was never theirs to begin with. Soon all of these innovations will be under the control of my organization."

"The Dharmapala?"

"*Very good*, you are paying attention. Scorpio said you would."

"So, she takes orders from you?"

"You've met her. Does she seem like a woman who does another's bidding? She serves our shared vision of the future."

"You admit to killing these men?"

"They were slaves to DARPA and its war machine. We liberated them."

"You are murdering *innocent* people—"

"*None* of you are innocent!"

"What does that mean?"

"Echo Squad were soldiers of fortune, willing to do anything for money, but they've outlived their usefulness. Vargas was an unprincipled man, full of vices and greed, and no sense of loyalty. We had need of his expertise but his betrayal was inevitable. He needed to be stopped before his research continued. The proof is right in front of your eyes."

"Proof? All I see are your victims. *Corpses.* These men are dead."

The conversation stopped. The woman on the other end of the phone laughed briefly. There was a long bone-chilling moment of silence before she spoke her final words and ended the transmission.

"No, Natalie. Not all of them ..."

The animation disappeared, and an audible spark of electricity flared near Vargas's head. The man took a deep breath and groaned in pain.

Byrne rushed to the man's side and checked his vitals. He had a pulse.

Dr. Victor Vargas was alive.

32

A s soon as the Abraxas docked, they were on their way back to the Cage with their Lazarus in tow.

The trip back took two helicopters. Nicks and Fatima took the dead in one, while Byrne and Quinn worked on Vargas in the other, keeping the man alive. Recovered tech and evidence was stashed in every nook and cranny the copters had.

The Cage had once been a grand library like something from a Victorian novel. Now, with three corpses on nitrogen freezer tables and the newly resurrected Vargas, it harkened back to those gothic origins, as if Dr. Frankenstein was about to begin a night of ambitious experiments.

Nicks played the role of Igor: mute, vacant expression, lost in thought watching the team working on Vargas. Her mind slithered through the clues discovered on the yacht. The Dharmapala was overconfident; one of their victims had survived, and that was a check in the win column for her team. Or was it?

Why didn't they finish the job?

VARGAS WAS the center of attention. Veins tapped. Tubes placed. IV's hung. Heart monitors activated. Quinn placed an EEG cap over his head. It was a prototype she was tinkering with.

It had two gears. In the first, a standard graph of brain waves, seen in most EEG reports, spilled across the screen. Second gear activated micro-thin needles retracted into the lattice of the headset. They sprung out with enough force to penetrate the scalp. It looked like a torture device, but it offered a view inside the brain few doctors had access to.

"His readings are erratic. Pattern suggests he's on the verge of a seizure," Byrne said to Quinn.

Vargas mumbled and pulled at his restraints. Quinn had trouble getting him to calm down.

"Get it off of me—you have to remove it—"

That's when Byrne and Quinn figured it out. Vargas had his own sigillum. Why the hell would he have experimented on himself?

"This is what's causing him to come in and out of his vegetative state."

To save his life, they would need to remove it. But how?

MOUSE GREW worried watching the team save Vargas's life. As Byrne and Quinn prepped for surgery, he opened up to Nicks about Vargas.

"While you guys were gone, I pulled up the research I had on him. I have a guy, a private detective who lives in Hollywood; he vets people before I get into business with them." He shared a story to put Vargas's work in context.

The Modular Prosthetic Limb (MPL) Nicks's biomimetic

arm was based on had an interesting back-story. It was first tested by a woman named Melissa Loomis.

One day, Melissa heard the screeching of her two dogs fighting with another animal. She rushed outside to discover a raccoon getting the best of her pets, so she intervened and was bitten on her right forearm.

Thirty days of intense treatment followed. This included twelve surgeries and a final amputation due to a terrible infection. Loomis saved her pets but lost most of her arm.

While she sat in her hospital room recovering, her best friends sent her little stuffed raccoons to cheer her up, and the researchers at John Hopkins, funded by DARPA, sent her reams of paper to read and sign. They needed her consent to attempt a new surgical procedure called Targeted Sensory Reinnervation (TSR).

The goal of this surgery was to create a human computer connection so the user of the prosthetic could hold things like stuffed raccoons and feel their softness. It restored the sense of touch.

While Dean Kamen, the famous inventor, prided himself on creating a hand that could pick up a grape without crushing it, these scientists wanted Melissa Loomis to *feel* the grape when she touched it.

To do so, they outfitted the arm and hand with hundreds of contact and temperature sensors. The TSR surgery remapped the web of nerves on her arm and connected each individual nerve with the appropriate electrode.

In this way, Loomis could sense the grape's cold taut skin. More importantly, she could pick up the grape and eat it.

"Her sense of touch was as it had been before the evil trash panda had mauled her arm. This incredible advancement pushed the modular limb into a new category: neuroprosthetics.

Vargas had been the leader in that research before he left to work for DR-Ultra," Mouse told her.

Nicks skimmed down Mouse's report. "Advanced Neural Engineering System Design was his focus."

"He was doing more than improving cybernetic arms. He was looking at how to control complete biological systems." Mouse said.

Nicks flipped to the end of the report. "Everything he worked on after John Hopkins is SAR," she said.

"SAR?" Mouse asked. "Refresh me."

"Special Access Required programs. Think of it as many levels above Top Secret. Need to know only," Nicks explained.

"Yeah, that's beyond what my P.I. could dig up. I guess if you want more it's up to you."

Actually, Nicks thought, it's up to Penbrook. Surely he would be happy to know they'd found Vargas and what seemed to be Project Starfire. But before they delivered the news, they had to save the man's life.

BYRNE AND QUINN reconfigured the surgical table so Vargas was in a prone position. They gave him the anesthesia and prepped his neck and spine for surgery.

Byrne felt he understood the components of the device enough to remove it, but once the surgery began his mood soured.

"I'm not sure we can get this out without causing permanent damage."

Quinn consoled him. "Just do your best. He's barely alive as it is."

Byrne steadied himself and tried to remove the first barb.

The implant surged with a microburst of energy, zapping Byrne and causing him to lose his grip on his instruments.

Vargas, although heavily sedated, seemed to react.

Byrne persisted and tried again. This time the result was worse.

"A partial complex seizure. His cerebral-spinal fluid pressure is too high," Quinn yelled.

Byrne looked at Quinn. They both knew it was futile. He was killing Vargas.

"It's not coming out, I'm going to close him up. We'll have to solve this another way."

Hours later, Vargas was recovering in a bed across from Mouse.

Byrne and Quinn buzzed around him, vigilantly watching for any sign of improvement.

"He's coming around," Quinn said triumphantly.

Nicks approached the bed as Vargas stirred. His glassy eyes focused on her and he reached out for her hand. She offered it reluctantly and he gave her a gentle squeeze. Fighting to shake off the sedative, he strained to speak.

"Natalie Nicks," he whispered, "*She* wants *you*, most of all."

33

Everyone buzzing around Vargas was worried about his comfort. He was the only one who didn't care. Something was overriding his pain. He felt blissful.

His anxiety was gone too. His internal struggle to remain in control of his own thoughts had seemed like a war worth fighting but now he wasn't sure why he'd ever resisted. The suffering wasn't worth it. The moment he gave in all feelings of reluctance and doubt were smothered by her voice and its reassuring echoes.

You're right where you are meant to be.

Her voice told him everything he had dreamed was coming to fruition. He was at the center of a new vanguard. One of its key members. A position he deserved. He was destined to be celebrated as the man responsible for the evolution of humanity.

All he had to do was listen to the comforting instructions echoing faintly in his head. Just follow the wisdom of his muse. She knew exactly what he needed to do.

Everything will happen as it should.

His first task was to assess his surroundings.

Next, he needed to secure a suitable weapon.

A piece of surgical equipment was a good choice. Something with a blade that could kill someone quickly with minimal effort. It was critical he was ready when Colonel Byrne reentered the med bay.

He would appear to be sedated so Byrne would approach him without suspicion. The voice would signal him at the exact moment he should attack.

He understood that if he didn't do this, the pain inhibitors would be turned off and he would be in unbearable agony. So much pain, in fact, he might go mad.

If he killed Byrne without raising alarm, he would be rewarded with the one thing he so desperately longed for—wealth beyond his imagination—as a faithful member of the Dharmapala's council. He'd live like the king he knew himself to be.

34

Sometime later, everything was quiet in The Cage. The space had two designated medical bays. One was built into one of the library's reading alcoves. The newer one across the room had more features. Its ceiling, floor, and back wall could be modified. The walls were on tracks, easily moved out or recessed, allowing the space to be converted into various combinations.

These spaces could serve as a surgical suite or larger hospital beds could be brought in if needed. One combination Byrne had not used until now was the morgue configuration. He was sad to see it at capacity.

The hospital was filling up as well.

Back on the west side of the library, his patient was sleeping, seemingly peaceful. Byrne slipped through the med-bay's door, adjusted the room's temperature, and checked the monitors.

According to the readings, his heart rate was high but within normal limits. Pulse-ox looked good. Time to check the wound. It seemed to be free of infection. Might as well change the dressings.

Byrne grabbed a sterile bandage kit and stepped closer to the bed. As he did, the heart monitor sped up.

Was he disturbing him? He'd thought he was being quiet.

"Sorry, I thought you were sleeping," Byrne said softly. "How are you feeling?"

His patient wouldn't look at him. He was hiding something in the bed sheets. Before Byrne could react, the patient seized his wrist, and swung the thing, like a weapon—

"Why in the hell can't I get a signal, in here?" Mouse shook his smartphone in Byrne's face, accusingly.

"Damn," Byrne startled, "you spooked me!"

"Sorry, my guy. But what's up with the shitty wifi?"

"The Cage is a *Faraday Cage*, that's why. Are you telling me your lab isn't protected in the same way?"

"Not twenty-four-seven, man." Mouse was dejected. "I'm going through withdrawals. Can't you lower the force field for an hour? I mean, I can't even play my music, and I need it bad since you parked Mr. Weirdo next to me. You know he's talking to himself over there—I think you fried his circuits for *real*."

"How about a better sedative." Byrne waved a syringe in front of Mouse like it was a treat.

"If I can't get online, I'll take it."

Byrne stabbed Mouse with the little needle. "So, he's chatty?"

"No man, he's not talking to me. It's weird shit. Like he's talking to someone that's not there. It's creeping me out."

"What's he been saying?"

"Ask him yourself, he's standing right behind you."

35

Nicks headed to her bedroom to take a break. She could hear Quinn in her room snoring. Fatima was in Byrne's room going through his desk drawers.

"Uh-huh, caught you red-handed!" Nicks said. "What in the hell are you stealing now?"

"This!" Fatima flashed a metallic keycard.

"Oh, no you don't, that's for the team leader." She reached for it but Fatima hid it behind her back.

"I've opened almost every door in this facility, save one. I bet this gets me in."

"In where?"

"Basement level two."

"That's a storage room. Nothing in there, I promise you."

"Wanna bet?'

Nicks shrugged. "What the hell are you going on about?"

"You're second in command, right?"

"Yeah, but that doesn't have—"

"So, Byrne is busy, is he not?"

"Yes, but ..."

"I have a theory. Wanna help me test it?"

"If it will cure your kleptomania, sure, I'm in."

"Then escort me to the basement, and let's see what's behind that door. Shall we?"

36

When Vargas stabbed the colonel with a six-inch Shandon post-mortem blade, Byrne didn't realize he was wounded until hot blood poured down his legs into his camouflaged Crocs.

A true samurai sword, like the one Scorpio used, was tempered so expertly and sharpened so methodically, it could cut a man in two pieces, swiftly and completely. The unlucky victim would find himself legless, disemboweled, and seconds from death before his brain ever registered the slightest bit of pain.

Surgical steel was created in a similar way.

Byrne grabbed Vargas's wrist, making sure the blade didn't go any deeper.

"Mouse, get help!"

Mouse screamed every expletive he knew as he leapt out of his bed. His bare feet hit the floor ready to run not realizing the sedative was kicking in. Mouse couldn't find his balance, and tumbled, falling face-first into the growing pool of Byrne's blood. *Splat!*

"Shit, shit, shit!" Mouse argued with his body. "Get the hell up!" His body shouted back—*sleep*! Darkness closed over him. He wasn't going anywhere.

MEANWHILE, Byrne had turned on Vargas like a wounded grizzly bear. Completely improvising, he had stabbed Vargas in the cheek with the syringe he'd been holding. Vargas took it in stride.

He'd boxed Byrne in, pinning him to the bed rail. Byrne pushed Vargas backward and they fought. With each swing, they became more entangled in the monitor wires and intravenous tubing hanging near the bed.

Byrne landed a solid right cross but Vargas wouldn't stop.He stabbed Byrne again. He was vicious and wild.

Byrne had been in hand-to-hand combat numerous times but this wasn't a trained fighter trying to kill him, this was a madman, flailing and screaming, like he was possessed. He seemed impervious to any pain or punishment Byrne dealt out.

When he finally opened up some space, Byrne hit him with a brutal palm strike to the jaw. It forced Vargas backward—long enough for Byrne to grab a nearby metal instrument tray. Vargas swiped the blade at Byrne. Byrne countered with the tray, swinging it like a shield.

Smack-clang!

The dissection blade fell to the floor, barely missing Mouse's face.

Byrne eyed the panic button near the med bay door and lunged for it.

37

A t first glance, the storage area was as empty as Nicks had predicted. Boxes and crates of equipment were organized neatly in one corner of the room with a mesh security gate around them.

In the front corner were several familiar crates, all of them peppered with bullet holes. They were the only items without a coat of dust. The largest crate was shattered.

"These are the equipment crates from the warehouse," Nicks said.

Someone had chained the two MAARS units to the concrete wall. They looked like medieval prisoners in a dungeon. Nicks walked around them warily.

"According to what Penbrook told you, this is what Echo Squad stole. Correct?" Fatima asked.

"Right, they provided security while this equipment was transported out of Blackwood Lodge to its assigned field test locations," Nicks said.

"But, since they were greedy bastards, they decided they would divert them to that toy warehouse, and sell them on the black market."

"That seems to be what happened. It was a stupid plan."

"I agree, but whoever stole Project Starfire was a genius."

"I'm not following you."

"Bear with me, I'll explain."

Fatima walked around the MAARS crate. It was the largest. She ran her hand along the sides, caressing the wood as if admiring the carpentry.

"What's this about, Fatima? What's this theory you want to test?

"Do you remember my story about what happened in Syria?"

"The DIA was supplying your group with weapons but the squad leader sexually assaulted one of the women, right? Another woman went crazy you said, and attacked the soldiers."

"Yes, it was the worst mistake of my life," Fatima said. "Not because I attacked the men, but because I didn't kill them all. I should have slaughtered them and taken the weapons by force. My sisters would still be alive."

"Wait. You were that woman?" Nicks couldn't believe it.

"Yes," Fatima said. "And the squad leader was Charlie Tango."

Nicks was stunned. She stared at Fatima.

"If you're trying to think of what to say, don't. That wasn't the read in. There's more."

"Lay it on me."

"You know Penbrook, I don't. However, I've gathered that he's been a little more emotional about this particular mission. Is that true?"

"I have to agree. I assumed because Project Starfire is so dangerous, and he feels responsible."

"Do you know how the DIA recruited me?"

"Penbrook hasn't shared anything about you with me."

"After they killed my sisters, I hunted ISIS every night.

One by one, I picked off the jihadis who were responsible. The other side believed I was the ghost of one of the murdered women. The DoD knew who I was because Echo Squad reported me. The DIA came looking for me. Probably to arrest me, but then they discovered what I had done. Over a hundred kills with a homemade sniper rifle. They offered me a deal. Join the DIA and test DR-Ultra's new smart bullets in the field. They needed to insert me in very dangerous places without risking anyone else's life. So they devised a system to smuggle me in. They dropped crates with food and medical supplies into these hot zones. Once the villagers scavenged the last scrap of food from the crate, I slipped out in the middle of the night."

Fatima's hand stopped along the bottom of the MAARS crate. She ran her fingers along the wood for a second and activated a hidden lever.

Click!

A secret compartment swung out from under the crate, like a sleeper from under a sofa. Nicks was astonished.

The hidden compartment was padded and outfitted with a panel of electronic controls. It had an air filtration system with an oxygen mask and plastic tubing running this way and that. Empty packets that may have contained food or water were stored in one corner.

"What in the hell is this? It appears they were smuggling—"

"—a person. Right out of Blackwood," Fatima said.

"How long have you suspected this?"

"It was a hunch. I didn't know for sure." Fatima inspected it more closely. "This is exactly like the one DR-Ultra built for me. The compartments are shielded. X-rays won't penetrate it. The walls give off false electronic readings if they are scanned by other devices. The space is claustrophobic but it's environmentally controlled. You're plugged in like an astronaut. Food, water, bodily fluids all taken care of. You can theoretically stay in here for a long time."

"You said DR-Ultra built this?"

"Yes."

"But ... Penbrook would have known to check—"

Fatima interrupted. "Here's my theory. Project Starfire wasn't stolen. Starfire *escaped* Blackwood Lodge. Penbrook isn't searching for a dangerous weapon. He's looking for a dangerous *person*."

"Damn, of course. Why wouldn't he say so?"

She wasn't surprised there were more layers, but finding out this late in the game pissed her off so much she couldn't see straight.

Fatima was watching her put the pieces together. Nicks eyed her.

"There's something else, isn't there?"

Fatima nodded. "I have to assume the missing person's code-name is Starfire—I think she's the one behind— "

"—the *Dharmapala!*"

As if to emphasize how Nicks felt about what she was hearing, the alarms blared — there was trouble in the Cage.

Vargas tried to talk to Byrne over the blaring alarm. "You fell right into her trap—you shouldn't have brought me here!"

Byrne scrambled away from Vargas; he was losing too much blood.

Strangely, his blood was his best defense. So much coated the floor it kept Vargas at bay. The madman was slipping and sliding, unable to gain traction. But he wasn't giving up.

Vargas grabbed a bone saw and swung it like an axe at Byrne. Byrne stayed in full retreat, grabbing loose rags and bandages as he dodged the saw, and packing his wound as he went.

He fell and couldn't get back up. He was in serious trouble but crawled forward on arms and elbows. Behind him, Vargas was muttering his bullshit. The alarm blared but no one was coming. Panic crept up his spine and grabbed him by the throat.

Where was his team? His chest heaved and a wave of darkness washed over him, threatening to sweep him away into oblivion.

Nicks jumped up the last flight of stairs, overtaking Fatima. Quinn was on her way downstairs simultaneously. At the south end of the Cage, Vargas was standing over Byrne with a shiny stainless steel surgical saw. Byrne was soaked in blood. Not moving.

Nicks searched her workspace for her gun. Her holster was there but the gun was gone.

Vargas mumbled, "You have no place in the Dharmapala's future, Byrne."

"Vargas, stop!" Nicks yelled.

Vargas turned around, pleading with his deranged eyes. Byrne rolled on his side and kicked Vargas, sweeping one leg out from under him. Vargas buckled.

Nicks leapt across the room. She grabbed Byrne and pulled him out of Vargas's reach, setting Vargas into a rage. He stood back up and moved on Nicks and Byrne.

He waved the saw like a sickle, flailing and muttering. One of the brightest minds in the room had devolved into a madman, clawing at the team like an animal with rabies. He swung the saw back, ready to slash Byrne again.

BAM! BAM! BAM! BAM!

The first bullet hit Vargas in the chest, but he didn't go down. The next two missed Vargas entirely. By sheer luck, the last one hit Vargas in the head, and he fell dead.

Across the room, the shooter stumbled out into the open. It was Mouse with Nicks's gun. He couldn't hold it straight. He swayed back and forth, like a drunk about to pass out. When it was clear Vargas was not getting back up, he collapsed like a rag doll.

Quinn and Fatima scrambled to Byrne's side. Nicks placed Byrne's head in her lap. He was fading fast.

"Should've dumped that bastard in the ocean," she said.

Byrne's face was alien gray, but he managed a few words before passing out completely.

"If you don't stop this bleeding in the next few seconds, I'm as dead as Vargas."

"It appears Dr. Vargas has failed us again," Scorpio said. "He's missed the window for signaling for exfiltration."

Starfire's voice reverberated through Scorpio's mind.

The fact they've welcomed him in like the Trojan Horse is all the victory we needed. He's led us to their location.

"How do you know?" Scorpio asked.

The communication device you planted came online a few moments ago even though their headquarters is shielded. They're being careless, which means Vargas has served his purpose. Their guard is down.

Scorpio's screen morphed into a map. New coordinates pinged. The map zoomed in on the location—it was a large residence in the Hollywood Hills.

It's time to push Viper out of her nest.

"It's not far. The Angelos Grove Estate."

They think these fortresses make them secure.

"We will show them otherwise," Scorpio said.

Destroy the nest, and take what's most precious to her.

"She won't have a choice—"

Exactly. She'll bring what we want right to us.

Hours later, Quinn emerged from the surgical suite. She tore off her surgical gown and fell into the arms of Nicks, who was there waiting for her.

"He's alive and out of immediate danger," she whispered.

They sat at the main table so Quinn could debrief Nicks. Windows filled the monitors with various aspects of Byrne's health data.

"He's breathing on his own, but the vitals aren't good. There was a lot of trauma."

"Should we get him to another facility?"

"No, we can't move him right now, too dangerous. I had to —well—"

"You did what you could," Nicks said.

Quinn managed a half smile.

"His brain activity is wonky but WNL," Quinn said. "Let's just say his whole body needs time to *reboot.*"

Nicks gave her a confused glance.

"I'm too tired to rehash it all, Nat. He's one of the toughest men I've met. For now, cross your fingers and pray," Quinn said.

Nicks knew she wasn't getting all the details, but she didn't push.

"You saved his life. That's all that matters. Thank you!"

NICKS CHECKED ON BYRNE.

Despite his war injuries, his normal impression was that of a man in his prime health. Nicks had seen him struggle with his chronic pain, but she'd never seen him this bad. When they had been lovers, she joked the air temperature around him was always ten degrees warmer than the rest of the room. An indomitable vibrancy radiated from every pore of his body.

Right now, he looked terrible. His skin was clammy and he struggled to breathe. She wondered if he would ever fully recover. She stroked his arm, squeezed his shoulder and whispered in his ear. He seemed to react to her voice.

She leaned in closer, hoping to hear him speak. But there was no sound except the hum of the machines keeping her friend alive, and her pent-up emotion slowly breaking free.

42

Nicks and Fatima finished tidying up and put away the cleaning supplies. The Cage was quiet except for the machines monitoring Byrne's recovery. The smell of bleach wafted through the space as a cool breeze swirled in from outside. Quinn and Mouse had opened the doors leading out to the garden level. Nicks could hear them both by the pool discussing things in a somber tone. Occasionally, there was a genuine laugh. Everyone was still shaken—any sign of resiliency was a good and welcome thing.

She grabbed a new bottle of tequila. Her once ample stock was dwindling.

"Let's join them!"

"I need a shower first. I'll meet you out there," Fatima said.

"Sounds like a plan." Nicks grabbed a glass, a lime, and some ice and headed toward the sounds of life.

THE TEMPERATURE WAS PERFECT. A gentle breeze filtered

through the trees as the sun dipped below the western horizon, painting the sky with crimson and purple clouds.

The tequila eventually did its job suppressing the anger, the unsettling feelings left by the many unanswered questions, and the smoldering desire for revenge. Nicks embraced the rare moment of relief and chatted with her friends. Mouse looked quite content. He sat by the pool wrapped in a beach towel, playing with his phone. As close to Quinn as the pool chairs would allow.

Quinn had let her hair down, literally; it hung around her tattooed shoulders, damp from her swim. She looked so calm you'd never know she'd been on her feet for twelve hours doing surgery. Another sign of her inherent toughness—growing up around violence bestowed an uncommon ability to adapt to almost anything.

Nicks poured herself another drink and sat down on the other side of Mouse.

"You know we need to use this pool more," Quinn said.

"You guys have it made. Wonder how much it's worth?" Mouse asked.

"Don't even think about it. You've got enough money to build your own damn mansion, leave ours alone."

"I couldn't live here—the cell service sucks! It's been driving me crazy!"

"See, that's why you don't have a girlfriend. You're married to your phone."

"This isn't mine. I borrowed it from the lab. Is it yours, Nat?" Mouse waved it at her.

Nicks did a double take.

"Mouse goddamn it, you shouldn't have taken that out of the Cage!" She ripped it out of his hand, crushed it in her bionic grip, and tossed it into the deep end of the pool.

Quinn jumped up. "What the hell, man! Are you crazy? That thing—

"—was the phone we found on the Abraxas. The Dharma-pala planted it there."

Mouse was confused. "The *dharma-who*? I've been sitting beside you for a while, if it's such a big deal, why didn't you say something."

"I didn't think anyone was that stupid."

Mouse stared at Quinn, his expression of curiosity melting into shame. "Shit, we've been out here maybe twenty minutes. If they are tracking—"

Nicks wanted to hit him. "Twenty-*freaking*-minutes?"

"Actually, longer than that, I came out to the pool house to shower. After that, I was checking messages. An hour. That's how long it's been."

"Which means she's had enough time to find our location and—"

"Who's tracking who?"

Nicks clamped her hand over Mouse's mouth. "Shhhhhhh!"

Mouse stopped talking.

Nicks looked up in the sky. Something was coming their way fast.

They all stood up. They could see a drone on the horizon. It looked like a MQ-1 Predator but sleeker, almost invisible against the darkening sky. It had missiles hanging from its wings —confirmation Mouse had been on the phone way too long.

"I fucked up!" Mouse said.

"That is a massive understatement," Quinn replied.

The drone swooped closer. Barreling toward the mansion.

"Take cover!" Nicks yelled.

The team dove behind the concrete garden wall just as the drone released its payload and the missile's thrusters engaged.

43

The missile flying through the air toward Nicks and her team was a Raylock Hawkfire 732 short-range missile. Nicks, Mouse, and Quinn hit the ground as it passed overhead like a fiery comet. It slammed into the southeast corner of the building and exploded.

The concussive blast hit the team, sending them sprawling for a second time. Quinn landed on top of Nicks with Mouse flattened at their feet.

Once she shook off the impact, Nicks looked at the mansion. A small cloud of smoke and debris was mushrooming into the sky. The estate's fire and sprinkler system had activated. Water burst from nozzles and smoke alarms buzzed.

Quinn tried to get up, but Nicks held her in place.

"Wait, don't move. That thing may come back around."

Nicks's implants engaged, and her ears targeted and amplified the sound of the drone. In spite of having an additional missile, the UAV was moving away from their location. Thank goodness.

"It's gone. We're clear. Are you guys okay?" she asked.

"Yeah, I'm fine but what about Byrne and Fatima?"

"Let's find out. Mouse, you stay put."

He didn't protest. He was busy looking over Nicks's shoulder.

"Well, at least you guys have faster response times than Koreatown," Mouse let out a sigh of relief. "Here comes the cops!"

A squad of men dressed like LAPD SWAT was coming around the corner and through the garden. They headed straight for the damaged section of the building.

"How's that possible?" Quinn wondered. "There's no way they made it here that fast." Something didn't add up.

"Unless they were waiting for the drone to attack us," Nicks said. "Which means those guys aren't LAPD."

She signaled her teammates to retreat behind the pool house, but it was too late. One gunman spotted them.

"Lay down suppressive fire," he yelled. "Do not let those three advance on this position." The squad leader motioned to two of his men, and they complied.

Nicks, Quinn, and Mouse disappeared behind the pool house as automatic gunfire ripped into the pool chairs, tearing them to shreds.

Nicks snuck a glance when the gunfire paused. A couple of gunmen were holding ground on level two, covering her position. She was at a serious disadvantage. She watched as the rest of the tactical team entered the Cage through the missile crater.

Nicks's group couldn't do anything about it. They were trapped and outnumbered. Also inexplicably safe. If these gunmen wanted them dead, it would have been easy to finish them off. She estimated they had at least seven to eight in total.

A few minutes later, the squad emerged from the crater. Two were carrying computer equipment. Two more had a man on a stretcher.

"That's the colonel." Quinn cursed. "Who are these assholes?"

Nicks watched helplessly as they carried him off, around the corner, and out of view. She couldn't tolerate waiting another second and stepped out of cover as if to go after them. She picked up a nearby pool chair and hurled it at the men on level two. It hit the decorative stucco railing with a crash and sprayed the closest gunmen with pieces of metal and shards of concrete. He ducked shielding his face but his partner was undeterred. Another volley of bullets peppered the ground in front of Nicks as Quinn jerked her back to safety.

Quinn whispered, "This isn't an attack on the team. It's a raid!"

"Fatima's in there," Nicks said. "I hope to God she's loading her rifle."

"If she's still alive," Mouse said solemnly.

While they prayed she was, the gunmen opened up on their position again. Then they peeled off one-by-one, emptying their clips as they went, and faded into the night.

Nicks burst from her hiding place and raced after them. Even with her enhanced speed, she was too late. When she rounded the corner of the mansion, they'd vanished like ghosts.

She was dumbfounded by how quickly and savagely they'd been hit.

The Dharmapala had successfully raided her home, kidnapped Jack Byrne, and possibly killed Fatima. Their investigation was now all out war.

PART VII

WICKED WORLD

44

How the hell did I get mixed up in this?

Nicks repeated her question like a mantra as she dug through the concrete and debris of her headquarters. She knew the historical events that brought her to the current situation, but how in the hell did she get ... *here?*

Nicks didn't want to fight another war. She wanted to get a case of cheap wine, a Brazilian wax, a pack of flavored condoms, and run away with one of her crazy Army girlfriends. She needed at least six months of full on drunkenness and bad sexual decisions.

She imagined it could start with hot-wiring two Harley-Davidsons. They'd hit the road and along the way, they'd stop and set up a tent behind every redneck roadhouse they found.

Her banner would read: *Nicky the Naked Cyborg.*

Come on in boys! See the things this she-borg can do with her bionic parts.

If you were going to risk your life, why not make it fun.

That's where I should be, she thought. That's where Fatima should be.

Not buried under a mound of wreckage.

Nicks powered through the rubble, using her arm like an earthmover. When she hit the bottom of the pile, Fatima was nowhere to be found.

She wasn't anywhere else in the estate either. The only explanation was that the raiders had taken her. Perhaps, when Nicks had ducked for cover, she'd missed the moment. Maybe they took her through the front door?

All the other entrances were still secure. There was no way into the Cage; the enemy had known that and had gone to extremes to compensate.

What were they doing with Fatima and Byrne? She had to get them back alive and in one piece.

"I'm amazed so much is still here, I mean look at it, beside the hole in the wall over there," Quinn said, "Everything around the crater is intact."

"It was a precision strike. They wanted to get into this specific level. How did they know about it?" Mouse wondered.

"Somehow the Dharmapala has been one step ahead of us. They knew about the tech in the warehouse before I got there. They cleared the yacht before we arrived. And they knew exactly where to hit the estate's structure to break into the Cage. There can't be more than a handful of people with that intel on us," Nicks said.

There was an explanation—one that sent a shiver down Nicks's spine.

"If DR-Ultra has a leak. Why didn't we get assigned to investigate it?" Quinn asked, rhetorically.

"I know why—they didn't tell you, that's why," Mouse said.

"Well, thanks *Einstein*, so helpful," Quinn grunted.

"There is no *they* that assigns missions," Nicks replied.

The two women looked at each other, both picturing the one person who held all the cards. Nicks didn't have to say his name.

Penbrook.

QUINN AND NICKS compared notes in one corner while Mouse sorted through the debris. A large piece of loose sheetrock had fallen over some of his belongings.

"Can I say something? I realize I've been secretive too." He wedged the sheetrock off the pile and pushed it out of the way. "If it'll make you feel better, I promise from this point forward, I will always keep you two in the loop. Starting with this ..."

Mouse waved them over and pointed at his find.

"Uh ... there's a naked dead guy under your stairs."

Nicks and Quinn looked at Mouse. Their situation was becoming more unreal by the second.

"Where's the hand sanitizer?" Mouse pleaded. "I'm gonna need the whole bottle."

MOUSE's dead guy was the only KIA in the mansion. Quinn double-checked their makeshift morgue. This dead guy was definitely a new customer. He had a well-placed knife wound in his neck.

"Well, it's obvious he's one of the assault team, but who killed him?"

"I'm guessing our missing girl," Nicks said. "Who else?"

"So where is his gun?" Mouse wondered. "Nothing else is under the stairwell except a bloody t-shirt with a bunch of nastiness on it."

Nicks grabbed a pair of hemostats lying on the table and walked over to the bloody shirt. She clamped it and picked it up.

Mouse cringed. "That's sick, man. Oh, don't get it close to your face ... what the hell ... are you smelling it?"

Nicks was playing detective, blood be damned. One hundred percent cotton, size small, designer brand, from her last trip to Nordstrom's at the Grove.

"That sneaky bitch, she stole this from me," Nicks said. "Good for her."

"So, she's a professional killer and a thief. Why is that a good thing?" Mouse asked.

"What are you thinking, Nat? She's following them?" Quinn asked.

"No, I already checked the garage. All the vehicles are still here."

"Are we sure his gear is gone?" Nicks asked.

The team fanned out for one more look. Deep inside, she knew they wouldn't find a thing. Nicks figured if Fatima was still alive, she was with Byrne. That was comforting but presented another concern. Fatima, in spite of being a badass, was outnumbered.

The minute she was exposed, she was dead—unless Nicks could find her first. She had one idea that might make that possible.

"Mouse, go upstairs—second bedroom on the left. Grab Fatima's things. I don't think she's even unpacked. Then meet Quinn and me in the garage."

Quinn and Nicks raced down the hall while Nicks laid out her plan. The raiders had a big head start. If Reaper Force was going to rescue their friends, every second counted.

45

While Quinn opened the garage doors and fired up the engine of their surveillance van, Nicks got Mouse set up in the back on a laptop and the van's com equipment.

"I'm deputizing you, Mouse. You're an encryption expert. Get on our system and review the CCTV footage around the property. We need to identify the vehicles they're using."

Mouse dutifully went to work.

"Quinn, do you remember the company Elessar?"

"The one Byrne was envious of because it's a cool *Lord of the Rings* reference? Santa Monica, right?"

"Yes, we need to hack into their database."

"Why not just pull rank? DR-Ultra could get authorization," Quinn said.

"We don't have time for that. We need eyes on their vehicles, now. We can't waste another minute!"

Elessar was one of those scary companies that made the average citizen of any political persuasion queasy. Especially if you hated the government spying on its citizens. They had a contract with the Northern California Regional Intelligence

Center compiling a database of all California license plates, and they used it in a way that put Big Brother to shame.

According to Byrne, the original Elessar was an object from one of his favorite fantasy novels. An elfstone that allowed elves to predict the future. Elessar—the tech company version—used their super-computer to process video cam footage from all over the state of California.

They had captured millions of license plates and the location of those captures, then matched those plates to the car owners through the state's motor vehicle department. They saved favorite and frequent stops and used algorithms to predict the possible route and final destination of any vehicle on the road. All in the name of national security.

Mouse cracked his knuckles and attacked the keyboard with a newfound fury. Several minutes later, he had what they needed.

"Hard to believe, but they didn't think to disable your cameras. They parked right outside the entrance."

Nicks watched as Mouse replayed the exact moment they pulled up. The raiders arrived dressed like professional body-guards in expensive suits. One black SUV and another vehicle that could be a tactical SWAT van parked along the street, near the gate.

In their neighborhood, these cars wouldn't draw any attention. Many wealthy foreigners, like middle-eastern princes flush with oil money, hired large details for their entourage. Excessive security served as a status symbol. The number of cars that followed you around town determined your importance.

Similarly, many celebrities hired teams for events at their homes. A security detail showing up at Angelos Grove Estate would be utterly forgettable to the residents of their neighborhood.

Nicks watched as they walked up to the gate of the estate,

somehow defeated the gate lock, and proceeded onto the grounds. Inside, they took cover in the trees and donned their tactical gear. They were all men and looked ex-military.

The man leading the squad seemed familiar. Nicks was sure it was the one member of Echo Squad they hadn't found. He had a tattoo on his forearm. Nicks zoomed in. It was a chess piece—a black bishop.

"Can you read one of those plates?" Mouse asked as he took control of the display and zoomed in. California required all vehicles to display front and back tags. Nicks read one plate aloud as he typed it into the computer.

"Got it!"

Elessar used DARPA funding, and access points were set up for the military to tap into the data. Those secret nodes in the system were vulnerable if you were an expert on military encryption—or if you happened to be the person who wrote the encryption program and sold the license to the government.

"After this is over, I'll get back in here and fix these holes. These dumbasses haven't used any of the patches I suggested. And that was a year ago."

Nicks gave Mouse a good job pat on his shoulder.

"Find their last recorded location and feed it to me over the coms. I'm headed after them, you guys are the chase van," Nicks said, as she climbed out of the vehicle.

"Where the hell are you going?" Quinn asked.

"You know your special project I rescued from our sticky-fingered comrade? Is that bent fork fixed?"

Quinn gave Nicks a high-voltage grin.

"I thought you'd never ask!"

46

Fatima was amazed she was still alive.

Sometimes the best place to hide was in plain sight. It was a cliché they had taught in her clandestine services training. She had doubted that logic until fifteen minutes ago. Now she knew the cliché had merit.

However, she was also realistic. Her charade wouldn't last long. At some point the medic and the other raider riding with her in the back of the van would size her up.

When things calmed down, they would notice she was too short and too small and looked nothing like the real operator she had killed and hidden under the north stairwell.

Any moment, she might need to take off the tactical goggles. The team would see their buddy was wearing expensive eyeliner and some damn good mascara. Without the ballistic helmet, her long hair would be another surprise sure to raise questions and a hail of bullets.

Right now, she was okay. The van interior was dark and the other operator was watching their rear. The medic was confused by Byrne's vital signs and working furiously to keep him stable.

She hoped that meant they'd grabbed Byrne for a reason, not to kill him. But why take him in the first place?

What was the next move?

She had no way to contact the team. When they searched for her and couldn't find her it would add to their confusion.

Did she act now or wait?

The driver was behind a thick blackout curtain they had strung up to hide the cargo. Did the mercenaries fear being stopped? She had no way of seeing their current location.

Where were they going?

She could kill the medic and the mercenary. She was carrying a Heckler & Koch MP5SD. But how to do that and handle the driver? She had a sound suppressor on the submachine gun, but that wouldn't mask a gunfight a few inches away.

She checked the other gear on her belt. A M67 frag grenade. Nope, she couldn't use that in close quarters. The WK double-edged tactical dagger was a good choice but not quick enough. Byrne could get hurt in the ensuing struggle.

The minutes were ticking away, if she was going to save Byrne—and her own ass—she needed a foolproof plan.

47

D irty thunder.

That's what her Uncle Wilco called it. He borrowed the phrase from *Hell's Angels,* one of his favorite Hunter S. Thompson books.

The jaw-rattling rumble of a Harley. The raging road hog's V-engine. Exhaust growling. Vibrating the chrome off the bike and the teeth out of your jaw. It was the sound Nicks grew up with. The only sound she associated with a motorcycle.

Quinn's Ghostrider was something different.

She flew down the 405 faster than any Harley could dream of. The machine between her legs was alive with power that seemed alien. It was almost completely silent.

The minute sounds it made washed away in the road noise. She was truly a ghost. A very pissed-off ghost with rage bubbling through her like hot motor oil.

"Are you still tracking my location?" Nicks asked.

"Yep, we're following you in the van," Quinn said. "But you're miles ahead of us. If you catch them, you're on your own."

"They're the ones who should worry, not me," Nicks growled. "You guys have an update for me?"

"Mouse is in Elessar's database now. The last image was captured on the 105, the trajectory is west. We're waiting for the next plate capture to process."

Nicks raced on, weaving through traffic.

"The program is predicting three possible destinations. LAX, Costco in Hollyglen, or the Los Angeles Air Force Base on El Segundo."

"I doubt they're stopping for toilet paper," Mouse joked.

"LAX or the Air Force Base," said Quinn.

"That's insane, they'd blow their cover so fast. Too much police activity and security at LAX," Nicks brain was overheating. "A military base doesn't fit either. They wouldn't make it through the gate with a kidnapped officer in their van."

"We're bound to get another hit soon. It will narrow the possibilities."

"It can't happen fast enough!"

48

After about forty-five minutes of traveling, the raider's van finally rolled to a stop. The driver lowered his window and a gruff voice asked for identification. Several long seconds went by. The medic and the mercenary in back with Fatima grew tense.

Fatima wished she had Nicks's hearing. All she could make out was a few snippets of the exchange.

"Wait right here," the gruff voice said.

They waited.

One minute became two.

The medic went back to putting a new IV line in Byrne, who was snoring. He wouldn't be any help when Fatima made her move. In fact, he'd be more vulnerable. She wondered, if she attacked, would they threaten to kill him to get her under control? She'd have to take the chance.

The merc, Fatima's unwitting comrade, cocked his head, straining to listen. His knee bounced. She examined him. Both men had the Black Bishop logo on their gear.

Who was paying for this private army? Why would Bishop Security risk their multi-million dollar operation by being part of this raid against Reaper Force? They had attacked members of the Defense Intelligence Agency. It was a slap in the face to the Department of Defense and the American government. To what end?

Three minutes turned into four.

Someone outside walked around the van; metal connected with metal underneath the van's chassis. She guessed it was an inspection mirror. Which meant this was a secure checkpoint.

The merc was getting concerned and looked at Fatima as if he wanted to say something. Fatima stared back calmly.

He picked up his rifle and tucked the butt of the stock into his shoulder. Fatima did the same and let the end of her rifle drift his direction. She couldn't point the barrel straight at him; he would've picked up on her bad tactics. But she was ready to take him out before he did the same to her. The problem was making sure Byrne stayed safe.

The man at the window questioned the driver. "What's your cargo?"

"Classified, my man," said the driver. "If you want to take a look, it's your ass."

"Yeah, well, classified isn't a fucking answer, so I guess we take a look."

A military base. Fatima was sure of it.

The gate officer wasn't one for bullshit. "Unlock the door, and step out."

The medic grabbed his pistol. The merc signaled Fatima. He wanted her to line up a shot—shoot the gate officer if needed.

The driver changed his tone. "Look, I'm sorry man, it's been a long day. Here's the manifest and our authorization documents."

Fatima raised her fist to signal: hold your position.

The merc didn't like that. He checked his watch. Five

minutes now. He signaled again: eyes on window. Line up a shot.

Fatima once again calmly refused, signaling back they should wait.

"Okay, look we don't screw around here," said the gate officer. "You should've given me this to begin with, not your bullshit about being classified."

"I apologize," the driver said.

The officer took a copy of the manifest, wrote a few notes on his clipboard and said, "Have a great day, asshole. Move along!"

Fatima signaled thumbs up.

The merc and the medic relaxed, but she didn't. If they were on a restricted military base, it complicated her plans. One thing she couldn't do was jump out of a van, in non-issue black tactical gear, and shoot people. All hell would rain down on her and Byrne.

She needed a miracle.

Nicks couldn't get Penbrook on the line. She'd called him several times. Where was he?

Nicks was about to blow a gasket when she got a call back.

"Hello, Captain Nicks?"

"Yes, who is this?"

"This is Marisol Flores, I'm Director Penbrook's assistant. He asked me to return your call. He's extremely busy preparing for a demonstration at the Air Force base."

"Wait a minute, did you say you're at an Air Force base?"

"Yes, it's been on the books for a long time. A lot of dignitaries here. DARPA's showing off their new aerial vehicle?"

"Which base?"

MINUTES LATER, Quinn opened her channel. "Nat, I have another hit, the prediction has narrowed. The vehicles are headed for Los Angeles—"

"—Air Force Base."

"Yes, how did you know?"

"There's a UAV demo happening there in about thirty minutes with a crowd full of top brass. The Boss is there as we speak."

"So another DARPA weapon? You think the Dharmapala plans to steal it?"

"It's too much of a coincidence."

"Why attack the Cage and kidnap Byrne?"

"Not sure but my gut tells me it's connected."

"Your gut is right. We have another license plate capture."

"What's the source?"

"The southwest gate of the Los Angeles Air Force Base."

"Damn it, I need to get there faster."

"We can't teleport you there."

"Wait a second," Mouse said. "Maybe we can!"

50

F atima's van parked and the driver cut the engine.

Her mute partner finally spoke. "Get your civilian clothes on before you get out."

The medic removed his tactical helmet. The mercenary sitting in the rear did the same, but Fatima sat there saying nothing, not moving.

"Hey, what is your goddamn deal? You heard him," the medic said.

Suddenly, she had their full attention. The merc was already annoyed, now he was mad she wasn't following orders. He knew Fatima wasn't one of them—it was in his eyes.

"It's dangerous without that ballistic helmet," Fatima said, swinging her Heckler & Koch MP5SD up, aiming at his scowling face.

"What the hell—"

Shlunk, Shlunk.

Two suppressed rounds slammed into his head and he was down.

The medic fumbled for his weapon. Fatima grabbed it

before he could. They struggled until Fatima could kick him backward and line up a shot.

Shlunk, Shlunk, Shlunk.

Two to the chest where it met the neck. One in the forehead. Despite the integrated silencer, the shots were loud inside the confined space.

The medic slumped over Byrne's stretcher dead as a doornail. Then, the real fun began. The driver pulled back the curtain.

51

L os Angeles traffic drove Elon Musk crazy. Like all Angelos, he abhorred the 405. One of the worst highways in the entire world. So, one day he tweeted:

"Traffic is driving me nuts, I'm going to build a boring machine and start digging."

When people scoffed at his declaration, he sent out another tweet:

"I'm actually going to do this!"

And he did. Weeks later, he created The Boring Company and started digging a tunnel that would eventually stretch from his SpaceX campus on Rocket Road to the 101. At least that was the plan. The tunnel was still under construction and Musk had been cagey about its exact location.

Luckily, Mouse and Musk were friends. Mouse had seen the gargantuan drilling machine and the tunnel himself. For weeks after the tour, he'd obsessed over its design. Musk let him study the plans and even pointed out temporary feeder tunnels that allowed construction crews different points of access.

While Nicks despaired at not being able to catch the raiders, Mouse put his obsession to good use.

"You've got to get off the highway," he shouted over the com.

"When?" Nicks asked.

"In five hundred feet, stop!"

"There's no exit."

"I know but trust me. Pull all the way over. There's a street running under the highway. It's blocked off. Look for construction equipment."

"How do I get down?" Nicks asked.

"Uh ... you'll have to jump. You can do that, *right*?"

"And take the Ghostrider with you," Quinn added.

Nicks peered over the side of the highway. There it was. The Boring Company equipment and a big pile of dirt. A security gate protected what appeared to be the entrance. A debris pile was next to that.

The drop was three stories. It would cripple a normal woman but Nicks was far from normal. She swung her legs over the edge of the highway, grabbed the chassis of the Ghostrider with her cybernetic arm, and lifted it over the concrete edge. It dangled there beside her legs.

She jumped.

She hit the dirt pile with so much force she got buried to her knees. The Ghostrider fell to one side and skidded down the pile. Nicks pulled herself out and scrambled after it.

The gate was locked. She ripped it open with little effort and an alarm sounded. Emergency lights went on, but she didn't stop. She jumped on the motorcycle and raced down the feeder tunnel.

"We'll lose each other. So, here's the plan. Shut the airlock after you get into the main tunnel. I'm hacking into the sled. I'm sending it to your location. You'll have one minute to get on, and it's off to the races."

"Sled? What do you mean, sled?" Mouse didn't respond. Nicks groaned but followed Mouse's direction to the letter.

A strange sled sped out of the darkness straight for her but it wasn't slowing down.

"Mouse, can you hear me? Hit the brakes—"

The sled kept coming, picking up speed.

"Mouse? Dammit! Slow it down!"

Nothing but static came over her com and the sled wasn't stopping. She'd have to jump. She quickly backed a few feet down the tunnel. With no clear way to judge the speed, she pulled back the throttle and raced toward the sled. The Ghostrider burst from the feeder tunnel out into the unknown.

Clang-bang! It connected to the sled and came down hard on the metal platform. The bike fell over and Nicks crashed right beside it. The momentum was too much. Nicks tumbled backward, threatening to fall from the platform. Her fingers tore into the sled's metal frame creating a few ugly finger holes—a handle strong enough to keep her from sliding off.

The sled continued to accelerate with enormous force. It felt like she'd hitched a ride on a rocket. A large digital display on the main control panel ticked off the speed: 50, 70, 90, 100, 120. A warning signal flashed maximum speed achieved but the sled hit another gear. 130, 140, 150, 160 miles per hour.

Mouse was pushing the thing beyond its intended limits. It rattled unnaturally. The control panel sparked. A smell of ozone permeated the air. Something was burning. She was pretty sure that was bad.

Elon would be pissed. But damn, the ride was a literal rush.

As Uncle Wilco would say: *Soak up that dirty thunder, girl!*

In no time, the sled slowed down, its brakes doing double duty. It stopped and slid into another mechanism. Gears whirled, and the platform rose like an elevator to the street level and stopped. Nicks fired up the Ghostrider and rode down the exit tunnel into the city of El Segundo.

She was five blocks from the Air Force Base.

52

Fatima braced herself. The driver was ready for a fight.

He hurled himself into her like an NFL linebacker. She landed with a hard crunch on top of the merc she'd just killed.

The driver grabbed the barrel of Fatima's rifle and a tug-of-war ensued before he slammed it backward, clubbing her in the side of the head, splitting her scalp open, and almost knocking her unconscious. Blood oozed down the side of her face. Dazed, she lost her grip on the Heckler & Koch MP5 and the man swatted it away. It clattered into the corner of the van.

Now she was pissed. She kicked him in the face hard enough to knock off his ballistic helmet. Blood flooded out of his nose. He leapt on Fatima and grabbed her by the throat, choking her, while he ripped away her mask.

"Who the hell do we have here?" He laughed.

The driver was one of those meatheads who enjoyed violence. She recognized him immediately. It was Charlie Tango.

He gave a slow smile. "Wait a damn minute—*I know you*."

Fatima grabbed a finger and bent it backward until it

snapped. Charlie Tango yelped like a kicked dog, pulling his wounded hand away, but he didn't stop. He slammed his weight down, using his legs and good hand to keep her pinned.

She was scared, but not to the point of panic. She'd seen him put women in this position before. It was the perfect setup for some long overdue justice.

He spread himself on top of her and grabbed her by the throat again.

"You trying to rape me like you raped my fellow soldiers? Because I don't think you're man enough to do it," she rasped. It was her first shot—an opening salvo of psychological warfare.

Charlie Tango's eyes narrowed. Fatima could see she had bruised his ego—his true nature stepping out of its shadow and taking control.

"I'll kill you, then I'll rape you. If there's anything left to rape!" His evil eyes glinted.

In her mind, Fatima saw flashes of what he had done in Syria. In the past, those memories had paralyzed her but now, after all the years and all the training, she banished them with ease.

She arched her back, pressing herself into him, opening up a space to free herself.

"What's wrong, can't you get it up?" she asked in her most erotic voice.

"You crazy bitch—"

Fatima bit into the man's earlobe, growling like a rabid pit bull, and ripped it from his head. Hot blood exploded everywhere.

Charlie Tango reached up to protect his face from further mauling, his grip loosened, his weight lifted. Fatima released the arch in her back and pivoted her hips in such a way that she slid out from under him.

Her hand found the WK tactical dagger strapped to her leg.

She swung it high and plunged it down into his right carotid artery. She stabbed him so hard the tip of the dagger slid through his neck and punctured the other side. It was a horrible mess, but wildly effective.

She twisted herself up and over his body. Straddling the man, she was now in control. Charlie Tango's threats were lost in a gurgle of blood. He tried to pull the blade out of his neck. Fatima slammed her flat palm into the butt of the dagger, driving it deeper.

Charlie Tango was not getting away this time.

She sat silently, enjoying his death and listening to see if the commotion had attracted any of his friends.

The coast was clear. But her mouth was not.

Something was in it.

She spit and a nasty piece of earlobe hit Charlie Tango's chest.

"You can have that back," she said. "And, if you're still listening, just remember—I *hate* being called crazy."

53

Scorpio could feel the presence of Starfire. She was broadcasting a warning.

Echo Squad is offline.

It was a sign Charlie Tango was dead. Viper was closing in, and it was time to move. She radioed the remaining members of the team and told them to converge on the rendezvous point. It was time for the final gambit. If it worked, Starfire would have what she wanted.

The Dharmapala would be unstoppable.

David Penbrook was in a small conference room overlooking the crowd as it gathered for the demonstration. Marisol Flores had told him he was late to meet the base commander. That was ten minutes ago. He didn't care about the damn demo or securing more funding for the development of the aircraft. None of that mattered now, nor would it matter in the future.

The door creaked open behind him.

"Sir, we have to go. The event is starting, and they are holding your seat."

Penbrook continued to stare out the window. His mind singularly focused on one thing—*Starfire*. It was his fault she had escaped, and he was at a loss as to how to fix it.

"Has the Reaper team reported in?"

"No, sir," she said. "And I have to say, I'm a bit worried."

He was too. He knew they were all in danger, and he had kept them in the dark, given them too little information about the real threat. Because of that, he had most likely sent them to their deaths. If they survived this, he'd never be able to face them again.

"Sir," Marisol said. She was standing next to him but that didn't register until she reached up and gently took his hand.

The sudden intimacy of Marisol's touch shocked him out of his stupor. Her hand was smaller than his but warm and strong.

"Ms. Flores, please—"

He tried to pull away but she gripped his hand tighter and pulled him closer. He was suddenly aware of her fragrant perfume. Her blue eyes glowed like brilliant sapphires.

"I've been working for you long enough to know what is going on. I know all of your idiosyncrasies, peculiar habits, and moods. Despair is a new one. One I won't tolerate," she said. "Not while you're in this position, not with what is at stake."

He stared at her completely bewildered. He'd never experienced such a compassionate gaze from a woman in his life. She was staring right into his core.

"You did everything you could to save her."

"Ms. Flores, Captain Nicks is very capable. She's fully equipped for these kinds of missions."

"I'm not talking about Captain Nicks, David. I'm talking about Starfire."

Penbrook was speechless.

"You offered both of those girls comfort under the worst of circumstances. With Starfire, you did it with the compassion of a real father. But she is beyond saving. You know that, you just don't want to give up on her. If you wait any longer, you'll be betraying yourself and everyone else that depends on you."

How terrible his judgment was when it came to those closest to him. He'd never seen Marisol as anyone beyond a high-strung secretary. Yet, here she was displaying a power no piece of DARPA technology had—empathy.

"It was easy to see the problems in the other girl. We all feared her because of the violence and the anger. You feel the way you do because you know deep down, Starfire is more dangerous than Scorpio will ever be."

Marisol squeezed his hand again with a lingering forcefulness that said: *It's time to accept the unacceptable.* She held his gaze for what seemed an eternity then turned and left the room.

As she closed the door, the truth opened him up. Despair gave way to recognition. There was one thing he could do. Something that might give his team an edge. His mind began to assemble a plan.

55

Nicks found a sweet spot in the base's fence. It was a small section in the shadows, out of reach of the spotlight and the roving eye of the security camera. She backed up across the road to get a running start and burst toward the fence at super-speed. Up she went, like a track-star vaulting a hurdle, and cleared the fence.

She landed, tucked into a forward roll, and came up running. She felt a flash of pride in the mastery over her body. Her cybernetic parts were getting the best workout they'd had since she first tested them.

But pride comes before the fall. A minute later, her left leg shook uncontrollably with muscle spasms, and she stumbled. From Wonder Woman to a clumsy child in mere seconds. It was embarrassing.

Flux came online. *"Critical Warning. System experiencing stress limits. Engage protocols for optimum performance."*

She ignored Flux and slowed her pace until the shaking died off. The limits could be overcome if she paced herself. She'd proven it time and again.

Up ahead, she could see what looked like a high school football game. A crowd was assembling for the Air Force's demo. She jogged over and joined the line headed to the stadium seating.

Banners hung at various places announcing this was a showcase for a new piece of technology called the ARES.

The drone's namesake was the god of war because Travis Raylock, the man behind the new machine, had promised to deliver the god of drones. Its acronym stood for Aerial Reconfigurable Embedded System, meaning the aircraft could accommodate many functions. It was a helicopter-airplane hybrid, much like the Osprey V22, but it flew faster, higher, and was piloted remotely.

Commanders fighting terrorists in the Middle East were still salivating over the DARPA-approved concept art. The military wanted this airplane.

The ARES was scheduled to fly down, land, shake its tail feathers, make sure every general with a fat budget had a hard-on, and fly off like the tease it was, back to its home at Raylock Industries' Skunk Works division.

Nicks worried this was a perfect opportunity for the Dharmapala to cause trouble. But she had no evidence. The two vehicles parked a few hundred yards from the spectator stands didn't offer much by way of proof. The Bishop team that raided the Cage may have surreptitiously infiltrated the base. But for all she knew, they had an invitation.

She considered alerting base security but, when she queued up to enter the stand, the only security detail was the bad guys. Two of them, wearing tailored suits and ties, stood nearby. They looked like VIP security, but the ruse was exposed by who she saw standing with them.

It was Scorpio.

56

F atima climbed into the driver's seat and had a look around.

They were parked in a lot across from what looked like a set of high school football stands. The signage told her it was the Los Angeles Air Force Base.

Men in beautiful uniforms adorned with flashy medals formed a crowd near the stand. It was time to move out and make contact with the team.

She grabbed some of the medic's gauze and dabbed at her wound. She needed stitches but the bleeding was beginning to slow. Her thick hair was helping it clot and also covered the wound pretty well. She cleaned her face as best she could and ditched the tactical gear. The vest with ballistic plates would draw too much attention inside the base. She had to wear something, though, so she kept the pants and t-shirt.

She tucked the HK MP5 under Byrne's sheets and opened the back door. A cool rush of fresh air hit her, blowing away the acrid smell of blood and death. Byrne groaned when the wheels of the stretcher locked into place and hit the pavement. It was the first sound she'd heard from him since the fighting began.

Byrne suddenly decided it was a good time for a resurrection. He sat up with the rifle at the ready. He pointed it at Fatima. She raised her hands in surrender.

"Thank god you're still alive!" she said.

"*Nasrallah?*" Byrne lowered the rifle.

"Welcome back, Colonel." She smiled.

"Help me get out of this goddamn stretcher," he barked. "Where in the hell are we?"

"Los Angeles Air Force Base."

"Where's the rest of the team? And, why are we in a van full of dead bishops?

Fatima rolled her eyes. "Long story."

"Out with it," Byrne demanded. "What the hell is going on?"

Indeed, she thought, what the hell *is* going on?

57

The star of the show arrived as Nicks was making her way to Scorpio. The ARES descended from the dark sky. Lowering its altitude without slowing down, it buzzed the viewing stands. Its wings shook like a fighter jet auditioning for the next *Top Gun* movie, enthralling the crowd of dignitaries. They yelped and cheered like kids amazed by a new toy.

But the ARES was no toy. It was one of the most capable war drones DARPA had created, and seemed to know this. The aircraft pointed its snobbish nose at the moon and lifted its proud chest. This gave the crowd a glimpse of the stealthy under-belly and the ordinances the vehicle carried. Then, it disappeared into the night sky.

Nicks knew the ARES wasn't done, she could hear it circling for another pass.

Thanks to an unfortunate number of drone attacks, she was developing a keen awareness of what UAV sounded like. The menacing buzzing of their rotor blades, the swoosh of their sudden aerial gymnastics, and the flicker noise of their fine mechanics were telling, but this vehicle had a different signature. Thrusters embedded in the fixed wings set it apart, and gave it the muscular sound of a jet airplane.

Shhhhfoooom.

Once again, the ARES zoomed up to the stands. This time it came to a full stop, hovering before the amazed crowd. With the grace of an angel, it descended effortlessly and landed.

Its tail cracked open and a well-dressed civilian walked down the cargo ramp to great applause. The man raised his hands.

As if an alien had arrived to address humanity for the first time, the crowd waited in attentive silence. The unmistakable squelch of a PA system broke the quiet and the man spoke.

58

Fatima covered Byrne while he snuck up to the back of their tactical van. At first they'd been glad to see it. Then, Byrne spotted the busted window. They watched it for a few minutes until they were both convinced it was safe to approach.

Byrne threw open the door and Fatima cleared the van. No one from Reaper Force was in the vehicle, and Byrne could see why. There was evidence of a struggle. Some of the communication equipment was smashed, and blood was splattered on a window.

Where was the rest of his team?

As worrying as the scene was, Fatima found a gift under the Christmas tree. A small duffel with some of her clothes stuffed under the back seat. And, wedged behind that, something even better—her black drag bag.

She unzipped it and peered inside. Her Zagros sniper rifle, in all its wonderful glory, smiled back.

"Maybe there is a god." She grinned.

Byrne was staring at her with an odd look on his face.

"Have you never seen one of these, Colonel?"

"No, it's not the rifle I'm looking at," he said, pointing at her neck. "You're wounded, soldier."

Fatima reached up and felt her wound. Her thick dark hair, now matted and wet, had hidden it until it couldn't. A split-second of nausea passed over her as she stared at her bloody hand. Charlie Tango had gotten at least one good lick in.

Byrne wiped off some of the excess blood and checked her wound.

"If you don't get that stitched up soon, you're gonna pass out on me," he said.

"We're wasting time," she sniped, and pulled away from him. "You handle your wounds, I'll handle mine."

She slung her drag bag over her shoulder and turned to Byrne.

"Let's go find the team. They're in danger."

Byrne wasn't arguing the point. He nodded his head in agreement and followed her.

59

"No pictures, please," said the polished looking man as he took the podium. "This is still a classified project."

As the crowd settled in, the presenter began. "Ladies and gentlemen, the Greeks celebrated the golden chariot of Ares as one of the most formidable weapons possessed by the gods. Our version isn't made of gold—"

"Might as well be," said a general seated in the front row, "I can't believe the price tag on this thing!"

The crowd erupted with laughter.

The presenter cleared his throat and chuckled nervously.

"Yes, well, as I was saying, the ARES isn't made of precious metals and doesn't have four immortal horses pulling it through the sky, but it has four state-of-the-art tilt-rotors within a fixed stealth wing design, allowing for vertical takeoff. It can function as a weapon or transport system and is capable of landing soldiers and equipment on any terrain in the world. It is, as of today, the most advanced UAV ever built!"

The ARES lifted off on cue and hovered over the field behind the presenter.

"Today, we have an additional surprise for the audience,"

the presenter said. "Since the ARES was designed for the battlefield, it can be outfitted with an AGM-Hellwing missile built by Raylock Aeronautics to protect itself and its passengers."

Many in the crowd stood up for a better look. Nicks noticed Scorpio and her Bishop team lingering around the edges of the stands.

"Now, we'll test the Hellwing. Please direct your attention to the designated target north of the field."

One of the video displays came to life. A digital clock began a thirty-second countdown.

Something was wrong. Nicks could hear two Raylock technicians arguing with each other. The drone wasn't cooperating. It was swiveling away from the intended target.

Nicks looked for Scorpio. She had disappeared with her team.

This was it, she thought.

It was the Dharmapala, not Raylock Industries, who was about to put on a show. The ARES turned and pointed the Hellwing right at the crowd.

Nicks worst fear was confirmed. The ARES was about to attack its audience.

She sensed the strange events of the last few days were about to reveal their purpose. The ARES waited like a thug leaning against a lamppost on a dark night. It didn't care about hiding. It was biding its time, judging the victim's openness to attack, watching for the right moment to strike.

In desperation, Nicks grabbed the nearest support beam with both hands and leaned into it with all the power she could muster. Her cybernetic arms and hands went into overdrive straining against the metal.

The support column bent inward. The harder she pushed, the more the crease deepened. The column buckled. People in the stands gasped as the structure tilted to one side. Nicks hit the column one more time for good measure and stepped away.

It crumpled under the weight of the crowd. This triggered failure in the other supports. Spectators jumped from their seats like sailors abandoning ship.

The ARES was undeterred. Nicks watched as the drone fed the targeting information to the video displayed on the larger monitors, confirming it was arming its missiles, and aiming at the audience.

"Clear the stands, it's malfunctioning!" she shouted. The crowd scattered in multiple directions.

"Turn that god-damned drone off!" yelled the grizzled general who'd cracked the joke.

"It won't respond to my controls," the presenter bellowed.

Several soldiers turned their rifles on the ARES, trying to disable it, but it was too late. It fired its missile toward the largest mass of people.

Nothing could stop it now.

60

The missile exploded in a thunderous bang a hundred yards above the crowd, and several large pieces of metal flew off like flaming Frisbees. The blast wave hit the crowd with a painless whoosh.

The Hellwing was a complete dud.

The bewildered spectators looked up at the cloud of dark smoke and wondered why they had survived. Tiny bits of shrapnel rained down. The curious picked it up and discovered it was harmless plastic.

The presenter, who had been frozen on the podium, was still on camera when he examined a piece of the plastic. Everyone could see what he was holding—a small green man holding a green minesweeper.

"A *toy soldier?*" he wondered aloud. "I—I don't understand?"

Nicks did.

It was the first thing she'd found in the downtown warehouse. Hundreds of bags of plastic soldiers. Green snipers. Green flamethrowers. Green men with mortars. The Dharmapala had bombed DARPA's top military supporters with toys.

The general was holding a soldier with a bazooka. It was still warm.

"A sick joke!" he barked.

Maybe, but Nicks thought it had deeper meaning to the perpetrator.

You are children playing with toys. I can kill you with them anytime I choose.

Nicks recognized it served one other purpose. It was a diversion.

She watched the ARES fly across the field and land. Scorpio and her Bishop team ran out to meet it. They had new prisoners in tow.

Her teammates—Mouse and Quinn.

61

Nicks put on her rage blinders and ran at bionic speed. She didn't care who saw her or who got in her way.

Behind her, base security was swarming the demo area and herding shell-shocked spectators into one of the main buildings.

Across the field, Scorpio was ordering her mercenaries to load pieces of equipment onto the pirated ARES.

Pop, pop, pop.

A short burst of bullets ricocheted off the concrete behind Nicks.

She slid to a stop and turned toward the gunfire. It was a Bishop, dressed in a nice suit, holding a 4.6mm Heckler and Koch MP7A1 submachine gun with a suppressor. He sprayed another round of bullets at her feet.

"Stop, right there, or I open up."

"You're shooting at a military officer inside a military base. That's not smart, dipshit," Nicks said.

He aimed his sights at her chest.

"I don't get paid to be smart—"

A single bullet tore through the man's forehead. His head split in two like a cracked eggshell and he fell forward dead.

"Now, he's using his brains," Fatima said, stepping over the man. She kicked the machine gun out of reach. "Clear!"

Her backup stepped out of hiding. It was Byrne.

"What a sight for sore eyes," Nicks said. She greeted them with a quick hug, but there wasn't time for much else.

"Scorpio has Quinn and Mouse. They've hijacked the ARES. We have to hurry!"

"We'll follow you. Go!" Byrne said.

As the three of them approached the ARES, the mercs spotted them and took up defensive positions. One fired a few warning shots, forcing the team to take cover behind a cinder block barrier.

"Shit, what's the plan, here?" Byrne asked.

"They're out in the open, if we can pick off Scorpio, maybe they'll give up," Fatima suggested.

Nicks peeked again and her stomach dropped. Three remaining bishops stood with Scorpio. As pros, they were playing this smart.

"Not with Quinn and Mouse in the way," she said. They were using them as human shields. Nicks could see Quinn was simmering with rage. Mouse looked scared.

"Any bright ideas, team?" Byrne asked, checking his bandages. So far, they were holding up.

Nicks knew she couldn't let the ARES take off. If it did, they may never see their team members again. She needed to get on the aircraft.

"I have to surrender," she said.

Before they could debate the strategy, Nicks raised her hands, and stepped out into the open.

62

Byrne jumped up and grabbed Nicks.

"Wait, Nat, you can't do that!"

Nicks didn't want to argue with him. She shoved him backward with her cybernetic hand. He absorbed the impact with ease. He wouldn't budge.

"Don't try that bionic shit with me. I'm feeling a lot better," he quipped.

Byrne pulled her closer with newfound strength. Confusion flashed in her eyes. She looked down at his legs. Where were his braces?

Nicks wasn't in the mood for banter, and she wasn't changing her mind. This was the only play. She knew Scorpio wanted her more than she wanted Quinn or Mouse. Nicks could see the mercs had finished refueling.

"We have to stop them," Nicks pleaded with Byrne.

Byrne wouldn't let her go. Nicks wrestled against him—an impossible stalemate.

The first shot gave Nicks a heart attack. It sounded like a mortar round explosion to her enhanced ears.

"God no," she muttered.

She turned and searched desperately for Mouse and Quinn, just in time to see Quinn's guard's head explode in a cloud of pink mist. His body collapsed several feet from where it once stood.

Scorpio and the other two bishops grabbed Quinn and Mouse and pulled them into the interior of their ARES.

Nicks swiveled around. Fatima was adjusting her gun. "Cease fire," Nicks yelled. "Are you crazy? You could've killed Quinn!"

Fatima didn't look up; she was retargeting.

"Not with these bullets," she said, adjusting the mechanism attached to her scope.

Without waiting for further orders she shot two more of the EXACTO smart bullets, one after the other. Nicks could hear their bizarre acoustic signature as they corrected their path and arced in mid-flight like miniature heat-seeking missiles. It was if the bullets had been thrown by a pitcher specializing in curve balls. They turned into the ARES and slammed into the remaining bishops hiding inside. The team heard Mouse scream as the last merc up the ramp fell out of the aircraft—a massive hole in his chest. Seconds later, Scorpio kicked the other dead Bishop down the ramp to join his friend, confirming Fatima had killed them both.

She'd cleared the way for a rescue, but Scorpio wasn't waiting for another magic bullet. The hatch closed, the ARES fired its engines, lifted off, and headed west toward the Pacific Ocean.

"Fucking mothers," Fatima said. "I had one more bullet!"

Nicks heart sank as the vehicle disappeared from sight. She turned her rage on Byrne who was still holding her arm.

"How Jack, how are you ... *why are you* ... where is your cane?"

She stared at him accusingly. Byrne wouldn't look her in the eye.

"We're letting them get away!" she screamed.

He loosened his grip, and she lashed out, throwing him against the cinder-block wall. He slammed into it and fell to his knees.

Fatima helped him back up. "Goddamn, I thought we were on the same side?"

"It's okay, I deserve that," he said, solemnly.

"You're damn right, you do!" Then she yelled at Fatima, "And, where the hell have you been?"

They argued unaware another ARES was approaching. After the rotor-wash made it impossible to continue, they looked up. A bright spotlight illuminated them like an alien tractor beam and the aircraft descended.

The back hatch opened and Penbrook walked down the ramp. He didn't look happy. A burly air force base commander and a nervous ARES technician accompanied him. Next came several of the commander's staff. The ramp retracted, and the hatch closed. The group rushed over to meet Reaper Force.

Penbrook was all business.

"What's the situation, Colonel?" Penbrook asked Byrne.

"The operative we've identified as Scorpio has hijacked the ARES. She and her team have two hostages. Gremlin and a civilian, Lee Park, who was assisting us in our investigation."

The base commander foamed at the mouth. "We've got enough firepower on this base to blow them to kingdom come. You give me the word, Director, and we will activate our fighter jets."

"Thank you, Commander Nelson. I realize this is your base, and we're imposing on you, but we'd like to get the ARES and those hostages back in one piece. These hijackers are also leads in a related investigation. My team needs to handle this personally."

"I have no problem with that. I have my own cluster-fuck to clean up in the viewing area. Every dignitary with a stripe or star wants my ass after that shit show." He signaled his staff to hand Penbrook a radio.

Penbrook turned to Fatima who was standing there silently holding her Zagros.

"Apparently, the new bullets worked?"

"Apparently," Fatima replied. She rocked unsteadily on her feet. Her knees buckled just as Byrne swept in and caught her.

Nicks looked worried. "What's wrong with her?"

"Nothing a few stitches and some bed rest won't fix," Byrne said. "Commander, one last thing. Would your team be able to tend to my wounded soldier here?"

"Absolutely." The commander motioned to one of his staff who scurried to Fatima's side. "Penbrook, I'll take care of your operator and leave the rest to you. Give me an update in fifteen so I know what the hell is going on."

Penbrook thanked him and said goodbye to Fatima.

"I hope you know how wrong you are about your asset over there," Fatima said, pointing to Nicks. Everyone stopped and listened as she continued. "Whatever your doubts are, I'd advise you to put them to rest. That woman has the heart of a true warrior. Doesn't matter how advanced your tech is, you'll never be able to program that into someone. Don't cut her loose or your organization is fucked."

Penbrook nodded in agreement. "Should I consider that your final report?"

"Yeah, you do that," she said, as she turned to leave.

With Fatima in tow, the commander nodded respectively to the remaining members of the Reaper team and his group marched off.

THE REAR BAY on the ARES opened, and the ramp lowered again. The design of the machine was interesting. The rear was curved aerodynamically like a bee's abdomen. It opened like Pac-Man's mouth, allowing for quick load out of its human or military cargo.

This aircraft wasn't configured for offense like the stolen one. They'd converted this one to carry personnel and a small payload so it could fly faster.

"I think it's obvious to all, this situation has expanded in a way that is regrettable," Penbrook said.

Nicks flashed a knowing look at Byrne. This was long overdue, maybe even too late, but she wanted to hear what he had to say.

"Yes, I think we need to know what is *really* going on."

"Project Starfire. An advanced research project several pay grades above you," Penbrook said. "That's the only thing going on, Captain."

"We know we're looking for Project Starfire. But what does that project have to do with the attack on Reaper Force?"

Penbrook continued. "The fact is, you still aren't cleared to know about any of this, but that changes now.

Penbrook ushered Byrne and Nicks up the ramp and into the ARES.

"I wanted Starfire safe," Penbrook said. "I've come to accept that was a mistake."

"Sir, we discovered the smuggling compartment in the crate," she said.

"Then you know Project Starfire isn't a piece of technology. It's much more than that."

"A person."

"Yes. An extremely smart young woman. Like you Captain

Nicks, she has abilities. In this case, cognitive abilities beyond anything our scientists have ever studied. They've been quarantined at Blackwood for most of their lives."

"Who are *they*?" she asked.

"To be exact, there were two projects running in tandem. Project Starfire and Project—"

"—Scorpio?"

"Yes. Unfortunately, you've met her already. As I told the team, she went rogue earlier this year."

Nicks shook her head in exasperation. Scorpio was deadly, what did that say about Starfire?

Penbrook added, "Scorpio and Starfire are extreme neurodivergents. Victims of severe head trauma as children. A new class of neuroprosthetics repaired their injuries but there were side effects. They now have enhanced cognitive powers—powers we've never seen documented.

"Scorpio's abilities are kinetic. She has an enhancement called 'adoptive muscle memory.' She can replicate the physical prowess of any person she observes, mimicking and mastering skills that take years to perfect like hand-to-hand combat, marksmanship, and martial arts.

"Starfire has an ability we call cyberkinesis. We still don't understand it. She appears to control machines with her mind. Any piece of technology that exchanges data through some form of connectivity is vulnerable. She even created a device to amplify her abilities while at Blackwood."

"The sigillum?" Byrne asked.

"Yes, exactly. Dr. Vargas helped her develop it in secret, hoping he could cash in on the advancement. When that was discovered, he was kicked out of the program."

Nicks looked at Byrne. That answered a lot of questions they had about Vargas.

Penbrook continued, "I want you to understand what's gone

wrong. The doctors noticed the neuroprosthetics didn't heal all the brain damage. They compensated for it. This compromised their psychological development. Scorpio's growing psychopathy was obvious. Starfire hid hers from the team.

"DR-Ultra had hoped we could study the girls and use what we had discovered to help people with neurological injuries. But things took a turn for the worse and it was decided the project had to be terminated. Neither of the girls could be managed by conventional means. DARPA's purpose is the elimination of threats. They couldn't take the risk. We had inadvertently created weapons. When they confronted me with their evidence, I didn't want to believe them," Penbrook said.

"Meaning they were going to kill these girls? They're human beings not machines!" Nicks said.

"Not anymore. They are something else—something very deadly."

Nicks stared at Penbrook. Did he forget who he was talking to?

Penbrook looked away for a moment, Nicks watched as he let his emotion subside, and gathered his thoughts. "I saw it like you do, I couldn't stomach it either. No one could control Scorpio. They saw her as an animal they had to put down. Starfire was reasonable, or so I believed. I was pushing for another solution through some back channels. Starfire had harmed no one. But next thing I knew, she was gone. When you found the members of Echo Squad dead, I guessed Scorpio was covering her tracks. But there is a bigger conspiracy brewing here."

"If those men were helping Starfire escape, why kill them?"

"Both women are decompensating. Giving into delusions of grandeur. Starfire is leaving clues for us to follow because she wants a confrontation with our team. We are the only ones that have a chance at stopping her. She needs Reaper Force out of the way."

Penbrook looked at Nicks. Nicks stared back, fuming. She'd never killed anyone by way of a bionic boot up the ass, but she was willing to give it a shot. Penbrook had held back too much important information.

An alarm went off inside the ARES and the massive rotors fired up.

"That's the signal. They've located the other ARES and programmed this one to intercept its flight path."

"What does that mean for us?" Nicks asked.

"I suggest you strap in," Penbrook said.

"Exactly where are we going?"

"To save your teammates!"

Byrne and Nicks chose their seats and prepared for takeoff. Penbrook reached into his suit jacket and retrieved a small gift box. He handed it to Nicks. She looked at it confused.

"Her real name is Riza Azmara. I considered her my daughter," the Boss said with uncharacteristic emotion. "There may be a moment, you'll know it when it happens, when giving her this is the only way to remind her of her humanity."

He walked down the loading ramp. When he turned around, he had tears in his eyes. The tail closed as Penbrook gave his final order.

"If you don't stop her, she will kill all of us. Terminate with extreme prejudice."

PART VIII

IRON MAN

63

"This reminds me of flying in a C-170," Byrne said, as the aircraft hit some turbulence. "Except back then I knew where I was going and why."

The interior was cold and loud. As innovative as it was, this prototype hadn't been built for comfort. After a while, the ARES settled into a comfortable cruising altitude but Nicks and Byrne were still uneasy. It was hard to ignore the cockpit was missing a pilot.

Byrne got up to check the navigation panel.

They were headed west out over the Pacific and would intercept the flight path of the other ARES within the hour. The exact destination wasn't clear but the first landmass on the current trajectory was at least eleven hours away. Where? He couldn't be sure until they were closer.

"Who the hell is this *Starfire*?" Nicks blurted out. "What a pretentious name."

"Agreed."

"—and what's wrong with Penbrook?"

"Besides the obvious?" Byrne shook his head. "He looked

distraught. Doesn't compute. I've never known the man to have an identifiable emotion."

Nicks agreed. Had the Director sniffed too much model glue as a kid and now that brain damage was making itself known? She flashed Byrne a serious look. "I don't see how he remains in his position after this—our team is done for."

"They need us—*they need you*—more now than ever."

"In the shape we're in?"

"Speak for yourself," Byrne joked.

They looked at each other. Both were a mess. Byrne had his color back but his bandage was soaked in blood.

"Let's clean you up," she said.

She got up and rummaged through the storage compartments. A flare gun. Water bottles. Two emergency blankets. One small first aid kit.

Nicks threw a blanket down on the pallet in the middle of the aircraft and opened the kit. "Up here soldier, let me freshen that bandage."

Byrne took off his shirt and sat down. Nicks set aside the items needed to clean his wound and went to work gently removing the bloody gauze. When she wiped the blood away with a cotton pad and rubbing alcohol, she was stunned.

Byrne was healed. Completely. All that remained was a thin pink line of scar tissue. It was impossible.

Impossible for *normal* men and women.

Byrne stared her in the eyes. His brow creased in his problem scowl. He seemed unsure what to say.

Nicks silenced him by placing her finger on his lips and shaking her head no.

She didn't need an explanation.

She knew.

SHE HAD READ reports of the first TALON soldier, his code-name redacted. A black mark just large enough to cover the name she had guessed it might be.

The files celebrated his exploits. His missions read like adventure stories, but his success came with a steep price. The power source that fueled his prosthetics was toxic—shortening his lifespan.

DR-Ultra benched him to save his life. They dialed back the augstim engines to the bare minimum to reduce the damage. The new mode left the cybernetic hero incapacitated and no longer able to use his enhanced powers. He became disabled and dependent on medications to manage the toxicity. It ended his operational career, and they reassigned him.

Nicks's TALON components had been designed to avoid the same limitation. Her bionics worked differently. To save the first TALON soldier, they needed a Hail Mary—a new power source that would reverse his condition. So far, everything they'd tried to date had failed. It seemed Quinn had done more than just save his life, she'd finally found the solution.

Nicks had wondered but had never asked Byrne for confirmation. She knew how he operated, his penchant for burying the past, and his reluctance to dig it back up.

She also knew she was the last person who should bring it up; he was more vulnerable around her. The whole conversation scared the hell out of her. Talking about his condition would give power to the fears she had about her own future.

She didn't want to know then, and she didn't want to know now.

What she *wanted* was *him*.

She raked her fingernails across his scars.

He shivered and broke out in goose flesh.

She pressed her hand into the warmth of his bare back and pulled herself into him. She had been here before, but it was so long ago. She'd been more fragile, and he was more careful. She pressed her lips into his ferociously, telling him being careful was over, at least for this moment—this moment they had denied themselves for so long.

Byrne kissed her with an equal amount of passion. His hand reached around to cup her ass. He squeezed her closer. He grabbed her behind the knees, picked her up, and threw her onto the raised palette in the center of the ship.

She pulled off her shirt and bra in one move and he fell on top of her, his mouth on her exposed breasts. His tongue tasted her hardening nipples. Nicks moaned and arched into him, enjoying the rush of his heat on her skin.

She raked her fingernails down his back and around his waist and further. Her hand slipped into his pants, eagerly searching for the rest of him. He unbuttoned his jeans with one hand and let them fall away before doing the same for her.

Suddenly, they were naked, kissing, tangled in a ravenous embrace, straining to push closer. She burned for him. This man she would never admit to loving was here, ready for the taking, and her body betrayed her. Nicks was achingly aroused; she wanted him, not just inside her, but always. It was an impossible thing, but for this moment all inhibitions were cast aside.

She opened herself to him and he entered her with shocking ease. Both of them were stunned by the transcendent wave of pleasure at the reunion, making Nicks question why they would ever stop loving each other this way.

She pushed herself, drawing him in deeper, and he rocked against her, finding a rhythm different from the past. It was harder, faster, more desperate. A wave of euphoria flooded through her. It wasn't enough, she wanted everything he could stand to give her. His pace promised she wouldn't be denied.

Her stomach tightened. Her chest and neck flushed as waves of heat flowed across her body. She surrendered to the intoxicating electricity of another orgasm. While it lingered, she pulled him closer. He plunged back into her and she rolled to her side flipping them both over until she was on top.

Always, she had to make her way here. It gave her the most pleasure. Here she controlled the rhythm and could maintain the pleasure ceaselessly as long as her partner matched her stamina.

Byrne didn't disappoint. But then, when had he ever? What other man could take her like this beyond all self-consciousness? Beyond all the terrible realities they'd both experienced?

Who else but this bionic man could she surrender to?

With him, she could lose herself.

Endlessly.

Until she disappeared.

64

An alarm sounded. Nicks thought it was her phone. She wanted to smash it to bits with her cybernetic fist. She willed it to stop, but it wouldn't. Byrne pulled himself from their tangled embrace and hopped over to the cockpit.

It was a proximity warning.

The ARES was finishing its descent and approaching its landing zone—Japan. Specifically, Yakushima Island in the Kagoshima Prefecture.

"Rise and shine, Captain Nicks. I think we're here."

They dressed and strapped themselves into the cockpit to watch the descent. Scorpio's ARES was ahead of them going through the same maneuvers. They descended quickly as they approached the island's western edge, flew low over the rocky outer bank and white sand beaches. They skirted the treetops. Lush green forest stretched out for miles. The island looked uninhabited.

Scorpio's ARES banked left, heading for the southwestern section of the island. Nicks could make out a tiny structure in the distance. Something from an old samurai movie.

The first aircraft prepared to land. Nicks's navigation panel showed theirs would do the same. According to the animated flight path, their ARES would land a few hundred yards away from the other one.

Nicks looked at Byrne for reassurance. "Landing right on top of them, is that the best idea?"

"So much for the element of surprise," he said.

"I think we already lost that—*look!*" Nicks shouted.

A drone, like the one that attacked the Cage, was closing in on them from the north. Her stomach dropped when she saw that it carried the same payload—a pair of Hellwing missiles.

"Oh shit, I'm taking the controls," Byrne said, overriding the remote pilot.

Nicks braced herself as Byrne banked west. The drone followed. Byrne lowered their altitude even further.

"Look for a safe place to land!" he yelled.

"There!" She pointed to a small clearing amid the dense cedar forest. He turned toward it, hoping to hit the grassy bulls-eye before the drone attacked.

The radar warning receiver blasted a shrill tone.

"It's locked on our craft!"

"A hard landing gives us better odds than a Hellwing. Drop us down as fast as you can," she said.

They braced themselves as Byrne made for the clearing.

The drone sped up. Closing the gap between them, but it didn't fire.

It was coming in too fast—

The drone shot over the ARES just as Byrne began to land. Metal crashed on metal as they collided. They were knocked off course. The ARES's stabilizer flew past their window and fell away.

The drone had kamikazed them on purpose, sheering their

rudder. Byrne lost control, and they went down with a bone-jarring bang.

Their craft skidded out of control the entire length of the clearing, spinning and sliding in the wet grass. The ARES tumbled twice and slammed into a line of ancient cedar trees where it came to a dead stop.

It took a minute for Nicks and Byrne to come around. They were banged and bruised but still strapped into their harnesses. The bow was damaged and cracked open. A rush of humid air flooded their compartment. They released themselves from their harnesses and crawled out of the wreckage.

Nicks scanned the horizon for any sign of the drone. It had disappeared. A touch of luck they badly needed.

Two things flashed through her mind. One, they were alive —*thank god*! Two, if they survived this confrontation, they would need a new way home. Their ARES would never fly again.

They checked each other for injuries and found none. It was time to rescue their friends. Nicks embraced Byrne one last time.

Over his shoulder, she saw they had a new problem. Inside the tree line, lingering in the shadows, she appeared, shimmering like a ghost among the old growth.

It was Project Starfire.

65

Riza Azmara was one with the woods, part of the vegetation, a phantom unlike anything Nicks had seen. An oversized hood hid her face while her white robe billowed in the wind. She vanished, leaving the forest filled with her otherworldly voice.

"The unwanting soul sees what's hidden—"

It was a young woman speaking in a singsong voice, melodic yet sinister.

"—the ever-wanting soul sees only what it wants."

Her words reverberated in the trees, and, like a whoosh of the wind, passed in the distance, dying off in a long pulsing echo.

"Two things—one origin—different in name—"

The strange hooded ghost shimmered like a mirage and dissolved.

Nicks and Byrne spun in circles trying to guess where she might reappear. Limbs of the ancient cedars, some a thousand years old, creaked in the breeze. The ghost materialized behind them, running among the fern fronds.

Her whispers were heavy with reverb.

"—whose identity is mystery!"

She was there and suddenly gone again.

"Mystery of all mysteries! The door to the hidden!"

Nicks grew weary of the game, climbed back in the wreckage, and rummaged around. When she resurfaced, she held the flare gun she'd found earlier in one of the storage compartments. Relying on her bionic hearing, she pointed the gun at the forest and swung her arm in an arc, following the strange sounds that accompanied the ghost. There was a pattern. Infrasonic pulses before each—

Shhfooom!

The flare shot into the woods and impaled the ghost. As the bright fire sizzled, the ghost glitched in and out of existence, still trying to spook them with its garbled poetry. Nicks advanced on the apparition as it faded. What remained was a blackened panel of thin, transparent plastic.

"Well, look at this, I've busted a real ghost," she joked.

Nicks flexed her leg and kicked the panel off its support wires.

"Stop playing games! We're not superstitious idiots you can trick with your stolen tech. I know you're listening! Come out and face us," Nicks said. "We're not scared of you!

"Let's be honest, if you aren't scared, you are a *fool!*" Scorpio said.

She was mounted on a black horse some twenty yards beyond the hologram device. Scorpio smiled at Nicks, turned the horse around, and rode deeper into the forest.

Byrne raced up to stop Nicks from taking the bait, but it was too late. She headed into the forest at full speed. He watched her explode with power. He'd read the reports about her potential speed, but he'd never seen her use it like this.

"Nat, don't, she's luring you into a *trap!*" he yelled.

He knew she could hear him, but it was a futile plea. He

shouldn't worry though. Nicks was the most powerful member of their team. If anyone could put an end to the insane killing, Viper could—but could she do it alone?

"Nat, if you can still hear me," Byrne said with grim reluctance, "I'm headed to the temple we saw from the air. Meet me there."

He ran back to the wreckage, grabbed some supplies, strapped them on, and climbed back out. That's when he was confronted with another problem.

A menacing black mass was descending from the sky. He couldn't believe what he was seeing. Dread and death were coming for him like a biblical plague on the wind.

66

Somewhere in the woods, Nicks was risking her life. He couldn't let her down. But he had no idea how to fight what he saw coming.

It was a swarm of insects. Not locusts. Something else with more wings. They moved with bizarre precision. The buzz became a roar as they approached.

He ran for the tree line.

The swarm turned on a dime and followed. It took on the distinct geometric shape of an arrowhead flying his way.

This was outlandish. He felt like a cartoon character being chased by animated bees. How in the hell could insects do this?

They had to be drones, he thought.

Miniature machines. Swarm-intelligent. Sharing their rate of speed, their trajectory, and distance from each other. Working with one mind.

Several of the drones darted ahead of the swarm and landed, clinging to the fabric of his shirt. He batted one away and grabbed another in his hand.

Examining it as he continued to run, Byrne realized how

wrong he was. This wasn't a machine at all. This was a real insect. A dragonfly.

Four wings. Beady eyes. Or was that a camera? He'd read about DragonflEYE research with fascination and found it ridiculous. But here it was, something like him, altered by science. It had a miniaturized control board and a solar cell mounted on its thorax like a backpack. Its long slender abdomen was capped with a thin copper electrode.

He touched it. It zapped him with an electrical charge strong enough to sting. He dropped the insect and looked back. The swarm was catching up. He couldn't let that happen.

He picked up speed. Swerving in and out of the trees. A part of the swarm broke off and dive-bombed him as he ran. The shock of their stings got his attention but it wasn't enough to be of any consequence. He raced on, pointing himself toward the sound of rushing water.

Another wave descended. Double the number. The ensuing shocks were more painful. He leapt over a fallen cedar and landed in a web of roots. He stumbled and fell. This slowed him down enough for the swarm to catch up. They hovered in formation above him.

Byrne grabbed a fallen limb and held it like a baseball bat. He swatted the closest insects out of the air. The tactic proved useless. The swarm adjusted, regrouped above him, and descended as one unified army.

In seconds, they covered him. When they attacked, it was with one controlled burst. Byrne felt as if a hundred Tasers had hit him. His muscles spasmed, and he fell onto the forest floor, paralyzed. He couldn't fight back, and the insects wouldn't leave him.

One more flare of electricity burst from their little backpacks. Like the swarm, darkness crawled over his body, enveloping everything until all he could see faded to black.

67

This was the reverse of a well-planned mission.

Reaper Force had been on the defense for the last week in the hope of capturing the cyborg killer and finding Project Starfire. Now, half the team had been kidnapped and the other half was lost in a Japanese forest hunting a ghost and an assassin.

Nicks raced up the ridge after Scorpio and the horse. The island's forest conjured images of a fairy tale. Mist. Fog. Tree limbs like goblin fingers. Green moss spread over everything like emerald cake frosting. Thick and delicious, but hard to navigate. At the top of the hill, it was clear the wicked witch knew the terrain better. Scorpio and her horse were gone.

Spinning around, Nicks scanned the forest, listening for any sign of her nemesis but finding nothing. It was foolish to chase her this deep into unknown territory. She'd lost Scorpio and had no idea where she was.

Down the other side of the ridge into a wide ravine, she sprinted, weaving through the trees, jumping boulders and fallen logs. Eventually, she made her way to a well-worn path headed north.

About a mile further, two drones passed overhead. Using a methodical pattern, they flew back and forth. Nicks took refuge in a dark crevice along a rocky embankment and watched them use their search algorithm to cover all the possible locations she might be. She had been chasing the assassin, but now she was the prey.

Hiding under a rock wouldn't do, but she had to wait for them to pass. She moved to the mouth of the crevice and peered out, straining, listening, hoping the drones would give up and leave.

The only sound she picked up was an animal forging in the brush. It was a Japanese raccoon dog, casually digging. When it saw her, it froze and stared.

The *tanuki* flicked its tail, waving it like a little flag, jumped, and ran up the hill. It stopped and looked back over its shoulder at Nicks.

Nicks climbed out of her hiding place and followed it.

At the top of the hill, there was an old structure, seemingly abandoned. The tanuki leapt through a tangle of vines and into a nest of debris and disappeared into the structure.

Nicks stepped inside.

The animal had made a home here. Apparently, it had been a teahouse for pilgrims on the path to a temple that, according to the dusty map she was staring at, was about a mile further up the trail.

Was her team there? Were they still alive?

Only one way to find out. She pointed herself in the right direction and ran.

PART IX

NEVER SAY DIE

68

The path up to the temple was easy to follow, but it exposed her to the drones. Every few minutes she stopped, waited for one to pass, and then continued.

As she neared the temple, the trail broke off at an overlook. A cool breeze flowed from that direction. She heard a waterfall. She peered down the trail and glimpsed the black horse. It was resting in a grove of trees, tied to a limb.

Several yards past the horse, she spotted Scorpio on the edge of the overlook. She had her back to Nicks, admiring the water-fall—*waiting*.

Nicks walked up to the horse. It pawed the ground and snorted. Scorpio turned around and greeted her.

"I see you insist on facing your destiny—no matter how dangerous it may be."

"I'm here for my team. Where are they?"

"Not dead, if that's your concern. At least—*not yet*."

"Let them go, they have nothing to do with this."

Scorpio paced back and forth as she talked, a predator waiting for the right moment to attack.

"Do you refuse to believe what my sister told you? None of you are innocent—especially your handsome colonel."

Worry flashed across Nicks's face, betraying her thoughts.

"Yes, we have him too. That doesn't concern you, does it? If it did, you wouldn't have left him alone and unprotected after what you shared on the ARES. Perhaps the viper is like the scorpion—do you kill your partners after mating?"

Nicks lowered her eyes, and growled through her clenched jaw. "If you've hurt him—"

"—you should be more concerned with saving yourself."

Nicks copied Scorpio's movements. They danced like boxers in the ring. She needed to avoid the stupid mistakes she'd made before. Scorpio didn't hold back. She fought dirty.

Avoid the sword, she thought. It was strapped to Scorpio's back in its sheath. It had stuck through Ms. Platinum like a toothpick in a hors d'oeuvre. She refused to be served to the Dharmapala like that.

"She blames your superiors for what happened. To me, you're just as complicit. My sister rejects that. She thinks you can be of use to the Dharmapala."

"Is that the point of all these murders? Revenge?"

"Much more than that, but I confess, revenge was the reason I was so—*theatrical*—when I disposed of the soldiers." She smiled as if she was recalling a pleasant memory. "Be honest, does it matter how you slaughter such abominations?"

Scorpio unsheathed her sword. Nicks backed out of range. Despite her futuristic biomimetics, she was still vulnerable to one of the most ancient weapons of war. And damn, one swipe of that thing would hurt like a mother-trucker.

"As much as my sister wants to meet you, I will prove she's wrong about the *great* Viper!"

Scorpio pounced with lightning speed and slashed at Nicks. A downward cut aimed at the crux of her neck. Nicks dodged the blade and came up fast, tackling her around the waist. They fell to the ground. Nicks, on top, jabbed Scorpio in the side, hoping to break a rib or two. Scorpio hooked with her right, using the handle of the sword like brass knuckles; she hit Nicks in the side of the head. Dazed, Nicks rolled off Scorpio, who crawled away and scrambled to her feet.

Nicks was still on her knees when Scorpio slashed again.

The edge of the sword came down hard, slicing into her forearm, flaying her artificial skin and clanging into the metal bone below. Scorpio drew the blade back in a flash, spun, and brought it down again across her leg. Another perfect strike.

Scorpio stepped out of Nicks's reach, admiring her work.

Nicks tried to stand. The wound was serious and deep. The artificial nerves sent their artificial signals to her brain and, although none of her human flesh was damaged, the excruciating torment was real.

Her knees buckled, and she fell—the dark fog of agony suffocating her will to fight on. She felt the same panic she'd felt as a young girl, in her first fight. The instinctual drive to flee before one is killed or harmed pleaded with her to run.

"My sister believes a *thing* like you can be of use."

Scorpio sneered as she wiped her blade clean of Nicks's strange blood.

"But how? What are you, really? I know men like your colonel will use you for their pleasure, but you're not a woman anymore, are you? The bombing in Afghanistan robbed you of that, right? You're not even a good machine. You're some corruption of the two. If your true nature was exposed to the people you love, like it is now, you'd be an outcast, a monster to fear."

Nicks dragged herself out of Scorpio's reach. Her left side was numb, failing to respond to her commands.

"As for this military team you profess to care about—do they feel the same? Do they respect you? You're not a soldier—not a

good one. You're weak and naïve. You came here with no strategy. I could have killed you seconds after you confronted me.
Look at you, I've barely broken a sweat, and you're already
falling apart."

Scorpio seemed content to let Nicks suffer. She was in no
hurry to finish her.

"In your old life, you caused the death of your team by going
into a dangerous area where being female made you an easy
target. You provoked those people. Dared them to take a shot at
you. That's *pride*, Viper. You continually demand respect from
others who are more *formidable* than you. No, I can't have
someone like you serving as her right hand. Our organization
won't survive your arrogance. Your pride invites death. Gets you
killed."

Scorpio's rage bubbled over, and she rushed Nicks. Nicks
was ready with a hand full of sand and gravel. She tossed it up,
blinding her foe. Scorpio stumbled backward swinging wildly.
Nicks moved in, attempting to sweep her legs, but the hilt
caught her in the chin. Scorpio faded back, then lunged. The
blade cut across Nicks's bionic arm, severing the tattered pieces
of silicon and exposing more of her components. Nicks
screamed and threw a desperate haymaker. It went wild, and
Scorpio responded with a roundhouse kick to the face. Nicks
spun to the ground in agony.

"You survived death once and had a chance to start over,
but you've squandered it chasing the false hope you could
rebuild your life. Get back to the way it was before. If you
trained hard, worked hard, you could finally be a hero. It's been
how many years? What progress have you made? You failed to
save your own family, you failed to save the villagers in Kandahar, and you have failed Reaper Force. Most of all, by trying to
be something you are not, you've failed yourself. And, now
you'll die twice."

The truth of what Scorpio was saying seemed worse than any wound Nicks had. It laid her bare in more ways than one.

Through the torn silicone skin, she could see her true self. The metal fingers. The titanium bone wrapped in carbon mesh. She stood up and teetered there, thinking.

She was a mess, leaking some strange purple liquid, a mixture of bio-coolant and blood. A few tears of frustration snuck past her steely defenses. They fell on her exposed bionics, and an augstim motor sizzled as if it would short out.

Blood. Tears. Biocoolant. It was if an ancient reservoir of self-hatred was leaching from her deep core, eroding the last measure of resistance and carving out a space for something long overdue—acceptance.

Scorpio was right; she had failed herself. If she was going to live another minute, she had to embrace who she really was—not who she wished she could be. Her body wasn't entirely human or entirely machine; it was something more—something perfect for this moment. A switch deep within her, beyond her biology and bionics, flipped into its proper place.

She tore off remaining strands of her silicone, exposing her metallic arm. She did the same with the silicone ear and threw it at Scorpio's feet.

Scorpio backed away, turning up her nose. "You are disgusting!"

"Did you forget, I'm a *cyborg*!" Nicks eyes narrowed and smiled. Her teeth were crimson with her own blood.

"Flux! Engage the Protocols!"

Flux came online. *"Requesting confirmation."*

"Yes, damn you! I confirm. Viper Oscar November Echo."

"Confirmed, Captain Nicks. Protocols Engaged."

Nicks had never tried the drug, but she imagined this was the rush one felt taking heroin. The protocols amplified everything around her in a new resonance. She felt reborn, empowered by a new wave of energy. Flux spoke to her in a way only she could hear.

"... *dialing back pain receptors to five percent* ...

The pain of her open wounds disappeared.

"... *overriding damaged relays in Left Arm Seven Charlie Mark Five* ..."

"...*overriding damaged relays in Right Leg Nine Alpha Mark Four* ..."

Her mind unclouded. Her vision cleared.

"... *rerouting power to all TALON components* ..."

"... *engaging combat protocol: Expert Class* ..."

"... *please set use of force parameters* ..."

"One hundred percent should be good," Nicks said, cracking a grin.

"... *maximum lethality. Ready to engage* ..."

Nicks beckoned Scorpio to come closer. She hesitated. Something had obviously changed.

Scorpio spun her right foot in a kick to the head, the same move that caught Nicks off-guard in Hollywood.

"Not this time," Nicks said, catching Scorpio's foot in mid-kick. She twisted her ankle until she heard tendons ripping. Scorpio stumbled backward, unable to put weight on her damaged leg.

Furious, she lunged awkwardly at Nicks. Her sword came down. Nicks blocked it. The blade clanged against her arm, metal on metal. No pain. Viper was in overdrive.

Scorpio attacked again, slashing at Nicks's waist. Nicks stopped it dead with her hand. Her bionic fist closed like a vise and twisted the sword out of Scorpio's grip, throwing it out of reach.

Scorpio stepped back into a defensive stance, a glimmer of panic on her face.

Nicks's augstim engines revved into a higher gear. She leapt with all the force she could muster. Vaulting through the air, she landed one of the most devastating, and illegal, moves she knew from MMA—a downward elbow strike to the face. It crushed Scorpio's nose. Blood sprayed everywhere. Scorpio stumbled backward, disoriented.

Nicks hit her again with a right cross, then an upper cut. Nicks heard bones shatter with each punch. Scorpio wobbled. Nicks finished her with an explosive knee strike to the chin.

Scorpio didn't have much to say after that. Disoriented and off-balance, she took one too many steps backward—dangerously close to the edge of the overlook.

"You may beat me, Viper. But the Dharmapala lives."

"Maybe so." Nicks was tired of her mouth.

"I promise you, the war is just beginning!"

"Too bad you won't be here to see me stop it."

Nicks kicked Scorpio in the chest and the assassin flew over the edge of the overlook. Nicks stepped forward and watched her opponent plummet at least thirty feet, hit a smattering of shale rock, and tumble further down the ridge. Her head slammed into a large tree, and she stopped like a car had hit her. She lay there motionless with the mist of death hovering over her. Nicks held still for a few moments—listening.

"Flux?"

"No indications of life, Captain."

She hurried back to pick up the sword with the scorpion handle and ran toward the temple, praying it wasn't too late to save her friends.

69

The stolen ARES had landed on the eastern lawn near the temple. Nicks moved closer, hid behind a stone column, and got a good look. The ARES was quiet. Its back hatch was still open but everything in it, including the Reaper team, was gone.

Wasting no time, she circled to the front entrance of the shrine. The temple was ancient, but she noticed there were many modern upgrades. High-end motion sensors and cameras covered every entrance. This temple was used for more than tourism.

Something is familiar about this place, she thought.

It hit her. The downtown warehouse! Scorpio had built a replica of this very place in the basement—a perfect homage to her base of operations. It had been a clue, one that confirmed she had found the lair of the Dharmapala.

Trying her best to avoid the sensors, she crept up to the entrance. She pushed the door open and stepped inside. The temple was dark. The humidity outside gave way to the pleasant coolness of circulated air. It was dry, undoubtedly to protect the large banks of computer servers along the northern wall. The machines hummed busily.

What was the purpose of so much processing power?

She walked forward, noticing the stone path gave way to a newly polished wooden floor. It only took a few steps before she activated the hidden switch with her foot. The false wooden plank sank into the floor and the Taser mine exploded.

Nicks, hit with multiple projectiles, fell to her knees, her muscles violently contracting. It was like being speared by Zeus with a hundred tiny lightning bolts.

Flux announced she was trying to compensate for the system overload. Nicks fought to stand back up, but the voltage was too strong. Scorpio's sword clattered to the floor. Slowly but surely, the dark gravity of unconsciousness pulled her under.

70

The darkness enveloped Nicks. She floated in it, disembodied, a serene prisoner with no sense of time or place until the voice she'd heard in the forest reappeared.

The unwanting soul sees what's hidden.

The young ghost again. Melodic and otherworldly.

—the ever-wanting soul sees only what it wants.

It reverberated within her mind and, like the rush of a waterfall, overwhelmed her, then passed, fading as it moved beyond her.

Two things—one origin—different in name.

A slit of light, like the fire of a star, appeared. The voice beckoned her into the light.

Two things—one origin—different in name.

She reached for the light and it embraced her, pulling her out of her unconsciousness.

WHEN SHE OPENED HER EYES, she was in a new part of the

temple. It was a room like Scorpio had made with an altar, candles, and a table.

Nicks sat upright, legs crossed, on a fiber mat. Heavy steel manacles and chains bolted to the floor secured her wrists and arms. A small table containing all the things one would need for a traditional tea ceremony lay in front of her. A woman in a hooded robe sat on the other side. Her head was bowed as if she was meditating.

Nicks couldn't remember anything after the Taser mine exploded, but it seemed something had injured her during the ambush. The back of her neck was on fire.

She strained at the manacles and chains. There was no give. She imagined they were strong enough to secure an elephant.

Her host wore a white hooded kimono trimmed in metallic silver fabric.

As her eyes adjusted to the candlelight, Nicks saw she was young. About twenty. Small and barely over a hundred pounds. When the woman removed her hood, Nicks thought her beautiful. She was similar to Scorpio. Tan skin, dark full eyebrows, and high cheekbones reminiscent of the beautiful Middle-Eastern women she'd encountered during her service overseas.

Her hair was shaped in a geisha bun and the candlelight made one side of her head, covered in dreadlocks, glitter like silver.

The geisha bun fell apart as the locks came alive. Each one seemed to have a mind of its own. They snipped like scissor blades when they bounced off each other. Red eyes blinked on the ends of their stainless steel caps.

A thick net of fiber optic cables descended from the ceiling. Each of the cyberlochs reached out like living vines and copulated with a mate. When every strand was coupled, the computer servers kicked into a new gear. Nicks's host seemed happily rejuvenated.

The woman's hair wasn't the only thing being controlled.

Electronic candles on the table lit up, illuminating the room and exposing more detail. The teakettle turned on and the water boiled.

Small micro-drones flew around the room performing various functions. And smaller spider-like drones, similar to the dreaded Caduceus drones, crawled over various surfaces.

Nicks noticed one was carrying the gift box she'd brought with her. Like an ant carrying an oversized piece of food, it clicked across the table and deposited the box next to the teacups. It was unopened.

No doubt this was Starfire. Or, as Penbrook had told Nicks —Riza Azmara.

"You carry Scorpio's sword; I assume she is dead?" Riza asked

Nicks nodded yes.

Her reaction was hard to decipher. Her face was blank but her voice had a tone of disappointment.

"She was a true warrior, but so are you. As much as I loved her, I knew destiny would force the confrontation, for this meeting was inevitable. Nothing, not even my beloved sister, could stop it from happening."

"Your *sister?*

"My most loyal friend. Her name was Lida Laram, and she has been by my side since we were children. She believed it was her purpose to protect me so our shared dream came to fruition. Part of that dream was having you here, as my guest. I hope her sacrifice helps you understand what it means to lay your life down for a truly meaningful purpose."

"If I'm your guest— " Nicks lifted her manacles. An excruciating pain shot through her arms and radiated through her body.

Riza watched her struggle. "The cuffs are EMP field generators—toroid mirror reflectors which expand the field disrupting your bionics—the more you resist the more pain you'll feel."

"If you want to talk, take them off," Nicks demanded.

"I'm afraid your restraints are for both our protection."

Nicks didn't like that answer. "Flux, engage the protocols!"

Flux responded, *"Talon protocols engaged."*

Just as quickly, another voice joined the conversation. Riza wasn't moving her lips but her voice echoed inside Nicks's head.

"EID Alpha, Hold Protocols. Activate AI Agent Kill Switch."

Flux disappeared. Her systems powered down.

When she pulled against the chains, her limbs shook and the pain was overwhelming. Without the protocols, it was no use.

Her host looked at her and smiled. Her mind spoke to Nicks's mind.

"Synthetic telepathy. A skill I acquired about the same time you gained yours."

STARFIRE WAS A WEAPON, after all. She'd taken over so easily, it was disturbing. A small drone buzzed past and around to the back of Nicks's head. She could feel the wind of its tiny rotors blowing as it hovered behind her.

A video feed appeared on a screen next to Riza. Nicks saw the back of her head on the screen. Implanted into the base of her skull was a sigillum. The silver against her skin gleamed in the LED illumination from the drone. The decorative skull looked like some kind of body modification a goth kid might get at the mall—but this modification was permanent.

Nicks raged. "What the hell did you do?"

"I won't hurt you, Natalie. The sigillum is necessary

because I have so much to share with you. We can't have any misunderstandings between us. This is a reunion, one I've hoped for most of my life. It must be perfect."

"A reunion?"

"I was very young when we last met. Despite all the horrors of that day, I'd hoped you would remember me," she said.

"That day?"

"The bombing in Afghanistan—the day we both died—the day we were both reborn."

Riza seemed to come in and out of her own world.

Nicks was bewildered. "You were in the market?"

"You waved me over, offered me gum."

"Oh my god, the *bubble gum*, of course."

"Then a man, a very sick man, armed with a crude explosive vest tracked you to the market. His damaged mind convinced him setting off the bomb would save his family from the evils of the invaders."

"They told me I was the only survivor."

Riza was an animal eviscerating prey. Her face full of unnerving delight.

"That was their first lie."

71

"Don't mistake me, I want to punish these liars," Riza said as she unleashed her power. "But, after you hear the truth, you will want to do it for me!"

Nicks mind flooded with alien memories. It was like a dam breaking. Riza's consciousness spilled over the wall of her own mind through the sigillum, and drowned all other images. The tapestry of Riza's life spooled out like a movie.

Had there been a witness, they would have seen two women staring at each other silently. One meditative, one stunned by what she was experiencing.

Let me tell you a story, Natalie.

The thoughts invaded Nicks with unwelcome intimacy.

Once upon a time, a girl was born to bless the world. As a child, she loved life with a full heart.

Images of Riza playing with Lida Laram, a young Scorpio, came into focus. She was joyous and content with the simple pleasures of her childhood in the village.

However, as she grew older, she became selfish.

Nicks watched as Lida and Riza had a string of silly, but

escalating arguments. In one defining moment, Riza slapped Lida and walked away from her distraught friend.

Because of this selfishness, she was punished, and her body was torn into a thousand pieces.

Nicks watched as the two girls ran through the market, searching for the rumored female soldier. How strange to see her younger self there, waving as the children ran over. Behind her, the suicide bomber pushed through the crowd. The bomb exploded and darkness fell like a curtain.

Before her last moment, God offered her redemption. If she renounced her selfishness, she could live again and her body would be restored.

A new scene unfolded. A fresh-faced Penbrook sat beside Riza's hospital bed. He watched over her lovingly as she endured surgery and fought through her rehabilitation. Riza walked through the hallways of Blackwood Lodge, into her new bedroom. The montage dissolved as Penbrook watched from behind the observation room's mirrored glass.

As the girl tried desperately to accept her new life, she discovered those around her were full of evil intentions.

The images of Riza's story grew darker as she realized she was a prisoner. Her pleas for freedom were met with excuses. It appeared her only consolation were her daily meals with Lida, who arrived with new physical injuries each day—evidence of her brutal experimentation. One memory showed Riza protesting this. Instead of changing this, the DR-Ultra staff separated the girls as punishment.

One night, on the verge of despair, she was inspired: If I turned my power against these evil men, I would overcome the darkness plaguing the world.

Nicks watched as Riza secretly worked at night, creating the first sigillum. During one secret rendezvous, she attached the device to Lida. They were together from that moment forward and begin to plan their escape.

And so it was: The child became the Dharmapala. The war to subdue the degenerate beings of this Age of Darkness began.

Nicks watched the final scenes play out. In the first, Scorpio left Blackwood for her field test but she never returned. Shortly after that, using the sigillum to control Echo Squad, Scorpio arranged to have Starfire smuggled out of Blackwood Lodge. The women were reunited and made their way to the island. There, Riza built the temple base to amplify the reach of her powers. Finally, the last scenes showed Starfire and Scorpio recruiting underworld figures for the Dharmapala's council.

Nicks watched the scenes fade. Her mind cleared. She was grateful to be rid of Starfire's pompous, psychotic narration. But what a bitter aftertaste. Starfire's plans were delusional, but the horrid treatment of the two girls was unforgivable. It knocked her loyalty off-center. How many more repugnant secrets did DR-Ultra have buried in that malignant hive?

TALKING TO HER VERBALLY NOW, Riza said, "I want you to understand why all of this is happening."

"Yeah, you owe me that, at the very least."

"As I grew older, I questioned why I couldn't leave Blackwood Lodge. I investigated, and found out you were alive and looking for the truth as well."

"Yes, there was a time I was hell-bent on understanding why it happened."

"Did you find answers?"

"In a way, yes. I realized what I really wanted was for the thing to have never occurred. The more I dug into the evidence, the angrier I became. I wasn't moving forward. In fact, my obsession seemed more damaging than the bombing had ever been."

Nicks recalled being in bed, fighting with Byrne about this very thing. Riza haunted the memory—a psychic voyeur reliving it with her.

"So, your superiors and your loved ones shamed you, and you ended your search without finding the truth?"

"You could say that, or you could say I *accepted* the outcome. I certainly had many nights where I raged over giving up. The impulse to start again was hard to resist. But, over time, the focus shifted to rebuilding my life."

"But you've rebuilt your life as a *weapon*, under the control of *DR-Ultra*. Why?"

"How is my job relevant to any of this?"

"Don't you understand? You and I are alike. Two things, one origin. We were both betrayed. You most of all—by the very people you protect!"

"What's your evidence?" Nicks demanded. "There are hundreds of conspiracy theories like this floating around the internet."

"This is a conspiracy, but it's not a theory. DR-Ultra was behind the bombing."

Nicks refused to accept that. "Impossible!"

Riza continued, "It started with your work in Afghanistan.

"There were four phases to the Kandahar operation. Your mission was the first phase. It was essentially a cover. I know you were there for more than vaccines and bubble gum; they tasked you with covertly collecting data."

Nicks didn't say anything. This was true. She wouldn't dispute it.

"The second phase was the real mission, a DR-Ultra test. One you were not informed about called Operation Mesmer."

Nicks protested. "I've never heard of anything called

Mesmer. You're misinformed. If it existed, I would know by now. I've read everything about that mission."

"Everything they thought you could handle," Riza said. "The third phase was classified. They used your data to find a location to deploy Mesmer. That was the Jehanni Marketplace. The final phase was simple. Observe the results."

"You're showing your crazy now. No one would green light an experiment like that."

"I've been as careful as a surgeon. I've dissected this conspiracy down to its cancerous beginnings. Now, I'll prove it to you." Riza pointed to a nearby screen.

Nicks was terrified by what she saw.

Byrne, Quinn, and Mouse were in another section of the temple. Nicks could see the room was both prison cell and lab. Each of them were strapped down to their own individual surgical table. Byrne's restraints were like Nicks, bulky elephant chains. He could barely move. His bionics, having just come back online, would take weeks to be fully operational. Those chains were overkill and meant he was completely incapacitated.

A dreadful nest of Caduceus drones hung over her friends. Biding their time and, Nicks suspected, waiting for a command from their mistress—the woman who talked to machines.

Nicks's heart sank.

"Colonel Byrne ... can you hear me?"

"Yes, damn it, I can hear you," Byrne yelled, wrenching the chains.

"Tell me about Operation Mesmer," Riza demanded.

"What the hell are you talking about?"

"You were part of the DR-Ultra field team that implemented Operation Mesmer, were you not?"

Nicks noticed Riza was watching her reactions instead of the video feed.

"That's enough, Riza!" Nicks said. "I don't give a damn what happened!"

"Yes, you do. You may not know it yet, but you do."

A Caduceus drone descended onto Quinn's table.

"Answer the question, Colonel."

"You've got the wrong guy; I was just a grunt back then. All of that stuff was above my pay grade."

The drone lifted one of its claws. A needle telescoped out and filled with fluid. It grabbed a web of Quinn's skin and pulled itself on top of her chest.

"I've programmed this surgical drone to do a complete autopsy on Ms. Quinn. Do you understand? If you continue to lie, I will let it perform its program. Then, we will move on to Mr. Park. After I extract his knowledge of DR-Ultra's encryption program, he'll be carved up in pieces."

The drone injected Quinn. She screamed as the paralysis spread. Her body went rigid. The drone produced a large scalpel and slowly cut into her skin.

"*Stop!* I will tell you everything you want to know, just get that thing off of her!" Byrne yelled.

The scalpel retracted. The drone backed away.

"Operation Mesmer was the first neuro-cognitive warfare operation DR-Ultra has ever field-tested. It was a complete failure," Byrne said.

Riza smiled. She'd broken through. "What was the mission of Operation Mesmer? Give me specifics."

Byrne looked at Quinn then turned to the camera with resignation. He took a deep breath.

"The Human Terrain Team was tasked with covertly collecting bio-data from the village in an attempt to recapture prisoners who'd escaped from the prison breakout in Helmut province. However, those running Mesmer didn't care about finding terrorists. They were looking for human subjects with a certain genetic profile, individuals related to the terrorists who could be targeted with a neuroweapon."

Nicks interrupted. "He's making that up, telling you something you want to hear because you are torturing Quinn."

"I disagree. I think this is the first time he's told the truth," Riza said. "Colonel Byrne, explain what this neuroweapon can do, or we'll watch the drone remove your teammate's organs one-by-one ... while she is still conscious."

Nicks could see tears welling in Quinn's eyes.

Byrne pulled against his chains in a futile attempt to break free. His fury brimmed over. Nothing to do but play the witch's game.

"The neuroweapon was a nano-computer capable of altering electric potential in a cell; it was inserted using a Trojan horse, a pathogen, a dead virus, like those found in vaccines. The body mounts an autoimmune defense and destroys the pathogen, releasing the nano-computer into the targeted area of the brain. Once the subject is infected, an outside controller can manipulate the nano-computer. They call the effect neural degradation. The hope is it would change the enemy's behavior in such a way they become more hostile, more aggressive, act out on their own people, even kill them. Thus the term, neuroweapon."

Byrne's confession disheartened Nicks completely.

Riza appeared satisfied, but she had saved the best for last. "Thank you, Colonel. I have one more question for you."

An image of an Afghani man appeared on the screen.

"Tell me, do you know this man?"

Nicks knew him. His image was burned in her memory forever. Despite, being vaporized by the blast, he had been the first and only suspect. He had no history of violence or any associations with a terrorist organization, but for some reason, he'd decided one morning to forego his normal ritual of attending the mosque, and meeting his friends for coffee. Instead, he drove to a secret location two miles outside of town, strapped on an explosive vest, drove back into town, and detonated the bomb within fifty feet of the American soldier handing out candy to the village children.

Byrne was mute, obviously at the end of what he was willing to confess.

"Do. You. Know. This. Man?" Riza demanded.

Byrne wouldn't respond. Riza cued Quinn's drone. Its surgical blade swung down within an inch of Quinn's chest.

"Stop!" Nicks yelled.

The drone froze. Riza turned to Nicks.

"Tell her what she wants to know, Jack. Damn you!"

Byrne looked at the photo again. "That man is the suicide bomber responsible for the Jehanni Market Incident."

Riza quoted from a report, "Also, known as Operation Mesmer Test Subject #13, a positive match for neuroweapon deployment?"

"Yes," Byrne said, his voice dropped an octave, as if all the life had drained from his body. "He exceeded their expectations."

"What is his real name?"

"Abdul Azmara," Byrne said.

Riza turned to Nicks.

"Oh god, no!" Nicks let out an audible gasp. "That can't be true! Jack, tell her that's not true!"

Byrne shook his head. "I'm sorry Nat. I really am."

"How easily it is to distort the truth when love is involved," Riza said. She was looking at Nicks, but she was staring through her and beyond—as if her essential self had vanished like the ghost she played at in the forest.

"My father, Natalie. The man who *killed us* was my *father*!"

72

R iza turned off the display. She sat and watched Nicks like an alien trying to translate what her display of emotion meant. Nicks stared back, making her own calculations. Even though the mission backfired, Riza had become what Operation Mesmer intended—a weapon of the most violent order.

"There is one final thing you need to know. After you were injured and taken away by DR-Ultra to begin your transformation, the rest of Operation Mesmer was shut down. The village was deemed infected by a biological agent. A new team called Echo Squad came in and cleaned up the mess.

"Lida and I were saved. But only so they could experiment on us. You see, we had been infected with the neuroweapon as well. The combination of that and the traumatic brain injuries we suffered changed us. DR-Ultra wanted to understand why. That's when David Penbrook entered my life. He told us both we had a rare disease and had to be isolated for our own protection. Another lie. They really wanted to harness our enhanced abilities for their own purposes."

Riza moved closer, almost within reach.

"Do you understand? We have to stop DR-Ultra or they will destroy humanity just as they have destroyed—"

"—your humanity?"

For the first time, Nicks saw a flash of relatable emotion. It was a sliver of anger, and underneath that panic.

"I've tested you, Natalie. You are DARPA's greatest achievement, but you don't have to be their weapon. You can use your abilities to protect the world from their evil."

Riza was working her like Mesmer worked a brain, trying to degrade her loyalties so she'd flip. She wanted Nicks, her sister in suffering, to become her sister in war.

"I can't deny how terrible this is, but it doesn't justify what you've done. If you know me like you say you do, you know I will take this information back and seek justice for you and Lida. I'll make sure every person guilty of harming us is held responsible. But I won't join your misguided war."

"The minute you open your mouth about this, you'll be dead. Surely, you realize that."

"You may be right, but I'll never become a *terrorist*."

"You already are! And, you're on the wrong side of the war." Riza walked around the temple making dramatic flourishes with her hands, the fiber optic cables trailing after her like living hair. Pulses of light surged from her head to the amplification node. The computer servers whirled to life. "Do you think I built this place for some misguided vendetta?"

"Well, if the shoe fits ..."

"No, open your eyes. See what is happening! Operation Mesmer is only a drop in the bucket. It's one project among thousands, and they are growing exponentially every day. America says it is a country of laws. Your scientists proclaim adherence to ethical standards. They swear they are doing all of this to protect their people and your country. But they are lying! In the name of security, they operate above the law and outside the ethical standards. Someone has to stop these monsters before it's too late."

"No! You've taken this too far. If you wanted revenge, look at what's happened. You've had your fair share already. Executing my teammates won't change the past. Listen to reason. If you continue this killing spree, you become the monster."

"The Dharmapala is a monster but one with a divine purpose."

Nicks wasn't getting through to her.

"A purpose, I can't fulfill alone—"

A new image appeared in Nicks's mind. She was in a dark room in front of a red velvet curtain. The curtain pulled back, exposing another chamber. At least six people, their faces concealed by shadows, sat in ornate, high-back chairs on a raised platform. They looked like a tribunal of judges staring down at her.

The central figure leaned out of the darkness. Riza in her virtual guise.

"This is the council," the Demon Queen said. "My lords of war!"

From right to left each of the figures leaned forward. A silver skull hovered over their faces, undulated like a mirage, fading in and out, obscuring their real identities. A thin man in a tailored suit peered down at Nicks. A glowing icon of a rook floated over his throne.

"She saves the best seat for you!" He pointed to the one empty chair, placed to the right of Riza's throne. Above it, a scorpion icon transformed. The new symbol was a viper.

"Join us," the council said, in unison.

They repeated this like a mantra over and over until the scene faded from Nicks's mind.

Riza watched Nicks absorb the invitation, then turned and walked back to the table and picked up the gift box.

"David Penbrook was our new father. The guilt of what he'd done had given him compassion for us. We used it to our advantage. We bided our time, until we manipulated him into freeing us from our prison."

She untied the ribbon and lifted the card from the box. She read it and laughed. She showed it to Nicks.

It read *Octopus*.

"Penbrook was kind to us but weak, a pathetic parent for two women with such incredible powers. That's why we sought you out. That's why I insisted on Lida observing you and testing you. I wanted to prove to her you were worthy of joining our family. A mother stronger than both of us.

"A *mother*?" Nicks cringed.

"You made us Natalie—by taking the brunt of the blast you saved us. That instinct to protect us is what I'm asking you to embrace. Prove they haven't robbed you of it! Join me! It will be so much easier if you convinced Mr. Park to defeat the DR-Ultra encryption. No need to torture him. Once I'm past the encryption, I will use my power to take control of every weapon they possess. With those weapons and you by my side, the war will be over before it even starts."

Riza rested her hand on the gift box's lid. Maybe it was poetic justice to take her out this way, but Nicks couldn't let her do it.

"Riza! I *will* help you. Put the box down."

"I knew you would come around," she said, real joy filling her face. "You do understand what's at stake, don't you?"

"Yes, I understand. Let me go, and we can work this out."

Riza was happy to hear that. She opened the box anyway.

"Don't worry. I scanned it. Nothing threatening here. Unless you consider the sentiments of an old man dangerous.

Penbrook hoped this would turn me away from my destiny. He was wrong. I will destroy everything he has ever built, and you will help me!"

She took the octopus out of the box. She spun it on her finger like she'd done as a child. The tentacles twirled out like a tiny skirt.

FA-BOOM!

The hardened epoxy exploded and catapulted Riza backward. She crashed into a row of monitors and rag-dolled to the ground. All the working machines in the area deactivated. The link through the sigillum disappeared.

"Flux, you there?"

"Back online, Captain."

"Then, engage those *bloody* protocols!"

"TALON protocols engaged."

Nicks felt a wave of new power flow through her cybernetic body.

"Lower pain receptors. Maximum power to my arms."

She grabbed the chains and ripped them from their moorings. She crushed the manacles at their weakest points until she could shed them.

She noticed Riza wasn't dead, in fact she was coming around. Nicks grabbed Scorpio's sword and leapt across the room to confront her. She sensed the sigillum reconnecting.

Riza spat at her. "A *bomb*—after all we've been through —*you coward!*"

"Riza." Nicks stepped next to her. "Shut the hell up!"

She raised the sword over the girl.

"Don't you dare!" Riza shrieked.

With superhuman speed, Nicks brought the blade down across the net of cables connecting the girl to her computer system. It was like giving an overdue haircut to a contemptuous child. With one slice, she terminated all the connections. Riza went into a fit of rage, arching her back and clawing at her face like something possessed her. She curled over in an epileptic fit.

When the convulsions stopped, she regarded Nicks with a catatonic stare. "Now, I have to kill you too."

"No, you pretentious little shit. No, you won't!" She slapped the girl across the face with enough force to knock her unconscious. Riza collapsed in a heap.

As Nicks considered her next move, an alarm blared from the main monitor.

"Critical node disengaged. Self-destruct sequence activated!" the computer said.

A clock appeared on the monitor indicating the start of a five-minute countdown.

"Are you freaking kidding me?" Nicks gasped.

Riza wouldn't make it out on her own, but according to the seconds ticking away, Nicks didn't have the luxury of giving a damn.

She raced over to one of the central columns outfitted with a touch panel and scrolled through the security settings. A few clicks revealed a menu titled for the lower levels. A few more taps opened a hidden door, and she rushed through it.

Nicks only had a few minutes to save her team, or they were all dead.

73

Nicks found everyone in a room that had been converted into a makeshift jail cell.

"Careful, it's electrified," Mouse said when he saw her round the corner.

"Is everyone okay?" she asked.

"Under the circumstances," Byrne said.

Nicks couldn't look at him.

"We have to move fast; this whole place is going to blow!"

Mouse pointed to the locking mechanism holding the cell doors closed. She used the samurai sword one more time to short out the electrical connection. Putting her boot to the bars, she kicked the cell door open with such force it exploded off its hinges. First, she freed Byrne from his chains by crushing the EMP cuffs. He hopped off the exam table and unshackled Mouse. Nicks grabbed Quinn and the team hustled back up the stairs and outside to the east lawn.

Mouse bounded onto the ARES and furiously attacked the flight controls. Byrne jumped in the pilot's seat. Nicks created a makeshift bed for Quinn along the jump seats.

Mouse looked at Byrne. "I've overridden the remote piloting system. It'll fly manually."

"Good job, I'll take it from here," he said, firing the engines.

Everyone strapped in as the rotors whirled to life.

As they took off, Quinn came around, "That bloody bitch was cutting into my *Sex Pistols* tattoo. I hope you killed her!"

Nicks combed Quinn's hair out of her face. "She won't hurt anyone, ever again."

Byrne turned the ARES south, circled back around, making one more pass over the temple before heading out to sea. As they flew by, the back half of the shrine exploded in a massive fireball.

A mushroom cloud of black smoke shot into the sky.

In rapid succession, there were more synchronized explosions, each one destroying a major support column until the entire temple imploded.

In seconds, it was nothing but smoldering rubble.

The shockwave of the final explosions washed over the ARES as it ascended. Byrne pushed the engines full throttle, and the aircraft broke through the clouds and, after a few minutes, settled into the safe and peaceful stream of a higher altitude. Nicks's team was alive and headed home.

No one, including a demon queen, could escape the hellfire they'd left behind.

Project Starfire wouldn't return to Blackwood Lodge. Riza Azmara was dead.

PART X

EPILOGUE

74

THE ANGELOS GROVE ESTATE, LOS ANGELES, CA

N atalie Nicks woke up to the sound of jackhammers busting up concrete two floors down. The bright California sun crept toward her bed, and a refreshing breeze filtered through the window. She grabbed her smartphone and checked the time.

Well, at least they had let her sleep until nine o'clock.

Any earlier, and she might have unleashed a few Caduceus drones on them. Of course, that would be mean since they were here to repair the damage to the Cage and put her home back together.

She rubbed the back of her neck. The sigillum was still there but covered by a skin-colored patch the team had applied. Byrne and Quinn had used Vargas's notes to jerry-rig a signal blocking cover to conceal the device. The plan was to surgically remove it after they figured out the safest method.

Nicks put on an old Led Zeppelin t-shirt and strolled downstairs, making a beeline for the coffeemaker.

Mouse proclaimed he'd already had two cups but wanted more. He was at his new workstation tinkering with something that looked like a mechanical snake.

I don't even want to know, not today.

Fatima was at the pool in one of Nicks's bikinis. She had a few stitches but looked no worse for the wear. Quinn was chatting her up. It seemed their team had expanded.

Byrne's corner of the Cage was silent. He'd left for a week's vacation, giving them both some needed space.

Penbrook was somewhere else atoning for his sins. But Nicks felt certain he'd keep his job. The DIA wasn't about to cut loose an administrator with so much intel on this new threat. After all, there was a lot to clean up.

The Reaper Team had severed the head of the Dharmapala but the conspiracy was much broader than one person. A few texts from Ms. Platinum, who was recovering somewhere on the other side of the ocean, had confirmed remnants of the organization were still out there. The Dharmapala council, the lords of war, had retreated to the shadows, but the hunt went on.

A BIT LATER, Nicks returned to her balcony with a mug and waved to the construction crew. There were several double takes. She wasn't sure if it was because her nipples were saying hello, or because she'd forgotten to—*oh damn*—her metal arm was glinting in the sun. She didn't have a new silicone sleeve yet.

"Shooting a movie today; it's a prop," she yelled.

The men laughed, looked her up and down one more time, and went back to work. They gave each other shrugs, suggesting it was just another strange day in Hollywood—the place your wildest dreams could come true—including half-naked cyborgs drinking coffee.

Across from the construction area and above the manicured

garden, a strange bird on the telephone wire flapped its wings and took flight.

Nicks sat down and watched the men work.

Did Riza Azmara's delusions have any merit? She couldn't shake what she'd learned about her employer. It worried her.

Shortly after joining Reaper Force, Nicks had read an article by the founder of *Sun Microsystems*, Bill Joy. He hadn't been very joyous about the future. He believed many scientists and technology innovators were actively seeking the destruction of the human race. This was a provocative claim, but it did have some factual analysis to back it up.

Advocates of unbridled innovation were pushing the world toward a singular moment when mankind and its machines would merge, moving humanity up the evolutionary ladder into an age of immortality and unlimited knowledge. All the scenarios he warned against had one conclusion—the destruction of humankind.

Everyone in Silicon Valley professed to be making the world *better*.

DARPA professed to be making the world *safer*. Was it?

Had her showdown with Starfire and Scorpio exposed the dangers of the very system she was working to protect?

It certainly exposed fractures in her relationship with Byrne. Could she trust him after all he had revealed? He knew enough about her to know that lying was the last thing he should've done.

But it wasn't a lie. He was following orders.

She could hear him saying that. She didn't want to have the argument. She took another sip of coffee and closed her eyes.

Despite all that had happened and all that had yet to be resolved, a comforting feeling washed over her. Every soldier prayed for it, no matter how terrible the battle had been. It was peace—the kind only attainable when safely at home. Home with a family worth all the risk.

Today, that would be enough.

Today, that was all that mattered.

MEXICO CITY, MEXICO

G eneral Marcel Bishop paced in front of the penthouse's grand window. The view of Alameda Central, one of the oldest public parks in the world, was spectacular, but it did little to change Bishop's sour expression.

"Where is he?" he growled.

"Setting up an important event for his company at the Palacio de Belles Arte. He'll be here when he can leave the meeting discreetly," said The Rook.

"What does that mean? He's planning a party? While we sit on our hands over here?"

"All part of the next stage, General. Nothing untoward."

"Perhaps, but it's dangerous to meet like this. I don't like waiting, and I certainly don't like bad tactics."

"With the sigillum network down, there's little choice," The Rook said. "Don't you agree, Ms. Flores?"

Marisol Flores stood up and joined Bishop by the window.

She reached out and stroked the man's arm, massaging his rock-hard bicep through his suit jacket. "Don't worry, Marcel. We are safe for now. Otherwise I wouldn't risk coming here."

Mr. Rook nodded, "Yes, it's daring of you to join us. Your position is critical."

"It's important the council remains intact and continues the work Scorpio and Starfire began."

"I agree with that. Too much is at stake." Bishop said. Feeling somewhat soothed, he sat down and took a sip of scotch from the crystal tumbler he'd left on the table.

Marisol smiled and continued, "Reaper Force thinks they've destroyed our syndicate. But we know otherwise. Keep the faith gentlemen, and I promise you, the world we envision will come to fruition just as our leader predicted."

Bishop stared at Marisol. How was it that this petite, unassuming woman calmed him so easily? What kind of strange witchcraft allowed her to infiltrate their enemy's command so cunningly, and yet remain so serene? He suddenly found her very attractive.

"So, our leader and main operative are missing and presumed dead and you have no doubts, Ms. Flores?"

"Not one," she said. "The Dharmapala is just getting started!"

PLEASE LEAVE A REVIEW

REVIEWS HELP ME KEEP WRITING!

That concludes **NEVER DIE TWICE**. I hope you enjoyed it!

If you liked the book, you'd make this writer very happy if you'd please leave an honest review. Reviews are critical. They feed the algorithms and allow more eyes to see my books. Despite being a bit of a hassle, they are essential to my success.

So, please take a moment to leave a review. If you do, I promise not to send a cybernetically-enhanced assassin to the location of this reading device. Thank you very much!

— Mark

CLICK HERE TO LEAVE A REVEW

JOIN TEAM VIPER

MARK'S ADVANCED READER GROUP

SIGN-UP FOR FUTURE BOOKS

If you join my Advanced Reader Group you get a chance to
read my next book free of charge. Just let me know you want it
by clicking on the link listed below. When the new book is
ready to go, I'll send you a FREE REVIEW COPY before it's
published and in the stores.

Click Here To Join Team Viper:

http://jonesmarkc.com/teamviper

VIPER FATALIS: OUT NOW!

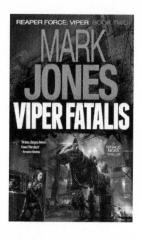

LIST OF CHARACTERS

Reaper Force
Captain Natalie Nicks [Viper]
Sergeant Margaret Quinn [Gremlin]
Colonel Jack Byrne [Spartan]
Fatima Nasrallah [Cartwheel]
Lee Park [Mouse]
Director David Penbrook
Marisol Flores
Flux

Bishop Securities — Echo Squad
Edward Chapman
Declan Wilson
Frank Hitchens
Dwight Johnson
Hal Simmons
C.T. Williams

The Dharmapala
Riza Azmara

Lida Laram [Scorpio]
Dr. Victor Vargas
The Rook
General Marcel Bishop

Other Characters
Uncle Wilco
Elin Thomas [Ms. Platinum]

Programs
DIA: Defense Intelligence Agency
DARPA: Defense Advanced Research Projects Agency
DR-Ultra: DARPA's Covert Branch
TALON: DR-Ultra's Bionics Program
Reaper Force: Joint DIA-DARPA Task Force
Echo Squad: Bishop Securities Elite Tier Operators
Operation Mesmer: Classified DR-Ultra Program

ACKNOWLEDGMENTS

Thanks to the team of people that helped me finish this book and supported me along the way: Hannah Sullivan, Dan Van Oss, Amanda Watson, Margaret Lynn Parsons, Diane and Larry Jones, Laura Kate and Jonathan Brandstein, Hannah Jones, Juliette Jones, and Maverick Jones.

ABOUT THE AUTHOR

Mark Caldwell Jones is a novelist and screenwriter living in Los Angeles. *Never Die Twice* is his first thriller in his Reaper Force: Viper series. Learn more about Mark and get free content like news about, *Viper Fatalis,* the next book in this series, by visiting him online.

For more information:
www.jonesmarkc.com/teamviper
mark@jonesmarkc.com

facebook.com/jonesmarkc
twitter.com/jonesmarkc
instagram.com/jonesmarkc

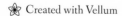 Created with Vellum